roll-back (rōl bak) 1. to re-up; to re-enlist; to return for a second tour of active duty immediately after completing the first; 2. to remember; to reminisce, especially about special missions and those fallen in combat, as in *roll back the clock*

SEAL TEAM ROLL-BACK

TIM L. "BO" BOSILJEVAC,
CDR USN, Former Commander of SEAL TEAM 4
and J. DEMAREST

AVON BOOKS ◆ NEW YORK

AVON BOOKS, INC.
1350 Avenue of the Americas
New York, New York 10019

Copyright © 1999 by Bill Fawcett & Associates
Back cover author photo by Kevin Dockery
Published by arrangement with Bill Fawcett & Associates
Library of Congress Catalog Card Number: 98-93785
ISBN: 0-380-78714-8
www.avonbooks.com

First Avon Books Printing: April 1999

AVON TRADEMARK REG. U.S. PAT. OFF. AND IN OTHER COUNTRIES, MARCA REGISTRADA, HECHO EN U.S.A.

Printed in the U.S.A.

WCD   10 9 8 7 6 5 4 3 2 1

Prologue

They were back where it had all begun for most of them, in Coronado, California, on the Silver Strand. It was the annual Fourth of July reunion at the local Irish pub. Nick Stine strode through the door and grinned as he looked around him at all the familiar faces, most of them younger. The place was packed to capacity and beyond, buzzing with loud talk and laughter. Someone shoved a frosted beer mug into Nick's shooting hand, spilling a little on the deck. *I'm home*, the SEAL thought, drinking in every sight, every sound, every scent.

The "old timers" had all served in Vietnam in one capacity or another. Many had done "roll-backs" after their first tours—re-oping for second and even third go arounds in the jungle. A few had seen action earlier, in Korea and WW II. Still others had been in places and fights no one would ever know about. Most were Navy SEALs or UDT, members of the underwater demolition teams. And all of them had fought in classified operations where there were no rules, where cunning, ruthlessness, stealth and deadly precision were all that mattered. They made the difference between death and an annual reunion.

"Hey, Nicky! Hey Nick! Over here!" Duane Mallon, Stine's old friend and mentor, beckoned him to a booth in the corner. Stine pushed his way through the gauntlet, catching several friendly slaps and punches as others recognized him. He reached the booth at last, and Mallon shoved a huge bear paw of a hand into Stine's stomach. Stine caught it before it reached its target, and the two gripped hands with bone-crushing strength. Their eyes locked and they savored the moment.

"Ya musta had the flu lately, Nicky. Yer feelin' a little weak!" Mallon felt Stine's upper arm with mock motherly concern for his health.

"Naw, one of the guys at the bar just showed me a picture of your sister. It made me kinda queasy." Stine laughed before he had the whole statement out.

"What? Who did that?" Mallon bellowed as he faked an attempt to get by Stine and fight whoever had the imaginary photo. "Point 'im out to me! I'll kill 'im! It was that intel weenie, wasn't it?"

One of the two "welcome outsiders," hearing the nickname he'd jokingly given himself, glanced over from another table and grinned. Tom Dickerson had been a Navy intelligence liaison officer, or NILO, back in Vietnam. He'd collected valuable intelligence to pass on to warriors like the SEALs, making their operations more effective. He was responsible for a lot of SEAL body counts, but Dickerson had never pulled a trigger. Thus the nickname "intel weenie."

Johnny Bison, a veteran FBI helicopter pilot, was the other invited outsider. He'd commanded a SEAWOLF helicopter detachment in Vietnam, the U.S. Navy crews who flew seat-of-the-pants missions in support of Navy operations ashore. The most harrowing ones were supporting the SEALs and UDT, often dropping them into the middle of a hot landing zone or snatching them out of a thundering firefight.

Mallon and Stine dropped into the booth and ordered a round. The Fourth of July reunion was the one time all year the whole group gathered to drink and reminisce, long into the night and louder than a brass band. As if on cue, Johnny Bison and Mike Boss started in on each other with their usual good-natured bellowing. Stine rolled his eyes and smirked; some things never changed.

"Oh, yeah?" Bison growled menacingly, his black eyes flashing. "Well, what makes you think *you're* so tough?"

"Could be the fact that I pulled your hairy hide out of a downed helo swarming with VC!" Boss shouted back, trying not to crack a smile. He almost succeeded.

"Oh, not *that* again! I'm never gonna hear the end of that! Okay, so you're my hero! *Are you happy now?*"

The two of them went at it for another minute or so until Bison gripped the SEAL in a playful headlock and kissed him on the forehead. The bar erupted with shouts and laughter as they were cheered on by their friends. Stine chuckled, then tuned them out and turned back to his beer. If it was anyone but them bellowing like that, he might have been looking for the quick flash of a K-bar knife. But Boss and Bison had been good friends for close to thirty years, and they had these teasing arguments whenever they got together over brews, usually two or three times in the course of an evening.

Stine studied the men around him, his eyes finally lighting on the dark, weathered face of Duane Mallon. The two of them shared a quiet smile at the traditional antics of the younger men. And Stine felt his memory reel back over the course of forty years and more, to their first assignment together in Haiphong.

"You're remembering it, too, aren't you?" Mallon asked him. For a moment they seemed to be the only ones in the room, and everything else around them narrowed and faded. "Haiphong," the old man continued. "The beginning. A time when you were younger than they are now, and every bit as wild."

"You know me too damned well," Stine grinned. "I find myself remembering Haiphong every time we have one of these get-togethers." Boss and Bison finally quieted down, and Stine launched into the tale, usually the first of many they traditionally told at their yearly gatherings.

1

First Man In

August 1954

Death surrounded him in a shimmering heat haze,
the overripe scent of lush Vietnamese jungle min-
gling with the stench of rapidly decaying corpses
from the last battle. Refugees fled past him by the
hundreds, carrying what little they owned in bundles smaller than grocery sacks. Lines of suffering
were permanently carved into the faces of even the
youngest of them. It was mass poverty on a level
that shocked and shamed him. It was war, totally
unlike anything he'd ever imagined. In the less
than two years that Nick Stine had been a frogman,
he'd never come this close to combat. The young
petty officer felt his California-carefree attitude
evaporating like water on a hot stove. Running a
hand absently over his short dark hair, he shifted
the weight of the gear on his shoulder a little, losing himself in his thoughts.

Alongside the shock in the face of so much suffering, the overwhelming aura of death and decay,

Stine felt a strange sense of quiet exhilaration, like a thin flame running under the skin. Danger made him feel alive in every pore. And the coastal city of Haiphong radiated danger, glutted with the dead, the dying, and the thousands who fled for their lives.

They were the reason for his platoon's mission, ostensibly. After an eight-year guerrilla bloodbath, France was finally abandoning a war she couldn't win. A cease-fire had been signed in late July, 1954, and the French were pulling out of North Vietnam. The U.S. Navy was trying to assist Vietnamese refugees fleeing the devastation and brutality of the war and the incoming communist system. The Americans were dispatched solely to assist with the evacuation; no military firepower was intended to be used.

Task Force 90 was a humanitarian mission under the command of Rear Admiral L. S. Sabin. Stine's underwater demolition team (UDT) detachment, formed under Task Unit 90.8.5, was assigned to the force under Commander A. E. Teal. The detachment's job was to support the evacuation of the refugees by reconning and securing an amphibious beach landing site on the Do Son Peninsula south of Haiphong.

That was the official mission. To avoid thinking about the other one, which was top secret and making him edgy, Stine let his mind light over the past for a while as he moved down the beach.

California was what he found himself remembering, naturally enough. Just before he'd been deployed overseas he'd been a member of UDT 3, one of the old underwater demolition teams based in

San Diego, and the lazy, easygoing atmosphere of the California coast had suited him. He and his platoon brothers worshipped Duane Mallon, their chief petty officer, who swept them in with tales bordering on the legendary and trained them from his experiences in the Korean War.

Mallon had served with the short-lived special operations group, organized for top-secret missions during the conflict. Some of the UDT and SOG operations were launched from U.S.S. *Horace A. Bass*, an amphibious surface ship modified to carry over 150 seaborne commandos and their landing craft. Mallon had also conducted missions from U.S.S. *Perch*, a conventional submarine from which UDTs, American Marines, and British Royal Marine commandos launched and recovered during their clandestine demolition operations into North Korea.

Other little-known groups like the "Scouts and Raiders" and the Navy combat demolition units had preceded UDT during World War II. One of the other old-timers in Stine's UDT 3 command told him and the younger frogmen incredible stories about the invasion of Iwo Jima and the missions of UDT men throughout the Pacific Theater during the period. These men were the true "Naked Warriors," the combat swimmers who sneaked ashore with only a knife at their sides, towing and dragging twenty-pound haversacks of explosives to clear lanes for the bloody Pacific Theater Marine amphibious assaults.

UDT men worked close to the enemy, close enough to hear them talking, to smell the smoke from sentries' cigarettes. Right under their noses, usually without so much as a firearm. They were a well-kept secret until the latter stages of the Great War. And they were everything Stine wanted to be—tough beyond normal human endurance, and totally without fear.

Two other men in Stine's deployed UDT detachment had helped train Nationalist Chinese in Taiwan for reconnaissance and sabotage techniques on the mainland, and they told stories of Nationalist raids into Red Chinese territory after the Korean War had ended. No Americans went with the commandos, or so they claimed, but they always said it with a knowing smirk that seemed to hint at secrets that had to be kept from the younger frogmen. Stine and his platoon mates knew better than to press for details. But to them it was like living in paradise. They loved life in the teams. It was an exclusive profession, a lifestyle, an elite brotherhood.

And that elite brotherhood soaked up a lot of beer in the liberty ports of the Far East, ripe for the barrooms and tattoo parlors overseas. They were filled with sea stories of Hong Kong, Subic Bay, Singapore, and Tokyo, and they were just as full of themselves. They couldn't wait to see it all and do it all, dreamed as if they had an open-liberty challenge to outperform each other and the frogmen who'd gone before them. And every one of them craved that challenge.

Then the operation came. It came without notice, but Stine was certain afterward that it had been building for some time. At that age, though, he lived like a stray cat, with little thought for anything beyond the next meal. Chief Mallon explained as much as he could to the men who now

showed a lot of uncertainty in the face of the unknown. They finally had a real mission, the challenge they'd sought.

The platoon was galvanized into action, and
Mallon had to continually remind them to relax
and act naturally. Their enthusiasm would flag at
odd moments, and there was always the possibility
that it could compromise their covert mission to
other sailors on the ship. The Chief cautioned the
frogmen to keep their mouths clamped shut, and
no one was about to cross him.

The UDT detachment conducted several daylight
administrative reconnaissance missions along the
coast. These actions were completely open and
aboveboard, and they gave the platoon a chance to
view firsthand the backshore area above the high
waterline. They recorded all the information ashore
as they walked slowly along the beach, just as he
was doing now, taking additional notes that only
the UDT men could decipher. To the refugees and
civilians ashore, nothing seemed to be amiss.

The Americans were lightly armed for self-
defense, but they were instructed to avoid a shooting incident at all costs. A small security team
carried M3 submachine guns on the beach. The .45-
caliber weapon nicknamed the "Greasegun" had
been with the unit since the latter part of World
War II. They also carried knives and all the sounding and marking equipment for the offshore recons.

The harsh August sunlight and tropic humidity
made it a steambath. The UDT men had taken time
daily to bask in the South Pacific sun onboard the
ship during the cruise, and Stine realized now that
it had prepared them for more than recruitment

poster photos. The all-day recons in the broiling sun, brilliantly reflected off the surface of the Tonkin Gulf, could easily hospitalize anyone unconditioned for the mission. After each day the men were totally drained of energy and slept deeply, skin roasted and lips peeling. Under the same conditions, a normal man would have been down for the count before the end of the first day.

Stine had actually been the first man to step ashore on the first recon. As part of the security team for the beach party, he jumped from the bow of the first boat and held the nose of the rubber craft by pulling tightly on the bowline. The entire group had been on edge, not knowing what to expect from the North Vietnamese. A few days of routine reconnaissance with no problems finally let them thaw out a little. After a while it was almost boring.

Then, on the fifth day, they bumped into a communist Vietminh patrol. The entire UDT detachment stopped dead in their tracks. The two armed groups eyed each other from a distance, fingering their weapons nervously. The Vietminh looked deadly and hardened, with none of the raggedness and desperation Stine had expected of them.

Fear slammed his heart into the pit of his stomach. His detachment was obviously outnumbered and outgunned. He could taste the sweat as it formed on his upper lip, felt it stinging his eyes as it streamed down his face. There was no way he dared take his hands from his submachine gun to wipe it away. The officer-in-charge and Chief Mallon stayed cool and kept the frogmen from accidentally shooting first.

If the Vietminh were trying to intimidate them into abandoning their beach recon mission, they had failed. The communists melted away as silently as they had come, and the UDT men completed their task, cautiously. Mallon assured his men that the communists wanted the Americans to know that they were being watched and that they were unwelcome. The land belonged to Ho Chi Minh and his forces now.

On the last day of the recons, the Americans received sniper fire meant more for harassment than for casualty. There were only a few shots, but they were a clear warning. That was good enough for Stine and the others; they didn't care to get any closer. They weren't Marines, and Stine had pretty much figured out at this point that he didn't like being shot at in broad daylight. Lousy frogman tactics, for one thing.

Finally the other mission became clear. At the end of the last day of the recons, part of the platoon was detailed to go ashore after dark. The covert operation was to be a quick and quiet one. At the time, Stine didn't know why they had to go in at night. Apparently the "indigenous personnel" they were supposed to escort ashore were as unwelcome in North Vietnam as the Americans. He knew very little and was told even less. Scuttlebutt in his platoon ran wild.

Two American officers from a unit called the Saigon Military Mission had come aboard the amphibious landing ship and briefed the UDT platoon commander, a lieutenant, and Commander Teal. Their names were Lansdale and Conien. That was more than anyone needed to know. The Chief told the platoon that the officers were probably CIA. Mallon knew the CIA conducted secret operations; he remembered a few of their exploits in Korea, while he was with the SOG. Stine didn't know much about the CIA per se, but he *did* know that the Vietminh would have a hard time seeing the frogmen and shooting at them in the dark. That suited him just fine.

Late that night, the frogmen quietly slipped two rubber boats over the side of the ship with the four Vietnamese agents. Laden with weapons, ammunition, and radios, he and his platoon mates climbed down a Jacob's ladder into the small black craft. Most carried small, heavy .45-caliber M3 Greaseguns. The weapons worked relatively well around beach areas but lacked the power and range of rifles. The UDT men had little choice, having nothing else in their inventory. Their best ammunition was stealth and concealment. "Sneak and peek," Mallon called it. Their success would be measured by how well they avoided a confrontation.

They paddled the small boats the few miles toward the beach, quietly, avoiding detection. They glided smoothly, the frogmen paddling together in a silent rhythm as they crouched low in the boats to conceal their silhouettes, synchronized like a finely tuned machine. They stopped short of the landing area by about six hundred yards. Two of the party's senior members slithered into the water with deadly grace and swam soundlessly toward the shore. Their reconnaissance ensured that the immediate landing area was clear of activity, both enemy and civilian. Using a red lens flashlight, they signaled the go-ahead, and the UDT men brought the boats in.

The surf was mild and the water was warm. As the boats grounded on the beach, Stine jumped out and held the first bowline securely. The Vietnamese, three men and one woman, all dressed in civilian native clothing and carrying small bundles, leaped from the boats and ran together into the darkness ashore. The UDT officer-in-charge immediately ordered the frogmen back into the boats.

As the Americans boarded the craft, Stine clutched his bowline tightly and peered nervously into the overwhelming darkness surrounding them. He had a bad feeling about Vietnam. The people they'd put ashore must have been some sort of spy team to be left behind as the French pulled out of the North. They could have been a sabotage or even an assassination team. Stine knew that he'd been a part of something uneasy, secret, important. And he couldn't shake the feeling that he hadn't seen the last of the darkened Vietnamese coastal night.

Someone hissed his name and Stine snapped out of his thoughts. He waded waist-deep into the water as the boats turned around, and he grasped an outstretched hand. It was the strong, solid grip of a teammate, a brother in arms. In a moment of emotional turmoil, it was a source of comfort. It was the hand of his lieutenant.

Stine couldn't help carrying a certain amount of unease with him from the events of the last few days. But the strength and cohesion he felt in UDT made him feel good about himself and what he was doing, in spite of everything. For the first time in his life he had a sense of belonging, of identity. The lieutenant helped him up into the boat, and the frogmen paddled silently out into the darkness against the mild surf.

No one ever suspected they'd been there. They left no traces on the beach. The UDT men were never allowed to talk about it. They never received medals or special recognition, nor did they ask for any. The mission was treated as if it had never happened. But Stine never forgot it.

When he returned to the Silver Strand at the amphibious base in Coronado, California, he had plenty of liberty stories to regale his friends with about the ports in the Far East. He also told them about the few days he'd spent conducting daylight hydrographic recons in Vietnam in support of the evacuation. His friends were openly, teasingly jealous of his good fortune, being used for a real mission on his first cruise, but they could never understand the odd pauses he made whenever he related his experience. Stine knew he could never so much as breathe a word of the real adventure. He could only hope there would be more top-secret missions to come.

And there would.

2

On The Cutting Edge

May 1962

"And that was where it all began," Stine concluded, reaching for the pitcher and refilling his beer mug.

"Nineteen fifty-four?" Dave Stone chuckled. "I was still fighting acne at the time."

"Don't remind me," Stine muttered, and his grimace turned into a grin in spite of him.

"Don't you dare start talkin' old, Junior," Stine's old sea daddy, Duane Mallon, mock-glowered at him from across the table. "You're gonna make me feel like a fossil." Stine laughed, letting everything settle into perspective as he drained his glass. He might have been an old-timer by the standards of a few of these cubs, but Mallon had been a seasoned veteran when Stine was still an unlicked pup. And while Mallon was living up a well-deserved retirement on the California coast, Stine still felt too badly needed to leave the teams just yet.

The years after Vietnam had almost decimated the special operations capabilities of the United States. Veterans of the war were greeted with coldness by a populace that no longer trusted its government, and SEALs and Green Berets in particular were seen as snake-eating assassins. America turned inward in self-imposed exile, reluctant to become too deeply involved in any international crisis.

The defense budget was cut. Some military forces were eliminated. Operational capability was destroyed. And there had been considerable talk of decommissioning the UDT/SEALs or banishing them to the Naval Reserve force. In the end it had just been talk, but Stine wasn't prepared to relax yet. He and his fellow old-timers were the glue that held the SEALs together, and they were constantly developing new techniques to train the younger frogmen on a shoestring budget.

Stine dragged himself out of his thoughts just in time to hear one of the old familiar refrains; they were starting in on Dave Knight again with the usual good-natured ribbing because he wouldn't drink with them.

"Yeah, but a *coffee*, Dave?" Tony Franco was teasing him. "C'mon, SEALs don't drink coffee when they can have beer! Just once before you die, let what little hair you have down and climb on the beer wagon with the rest of us!" The others cheered and pounded on the dark wood tables, but Knight regarded Franco calmly and quirked an eyebrow at him in an age-old gesture that redoubled their laughter.

"I haven't touched a drop in thirty years, and I

ain't startin' now." Knight grinned wryly, toasting his fellow frogmen with his sedate black coffee. "I remember the last time too well. And you were there, Tony, so I don't want to hear it from you."

The city of Da Nang was beautiful in the spring, especially in 1962, before the large American buildup, before the war bled all over the countryside. Located on the northern coast of South Vietnam, the city held a bay that curved like an embracing arm, protective, as if it guarded a jewel beyond price. On the tip of the point, the land mushroomed into a large mountain that seemed to rise from the sea like an image of Triton. The Tiensha Peninsula on which the mountain sat was known as Cap Tourane. To the south, on the seaward side, was a place Americans would come to know as China Beach.

The high point was called Monkey Mountain. The Americans built a high-security communications site at the top of the twin peaks on Cap Tourane. They and the South Vietnamese held the top and the bottom of the rock, which stood nearly two thousand feet, very securely. Guerrillas lay honeycombed in a vast tunnel network within the mountain's bowels. Before the Americans came, the entire country had been breathtakingly beautiful. The massive buildup wouldn't come for several years yet, but the American presence was still felt very strongly in 1962 and increasing rapidly. Advisors saturated the country as the far eastern contingent of the United States anti-communist policy slowly became a reality.

The Central Intelligence Agency was running the

show on the covert operations side of the house. They had conceived and built the First Observation Group, a cover name for a unit organized for a variety of special missions. The problem was that Agency expertise in maritime raiding operations was being stretched to the limit. Vast resources had been expended for Operation Pluto, the invasion of the Bay of Pigs, which had ended up monopolizing the vast majority of the CIA's maritime experts. Cuba and Castro continued to be the primary threat focus of the Kennedy administration; they were a lot closer to home than Vietnam. The Agency was spread thin, unable to cover all their global commitments. But for better or worse, the Americans had decided to make a stand in Vietnam, and the determination was solidifying rapidly to meet the communist threat.

The Kennedy administration was pressuring the Pentagon to develop guerrilla and counterguerrilla trained forces in the military. The battles of the Cold War could not be appropriately addressed with nuclear or large conventional formations, which the U.S. military had amassed in the 1950s. Unconventional capability was the new, innovative weapon, and Kennedy wanted a lot of them to face the new threat.

The Army had produced the Green Berets in 1952, and they were an overnight sensation. A cross between the old OSS Jedburgh teams (which organized resistance fighters behind the lines in World War II) and Army commandos, the Green Berets saw a lot of action in Central and South America, the Congo, Laos, and South Vietnam. The Navy wanted a small, secret team of hardened warriors to be prepared to execute similar operations in the maritime regions of the world's hotspots. SEALs were the Navy's way of answering the call for unconventional warfare forces.

In January of 1962, SEAL Teams ONE and TWO were commissioned. The name SEAL stemmed from the acronym "sea-air-land," all elements in which they were expected to operate. SEAL Team ONE was based in San Diego, and Team TWO in Norfolk, Virginia. They had a mission statement, but its ambiguities allowed the naval commandos to form very unconventionally, maximizing flexibility to meet any threat. Comprising handpicked, experienced UDT frogmen, the SEALs capitalized on adaptability and change, but always in or around water.

Within two months of the SEAL teams' formation, two Team ONE advisors were dispatched to Vietnam to assist the CIA in maritime covert operations. Their mission was to advise selected South Vietnamese commandos in tactics and techniques for seaborne raiding.

The Americans would also assist in reviewing targeting and advise the CIA paramilitary men. None of the SEAL advisors were allowed to accompany the Vietnamese commandos ashore into North Vietnam, their main target area. The fact that the United States was supporting such cross-border operations was classified. (Uncle Sam wasn't supposed to be conducting sabotage missions in Ho Chi Minh's front yard.) The advisors were, however, allowed to lead the commandos on training forays into communist guerrilla territory in South

Vietnam. It was good duty, and HT1 Dave Knight took full advantage of it.

When the call for volunteers first went out, Knight had been in the right place at the right time. A plankowner in SEAL Team ONE, he'd been one of the select frogmen who'd formed the initial command cadre. His experiences in UDT 11 and 12 on the California coast made him an ideal candidate. Knight was one of the best frogmen in the Teams, especially when it came to explosives. Everyone knew it, and given the choice, the commanding officer had picked the best he had available for Vietnam. The CO had been in Southeast Asia himself while he'd been in UDT, helping deliver amphibious craft to the Laotian government in 1960. He'd seen the situation firsthand, and now he cared enough to send the very best.

Knight was one of four men selected for Vietnam assignment. Two others were detailed to the mobile training team that was to begin in April. They served as trainers to the South Vietnamese Biet Hai commandos. The South Vietnamese were just beginning to develop maritime commandos, and the Biet Hai were the core of one group of frogmen. In the meantime, Knight and one other SEAL would be advising and leading an indigenous group already trained as frogmen and commandos assigned to the covert CIA cross-border operation. Knight knew that his job was going to be the more choice of the two SEAL Vietnam assignments; he would be leading his men on combat forays in the south and advising them alongside the CIA. He'd never been in combat before, but he was as ready for it as anyone in SEAL Team ONE.

Knight and his partner, BM2 Tony Franco, arrived in South Vietnam in March on a military flight out of the Philippines. They traveled to Da Nang after in-processing in Saigon and received initial briefings from CIA personnel. Their mission was classified; their cover story was that they were naval advisors assisting the South Vietnamese in a coastal patrol boat project.

The SEALs wasted little time in launching themselves into their work. It didn't take them long to figure out that their job wasn't going to be the cakewalk they'd anticipated in San Diego. The CIA seemed to be undercutting the South Vietnamese chances of success. Although the objective was to sting the northern communists, the Agency kept deniability as the primary focus in the commando actions. No matter how the South Vietnamese fared, the Americans had to be able to keep their involvement secret. The frogmen launched their missions from junks and other second-rate indigenous craft, and these were no match for the Vietcong patrol boats. There also weren't enough South Vietnamese frogmen to go around. It took a lot of time and effort to train and prepare a quality commando team. Too many of them had been captured or wiped out because of the tactics involved. Attrition meant the CIA had to call on mercenaries and other foreign forces to assist in the raids.

Nungs, Vietnamese of Chinese blood, and other foreign fighters were paid and trained to supplement the South Vietnamese government forces. Additionally, strong U.S. support of Taiwan compelled the staunchly anti-communist island nation to return a few favors from time to time as political payback. On some missions, nationalist Chinese frogmen were used, all quietly arranged and paid for by the CIA. Knight heard stories of UDT helping nationalist Chinese infiltrate Red China to facilitate a steady flow of intelligence agents and sabotage operations. He even knew two Army Special Forces men who'd trained Tibetan guerrillas in a mountain camp in Colorado for infiltration operations into China a few years before. The United States actively used whoever they could in order to touch their foes behind the Iron and Bamboo Curtains.

Knight thought after looking at several past maritime operations into North Vietnam that the raiding teams were being uselessly thrown away. The percentage of groups that never made it back from missions was far too high, and most of their objectives had been targets of little consequence.

Knight and Franco began an ambitious program to rectify the situation. First they conducted a series of training exercises to get to know the combat forces personally; they exercised alongside the men, raising their own credibility as warriors. None of the CIA paramilitary people had associated that closely with the commando groups. And the SEALs ran training operations in the immediate vicinity of the small base south of Monkey Mountain.

The first thing they taught their men was how to swim ashore silently without having to come in on a boat. That alone helped tremendously to keep their operations from being compromised at the beach landing sites. Because of their close contact, Knight and Franco were able to look for the natural leaders, the cliques that developed in the teams, and divisions due to long-standing prejudices along ethnic lines in the groups. Instead of wasting time attempting to break these down, the SEALs reorganized the group into small combat teams. And once they were reorganized, the teams worked more closely together to accomplish each task they were given.

Ocean swims revealed the strongest swimmers, allowing Knight and Franco to select their "scout swimmers." Knight organized a competition and bestowed the title on the best waterborne operators, and the teams learned how to send those first two men swimming ashore to scout a landing site before a larger group followed.

Weapons training was concentrated on older weapons, all World War II vintage. The SEALs were appalled that the commandos had been given such antiquated arms and were still expected to survive. Again, the Agency managers argued that there had to be deniability to all operations. If teams were caught ashore with the latest arms and technology, the finger could easily be pointed at the United States. After a few long and heated discussions, the Agency people allowed Knight to upgrade the weaponry to a degree. It was never enough to satisfy Knight, but he felt good when he won a few of these battles. He was beginning to wonder if the CIA wasn't a worse barrier to success than the Vietcong.

In April, Knight and Franco listened to details from one of the Agency paramilitary contractees about the debacle at the Bay of Pigs the year before. The reports they heard made them sick. The entire episode was a total failure because the United

States waffled the strongest military support in the most critical hour. Knight was determined not to let that happen to his project, and he vowed never to fully trust the professional Agency people. He felt closer to some of the contractee paramilitary men, former Green Berets and Rangers who never minded getting their hands dirty.

In that same month, Knight, Franco, and their men were scrambled for a possible rescue mission into the nearby hills of I Corps, the northernmost military region of South Vietnam. Four Army Special Forces advisors had been captured by the VC when the irregular unit they were training was overrun by an enemy force. The unit was riddled with infiltrated VCs, and they turned on their American advisors when they had the chance in the field. Two of the Green Berets had been wounded and were executed when the guerrillas determined they could not outrun pursuing reinforcements while carrying the wounded. The other two Americans were dragged off into a communist sanctuary.

For days, South Vietnamese units scoured the hills, believing they were chasing the communists toward nearby Laos. But they lost the trail. Knight and his men were ready to scramble for a rescue if a location could be pinpointed, but the trail had turned cold. Finally, three weeks later, the Special Forces captives were released as a gesture of goodwill. It was discovered in their debriefing that they'd been held in the jungles of nearby hills and had never been taken toward Laos at all. The VC had hidden them right under the Allies' noses.

The lesson wasn't lost on Knight; the cunning of

the VC never ceased to amaze him. He grew to respect them tremendously. The Special Forces men were the first recognized Green Berets killed and captured during the war, but Knight knew there had previously been others in Laos. That secret information was closely held, and it never addressed the additional CIA people, including contractees, who were missing or captured. Knight only wondered how many Agency people had made that list.

After two months of preparation, Knight wanted to move into the second phase of their training plans. As he prepared, another cross-border mission was launched. He watched as another group of frogmen was sent against the patrol craft at their berths at Quang Khe in the panhandle of North Vietnam. Without American advisors to lead them, they went ashore from sampans in the Gulf of Tonkin. The demolition teams, frightened and uncertain of themselves because of past team losses, gave a half-effort and never completed the mission.

The SEAL advisors were frustrated. Knight continued his training program, working closely with the targeting people in hopes of gaining permission to lead the groups on small combat patrols in I Corps of South Vietnam. After a while the SEALs got the permission they wanted, and Knight relished every operation. It was the reason he'd become a frogman and a SEAL; it was the reason he'd volunteered to come to Vietnam. He was a warrior. He knew that if he could lead a team into North Vietnam, they would be successful.

The first three training operations in the South were simple reconnaissance missions onto offshore

islands known to be Vietcong havens. The Vietnamese frogmen did better than he'd expected, and
Knight showed them that the daily tactics they
were drilling in worked perfectly in the field. No
contact was intended on the first training missions,
and none was made. Many of the newest recruits
were extremely anxious, never having been in combat before. The SEALs knew they had to conduct
these initial operations to give the new men confidence and make them all work as a cohesive unit.
Some of the other men were veterans of forays into
the North, but the key they all still lacked was dy-
namic leadership, an important factor in making
any combat unit an effective team.

All the initial training missions justified the mod-
ification of equipment and the use of the new
weaponry Knight and Franco had procured for the
frogmen. The commando teams became more comfortable, encountering small groups of VC on the
move at night. They only observed, never confront-
ing them, but it gave them confidence, finally
knowing they could move unseen and unheard in
enemy territory. When their confidence became
out-and-out arrogance, Knight realized it was time
to move into the third phase of their training plan.

Several small ambush missions were scheduled
and planned. The teams settled down and became
deadly serious. Two of the teams made no contact
on their first ambush missions. But on the third,
Knight watched as his team ambushed five Vietcong near a coastal settlement known to be sympathetic to the communists. It was a perfectly
executed operation, nothing fancy, all very simple
and straightforward. Five VC entered the kill zone;

five were killed. Each subunit worked flawlessly, and fire discipline was good. The search team recovered a few documents and personal diaries and left the site less than two minutes after the first shots were fired. They were treated as heroes by the other teams upon their return to base, and they gloated with the praise, proudly displaying captured weapons as trophies.

Intelligence from the captured documents set up the next two ambushes, and the teams were taught the importance of returning with any information available. Rather than wandering around aimlessly, the next two teams also made contact as a result of the recovered diaries from the first ambush. Then Knight threw in another piece to the puzzle. For real intelligence bonanzas, he taught them, always take prisoners.

It was easy to ambush small groups of enemy soldiers and cut them all down. It was a lot more difficult to deliberately keep one or more of them alive and bring them home. Knight showed his men how to use tear gas to help disorient their prey. He also showed them that tear gas could be a big problem when the team came in by water. It was hard to waterproof their gas masks and all the items they needed and make sure they stayed functional. And when the team members stayed wet for several hours after swimming ashore, donning gas masks always fogged the eyepieces.

An alternate technique was to use one or two marksmen to shoot selected enemy soldiers in such a manner as to wound them in the first volley of rounds fired in the ambush. If you shot your intended victim in one of the legs, it would effectively incapacitate him. It would also be very difficult to move the victim to the extraction site. Franco taught the men to shoot their targets in the shoulder; preferably the right shoulder, since most of them were likely to be right-handed and use their right shoulder to aim their assault rifles. Hitting them in the right shoulder would prevent them from using their weapons effectively against you, yet allow them to walk unaided to the extraction site. Carrying someone cost time, and in North Vietnam, you didn't have a lot of time to evade enemy soldiers and dogs scrambling to find you.

During one training exercise, Knight made the team carry him. He was considerably larger than his Vietnamese trainees, making it a monumental effort for them to drag him through the shifting sands to the extraction site on the beach. Needless to say, they got the point. In three ambushes that followed, the teams brought back a total of five prisoners who yielded important information.

Other tactical lessons were drilled into them as well. Some of the operations in the North called for the planting of mines. A handful of others called for the placement of sensors and beacons. The commandos didn't have to know how the electronics worked; all they had to do was activate them. A handful of the operations saw them infiltrating agents into the North under a classified program called "Plowboy." Most missions simply called for sabotage or harassment. The teams drilled in the ordnance and equipment they would be called upon to use. But regardless of the mission, it was always taught that it was valuable to bring back a prisoner.

Knight began to work hard to try to break the code on the targeting. The CIA managers kept him at arm's length at all times on the objectives. He was never able to penetrate the inner circle of men who decided where the next mission would be conducted. The frogmen would go on any mission they were assigned, but Knight wanted to make sure the targets were worth the effort, and the lives.

Four months into his tour, it happened. He went into Da Nang regularly to get supplies for the teams and to blow off a little steam after his epic battles with the Agency pencil necks. On the night of the incident he'd gone out alone, knowing it wasn't smart and not particularly caring. He was fed up and frustrated and needed to unwind. He'd holed up in one of the local bars for a while, had a few drinks, and flirted with the women who worked at the bar. A few hours later he'd staggered out, dumped himself into his jeep, and headed off.

On the way back to the base, he was flagged down by a young, pretty Vietnamese woman on a darkened and deserted road. Ignoring the warning note of instinct, he pulled the jeep over. The woman seemed frantic, but Knight couldn't understand a word she was saying. She rattled on too fast for his limited Vietnamese to keep up with, and the fact that he was slightly drunk didn't help. His senses were dulled.

The woman had his full attention when he climbed out of the vehicle. As he tried to calm her down, he suddenly realized there was movement to his right from behind. He turned and saw two Vietnamese in black pajamas coming swiftly out of the darkness at him. One had an SKS carbine with a three-pronged spike bayonet extended and locked out, while the other carried a bolt-action rifle under his arm, pointed straight at him. The SEAL's training immediately translated into instinct. Knight pushed the woman to the ground with his non-firing hand and dived behind the front of the jeep as he groped for the 9-mm Browning automatic handgun he always carried with him.

The first rounds from the VC went high and cracked and whistled into the night. As the SEAL pulled the Browning, two rounds hit the front of the jeep. The engine block guarded his upper body, and he used the front wheels to keep his feet covered as best he could. The Vietcong were only a few dozen feet away and closing in at a dead run, and if they made it to the jeep, he knew they'd be able to split and hit him from both sides. Their rifles were more effective than his handgun at that distance, but as long as they were running toward him, their chances of hitting him weren't that good. He had two targets, they had one. His mind raced, calculating his odds in a fraction of a second.

The Browning felt right in his hand, like a familiar favorite baseball bat in the hands of a designated hitter. Knight waited just long enough to listen to the VC approach as he peered under the vehicle to help him judge the distances involved, and then he came up low over the hood, using it as a cover. He hugged the vehicle, minimizing the amount of body he exposed as a target. Locking both arms out, he steadied the pistol on the hood of the jeep.

He couldn't see the front sight of the weapon

well enough in the darkness to focus for an aimed shot, so he unloaded half a magazine into the two guerrillas. Using each muzzle flash to silhouette the front sight, he adjusted each round. One man dropped quickly with a shot to the head. The second took five shots, and although he finally went down as well, Knight could hear his labored breathing as he fought to hang on to life. The SEAL's own breath came fast as the first wave of adrenaline coursed through him. His senses sharpened almost unbearably; he was suddenly stone-cold sober.

Just as he regained conscious and deliberate thought, his hands started shaking, and he heard the too-familiar sound of a spoon flying off a grenade. He turned quickly to find that grenade in the hands of the Vietnamese woman. Totally floored, he hesitated for what seemed like an eternity. Instead of throwing it as he'd expected her to, the woman jumped up and rushed him with it, screaming at the top of her lungs.

Knight immediately drew down on her and unloaded five more rounds, dropping her ten feet away. The grenade rolled away from her as she fell. Knight scrambled and dived over the hood of the jeep as a tremendous explosion rocked the ground. His ears rang as he felt dirt pelting his face. Rolling to a crouch, he shook himself repeatedly. He still held the Browning at arm's length, looking wildly around into the darkness for other targets. Scared and shaken, he was charged and totally alert now. Seeing no further guerrillas, he quickly dropped the magazine out of his weapon and inserted a fresh one with his free hand. Fighting to still his breathing, he looked around one more time. Nothing moved. All three VC were dead. Knight was still alive.

He knew he needed to get out of the immediate area. All four tires on the jeep were still inflated, and the vehicle started without a problem. He sped off toward the base. His legs were weak, and he felt slightly sick. He reported the incident, and later intelligence uncovered the fact that he and Franco both had bounties on their heads. The Vietcong saw the potent frogman force they were building, and they wanted it stopped.

And Knight came to a chilling realization, unable to wrench the image of the kamikaze Vietnamese woman from his mind. If the VC were that committed to their goals, this war was going to get worse. A lot worse.

The assassination attempt sobered the American advisors considerably. The Agency finally admitted to the SEALs that an American paramilitary contract man had disappeared after visiting a Da Nang brothel two years before. Knight was furious at not having been told beforehand. The CIA managers argued that they could never definitely prove what had happened to the man; he could simply have gone into business for himself, maybe even for the other side.

After the attempt on his life, Knight paid a bonus to two of his most trusted Nung frogmen to guard him at all times. He assigned two others to Franco. Knight and Franco never left the Nungs' sight.

A short time later, one of the maritime teams was lost on an operation in North Vietnam. Nothing was ever heard from them again. The Agency people acted as if it were business as usual, but Knight couldn't be so cold. He'd worked too closely with the frogmen, and he'd come to respect them. He hated the fact that he couldn't accompany the teams up North, felt the helpless guilt of a father who was unable to do the most he could for his sons. There was an emotional attachment forming there, and that was something the Agency men repeatedly cautioned him about. The commando team disappeared, and a single intelligence report later indicated that some of the men had been captured and transferred to a large, French-made prison in downtown Hanoi, called Hoa Lo. Knight knew it would be a long time before they were freed, if they were ever freed at all. He began to feel the first pangs of bitterness.

At the end of the six-month tour, two more SEALs, BM1 Julius Conrad and OS2 Jerry Eagle, rotated into the advisory positions. Knight and Franco had a lot of recommendations before they left the country, both for their teammates and for the CIA. They believed the South Vietnamese needed to consolidate their maritime commando forces into one unit. And they knew the targeting and mobility for the teams going into North Vietnam had to change. They recommended the use of torpedo patrol craft, similar to the PT boats used in the Pacific in World War II to increase mobility. They also recommended that Americans be allowed to lead the raids.

Knight couldn't help but smile at the naive enthusiasm of the SEALs sent to replace them. It had

from the beach along the north bank of the Dai Giang River as it emptied into the sea. The city was the southernmost major staging base in North Vietnam for the communist army. The city was cut in half by Route 1, which ran from north to south parallel to the coast. Tracks of the major national railroad came together with Route 1 at that point, having drifted in from further west just to the north of the city. The Song Dun River also emptied into the South China Sea nearby, about five miles north of Dong Hoi, but it was a much smaller river than the Dai Giang. On the south bank of the Song Dun near the beach was the small village of Ly Nhon Nam. There was nothing to the north, which is why the frogmen chose that particular spot for the beach landing site. From the BLS, it was a straight shot less than two miles inland to the bridge where the railroad tracks and Route 1 crossed the Song Dun River.

On that isolated, desolate shore a half mile north of the Song Dun River mouth, two figures emerged suddenly from the ocean blackness. The surf broke foaming around them and shoved them landward with each wave as they carefully drifted toward the beach. Only the dark shapes of their heads were visible against the white of the foaming surf, but even a trained observer in precisely the right spot would have had a hard time seeing them. Their approach had been slow and cautious, and they'd held their weapons just high enough to remain out of the water after they were in the surf zone, avoiding adhesion of minute and fouling sand particles to the working parts of their firearms.

As they touched bottom, they continued to move

easily toward the shore, squatting ever lower as the gradient shallowed so that only their heads and weapons were exposed. The UDT duckfeet fins that had propelled them toward land were now removed and their left hands inserted into the heel straps, allowing the fins to hang freely from their non-firing arms. Neither man wore a face mask. It hadn't been necessary, since they hadn't used scuba to come ashore. And there was the fear that the glass of face masks might have accidentally reflected a hint of light to be seen by the enemy.

Tan and Nguyen turned their senses in opposite directions up and down the beach, straining to pick out the possible presence of another human being or animal. Satisfied after a short time that the beach was deserted, they silently nodded to each other in signal.

As one man they rose and moved quickly to escape the final grasp of the sea. The waves gripped their clothing and pulled at their feet as they lifted their knees high for the final sprint ashore. They ran across the open beach for the safety of the dunes as if crossing a busy highway, moving up the slight gradient of a tiny natural tributary from the Song Dun. The stream would help to cover their tracks and the water that dripped from their bodies. The soft rush of the waves breaking on the shore covered nearly all the sounds made by their sprint.

Both Chinese Nungs dropped to their knees side by side facing opposite directions up the beach, careful not to kick sand onto their weapons in the process. They opened their mouths wide to help quiet their labored breathing as they listened for any sound indicating that they'd been detected. Their hearts pounded, not so much from their sprint as from the fear known only in combat when you finally touch down in your enemy's backyard.

They made their preparations in silence, nervousness gnawing at their vitals. They were deep inside North Vietnamese territory, alone and totally cut off from all support. If they were captured here, they were on their own. The leaders who'd sent them would never acknowledge their mission. They would never leave North Vietnam alive.

After a moment, Tan carefully opened the dust cover to the ejection port of his .45-caliber M3A1 submachine gun and opened the bolt to make sure it was ready to fire. To cock the bolt, he had to put his right forefinger in one of the holes and pull it back. He'd kept the bolt closed while in the surf to prevent churned-up sand from entering the upper receiver and fouling the blowback bolt mechanism. It was a heavy and old American weapon, a holdover from World War II frogman days, but those same heavy internal mechanisms and large tolerances made it fairly reliable coming out of the water and sand.

His particular weapon was manufactured in 1945 and had seen better days in the OSS. It had a two-stage silencer developed by Bell Labs. A thousand of the silenced barrels had been produced for clandestine operations by the OSS in World War II. But Tan knew nothing of the weapon's history. He only knew it was reliable and learned from the Americans how to use it effectively. At close range, the Greasegun could hold its own against home guard enemy sentries. It had a thirty-round magazine and was fairly compact. After he cocked the bolt, he extended the wire shoulder stock and tucked it snugly into the ribs on his right side.

His companion remained vigilant with a 40-mm M79 grenade launcher. The breach-loaded weapon fired a grenade-type round fairly accurately, much more so than a rifle grenade. It weighed about six and a half pounds loaded, and with such a big bore, the M79 was ready to fire right out of the water. Nguyen had fired enough rounds in training and combat not to worry about using the leaf sight over the top of the barrel at night. It was better in the dark to fire at closer ranges and sight by looking over the barrel using "Tennessee elevation."

An American SEAL named Conrad had taught him that technique. If they were forced to shoot and run, the M79 would be the first weapon they'd use. It would be harder for the enemy to pinpoint in the night, possibly giving the frogmen a few more seconds to reach the water and escape. Conrad had taught them that, too. Not even hardcore North Vietnamese soldiers would try to follow them into the sea.

Both scout swimmers traveled light. They were meant to run back into the sea if contacted, rather than stand and fight. They were a reconnaissance team. Their job was to ensure that the beach landing site was clear and to secure it for the main body of commandos. Only the main force would fight it out if it became necessary.

After five minutes of careful listening and searching the darkness, the scout swimmers concluded that they'd made it this far undetected. One at a time, they opened the inflation tubes on their gray UDT lifejackets and deflated them slowly and quietly, cupping their mouths over the ends of the tubes to silence the hiss as air escaped.

The horse-collar-shaped lifejackets fit around their necks and upper chests. When inflated, they kept a man's head above water to keep him from drowning, even if he went unconscious. The devices, developed for UDT men in World War II, could be blown up orally on the left side or very quickly by activating a small carbon dioxide gas cylinder on the right.

After they secured the heelstraps of their fins to the backs of their pistol belts, they helped each other to invert the fins and strap the blades underneath the back straps of their lifejackets. They were marked men if they were caught, and they knew it, but they both carried the bloodlines of generations of Chinese warriors. Like all men in their squad, they were branded with "Sat Cong" tattoos on their upper chests. The "Death to Communists" inscription would mean certain death if they were captured.

One at a time, they moved to the top of the nearest sand dune while the other man covered. From the top of the dunes they peeked over the sand, taking care not to silhouette themselves. They peered into the darkness away from the water in an effort to locate any enemy patrols, civilian activity, or animals wandering about. The final dune line made a walled barrier against the sound of the surf, and they were able to hear inland much better from their new position. Vehicular traffic which sounded like diesel trucks could be faintly heard on what they believed was Route 1, further inland.

A dog barked from the direction of Ly Nhon Nam, but there were no lights, and the North Vietnamese night was still.

All was clear, and after ten minutes of careful, methodical vigilance, Tan turned and signaled out to sea with a blinking red lens flashlight while Nguyen continued to watch inland and up the beach in each direction. The light was hooded so that no spillage of red could be seen on the sand near the scouts to be detected accidentally by anyone wandering the beach. All the light was directed into the damp night, but angled slightly left and right each time the signal was sent to sea to cover a broader area. The scouts waited and listened. Twice every minute the signal was sent seaward to guide the others in. In between the signals, they continued to watch for enemy activity.

BMC Julius Conrad picked up the signal easily the first time. His entire attention had been focused toward the shore for the last forty-five minutes, since he'd released the scout swimmers from the lead rubber boat. He silently signaled the others to paddle toward the red light six hundred yards away. The commando team had been dropped off by Nasty boats a mile from shore. The heavily armed speedboats had brought the raiders to that point from Da Nang after a sweeping course out to sea. The Nasties were fast patrol and torpedo, or PTFs, which had been designed and built in the 1950s. They resembled the PT boats which had raided and torpedoed Japanese shipping during World War II.

The first two PTFs came from old stock in the United States and were gasoline powered. They'd finally been transferred to Subic Bay in the Philippines in December of 1963, after several Vietnam raiding operations foundered and the need for such craft was identified. Subsequent purchases were made of an aluminum-hulled Norwegian vessel. By mid-1964, several were in service in Vietnam carrying commando teams into the North. Their forty-plus-knots speed and nearly one-thousand-mile range made them a good choice for the coastal raiders. They were a vast improvement to launching operations from Vietnamese junks, the typical method of insertion and extraction before the Nasties, back when the CIA ran the missions on Conrad's first Vietnam tour.

On this operation, the final ten miles were conducted at low speed straight from the sea to avoid detection. It was the large wake that the craft kicked up at high speed that would be most obviously detected on radar. The Nasties had withdrawn quietly to sea after they'd let off the commandos, remaining on-station for emergency extraction and fire support.

From the rubber boats, Conrad now guided on the intermittent red light signals sent by the scout swimmers ashore. So far the team was performing well. Conrad allowed himself a ghost of a smile. He'd devoted a lot of time to their training along the beaches near the base at Da Nang in South Vietnam. This was his team's furthest mission inland into the North to date. The risk was considerable, and he knew that if he personally was caught or killed, no one but the NVA would know, a thought that cast a chill breath over a heat-glazed night.

The commandos didn't expect to go up against

any hardcore NVA soldiers at the target, just a few well-trained home guard troops. But the commando raids conducted by the South Vietnamese and Americans that year, code-named "34 Alpha" and referred to as "Timberlake," had increasingly stiffened communist resolve. It was becoming harder to penetrate the coastline on each raid. Conrad and the other SEAL advisors were never authorized ashore with the South Vietnamese and other indigenous frogmen into North Vietnam. The Nasties were crewed by Norwegian mercenaries that the Agency had hired for their skill with the craft. Often, they were the only "round eyes" to go north with the commando teams, although the SEALs accompanied the men whenever they could, staying aboard the Nasties and gritting their teeth in frustration.

This mission created a special problem. The explosives expert from the Agency on this operation was a European contractee, not an American. The Nungs had never worked with the mercenary before, and there was no operational chemistry between them in the field. There was no operational feeling at all. The mission required the Frenchman's special talents because of his previous experience with the specially constructed Agency demolition charge and initiator. Additionally, the former Legionnaire had worked in this area many times before, during the French Indochina War in the early fifties.

The CIA didn't want to risk losing the Frenchman ashore. He could reveal too much about specialized explosive techniques which had taken years to develop. The Agency planned on using a lot of those techniques in the upcoming hostilities, and they didn't want to broadcast all their best methods to others, not even to the U.S. military. The CIA didn't want their techniques turned against them in this or any of the dozen other guerrilla wars fought at any given time around the world. To get the man securely to the target would take a well-trained indigenous team. Conrad's was the best at Monkey Mountain, but it would take the American's leadership to control the Nungs this far north, where sane men never ventured unless they had supersonic F-4s strapped to their backs. Few teams ever got out of the North undetected, and a lot never even got to their targets in early 1964.

The CIA had been in charge of such operations in the early sixties, but the Military Assistance Command, Vietnam had taken over that February. MACV created a studies and observation group to handle all covert cross-border and specialized operations. The 34 Alpha missions were a small part of the black side of the war. The CIA was still involved and had representation in MACV-SOG, providing intelligence, logistics, and supplies, and in some cases, mercenaries.

Although they studied and observed the NVA frequently, their real missions were special operations of the most dangerous kind. The Agency needed the SEALs in all their maritime raiding projects worldwide. Conrad had even heard that two of his friends in SEAL Team TWO were helping the Agency train Cuban exiles to run similar missions against Castro's Cuba from bases in the Florida Keys. The CIA was a busy organization.

Conrad knew a few SEALs and UDT men from the East Coast who'd actually done hydrographic reconnaissance and other missions into Cuba. They'd been there. The Agency definitely needed the experience of men like that.

As the year progressed, few over-the-beach commando teams were completing their missions into North Vietnam with the results the United States had hoped. The 34 Alpha raids had been a slow starter and had already precipitated a confrontation in the Tonkin Gulf between American and North Vietnamese naval forces during the summer. In August, the North Vietnamese had been chasing some of MACV-SOG's Nasties out to sea after a commando raid when they had turned and attacked U.S.S. *Maddox* and U.S.S. *Turner Joy*.

The White House now felt it was time to put the screws to the NVA. The Commander in Chief, Pacific, the senior military officer charged with operations in the Pacific Theater, badly wanted Conrad's mission and others like it completed. Only cumulative successful strikes would produce the political results the White House desired. On this mission, the Agency had also dropped a subtle hint to the American advisor. If the team ran into big trouble, the Frenchman was not to be captured alive. Conrad was expected to ensure that result.

MACV-SOG's operations department never batted an eye. It made Conrad wonder what they'd instructed the Frenchman to do about him.

He could only think of him as the Frenchman. Giving him a name made it too personal. It was easier to be cold. He'd have to watch his back all the way through the mission. All these factors resulted in the American SEAL being reluctantly sanctioned ashore. Just this one time.

Conrad was one of the most trusted SEALs that had worked in MACV-SOG and with the Agency. This was his second tour in Vietnam, his first having been as an advisor in late 1962 and early 1963, when the CIA ran the operations. He'd established a lot of credibility, and it made a difference when the MACV-SOG needed someone to go in with the Frenchman.

The initial training undergone by the Nungs was similar to Conrad's. First came underwater demolition training and acceptance into a Vietnamese UDT. Attrition among the South Vietnamese was almost as bad as in American training. Fifty to seventy percent of all trainees never graduated. The ones who did were trainable. But such small teams had a hard time keeping up with the fast pace and casualties of sustained combat operations.

Conrad had ten years under his belt as a U.S. Navy frogman, a lot more than any of his indigenous team. He'd completed several years in UDTs 11 and 12 based at the naval amphibious base at Coronado in San Diego with a lot of cruise time in the western Pacific and all around the Orient. When SEAL Team ONE was commissioned in January 1962 he'd been a plankowner, one of the first handpicked U.S. Navy SEALs. He'd been one of the first SEALs to help train South Vietnamese frogmen, called the Lien Doc Nguoi Nhia, or "soldiers who fight under the sea." Following selection as an LDNN, the South Vietnamese frogmen who showed the most promise in the field were skimmed off the SVN Navy for MACV-SOG. Conrad's was the only all ethnic Chinese Nung team.

Team Hun was their radio call sign. They'd been put together deliberately as an all-Nung team; they fought more effectively without mixing in other Vietnamese. Conrad ran them hard but treated them fairly, and they were paid well. He took great pains to see that they were taken care of, and he'd led them on many of their training and operational missions in I Corps, the northernmost sector of South Vietnam with the heaviest infiltration of NVA soldiers. And the team covered Conrad's back, like a pack of wolves protecting its leader.

The North Vietnamese were good. They had one hell of an intelligence network. SOG advisors suspected that many of their missions were being compromised by agents near or even in their Da Nang base. There was even the unspoken possibility that some of them were LDNN. Conrad had considered all this long ago, and he wasn't taking any chances. He remembered all too well the assassination attempt on another SEAL advisor he'd relieved in 1962. It was a lot safer working with an all-Nung team. They disliked other Vietnamese, northern or southern. If you paid the mercenary teams well, they were loyal. The SEAL didn't have to sleep with one eye open, as long as his Nungs were around him.

Conrad tended to accompany the team north of the DMZ on all the operations, though he was officially restricted to the Nasties. Sometimes he broke the rules and went ashore anyway, but he made sure no one at Monkey Mountain ever found out. Some of the people in the operations department probably knew or at least suspected, but they

never asked and he never told them. MACV-SOG
and the teams were coming under increasing pressure to complete missions successfully. All operations really wanted were results, and deniability in
case of casualties.

So Conrad did what he thought was necessary
and made sure his uniform and equipment were
always stripped of any sign that would prove
American origin. And where they could, the
Agency tried to provide a few foreign mercenaries
to MACV-SOG so that there was always deniability
if they were captured or killed. It helped cut down
the odds for the American advisors on the few operations they went ashore on.

This time, he wouldn't have to break any rules
when he went ashore. But if the mission was compromised, it was up to him and his team to get
themselves out. The only support they were going
to get was from the Nasties.

The rubber boats soon penetrated the surf zone
and each skillfully caught a small wave, propelling
them into shallow water. Near the shoreline, five
men got out of each of the four boats. They quickly
released and picked up equipment which had been
tied into the craft in case they were to broach and
overturn in the turbulent surf. The raiders moved
quickly to the scout swimmers' position. The boats
were hurriedly turned around, and the remaining
crews paddled them feverishly against the pounding surf into the darkness.

Conrad linked up with Tan at the base of a sand
dune. The Nung quickly gave him a hand signal to
let him know that the area was clear. The commando team passed the scout swimmers' position,

moved inland about a hundred meters, and set up a small security perimeter.

They stayed quiet for five minutes as they knelt outward in a circle until they were certain they were still undetected. On Conrad's hand signal, all weaponry and communications equipment, carefully prepared to survive the trip ashore, was now broken out and readied for use. Although they'd come in by small craft, the commandos had kept their fins on their wrists and at the ready. If they'd met a firefight on the beach, they could always have hit the water again, but they'd have needed their fins to do it. Now that they were too far ashore to escape by water, they strapped their fins across their backs and deflated their lifejackets.

Both Conrad and the Frenchman carried silenced M45 submachine guns. The 9-mm Swedish-made weapon, commonly called the "Swedish K," was top of the line. They even held original two-stage Swedish arms silencers, but Conrad didn't feel totally comfortable with the arms on this operation. They'd be in the open a lot, and if they got in a firefight, they'd need heavier firepower. The idea here, though, was to keep a low profile, sneak in, and slip out. If there was any fighting to be done, the team was to hit at close range, then turn and run. Run very hard.

Once they were ready, Conrad glanced at the map under a small red light partially obscured by his finger to allow only the slightest ray to show. He knew exactly where they were and where they were headed. The area for a mile landward was flat, with a lot of sand dunes and scrub brush. They would pass the southern tip of a lake on their right and traverse a coastal lowland marsh for the second mile. As they moved, they would pass within half a mile of the villages of Ly Nhon Bac to the south and Xom Phuong to the north. The target was near Xom Phuong. No signal was sent to sea to notify the Nasties that the team had made it ashore. Such a signal was unnecessary and further risked compromise. The Nasties would signal Da Nang when the rubber boats returned to them and verified that Hun had made it in.

Conrad made sure the group was ready to move out after pinpointing their location on the map. When the compassman had the proper azimuth, the SEAL signaled for the team to pick up and move inland. The area was too flat to use terrain association reliably as a navigational technique, offsetting from obvious geographic fixtures which could be seen from long distances. They would have to move on fixed bearings for given distances. He'd taught the Nungs how to estimate the distance they'd traveled by knowing their stride and counting paces, but they'd never been that great at it, and movement in the shifting sands made it trickier to judge. He'd have to stay alert and make sure no mistakes were made.

He kept the Frenchman close as they patrolled inland toward the railway. Several times he caught the other man staring at him, and it irritated and distracted him a little. The movement was easy because the terrain was sparsely vegetated, but they took their time and stopped frequently to remain undetected. The compassman was right on the money, but Conrad continually double-checked the bearing while patrolling and kept track of the pace count.

The team stayed clear and north of the Song Dun River, wary of the possibility of river traffic, even at night. The vegetation would undoubtedly be thicker there, too, making movement louder and more difficult. After about a mile, Conrad saw the lowground of the lake to the north. They slowed their movement even more during the final mile. A bend in the Song Dun passed on their right. A very dim light could be spotted at the hut at the switching station. Hun had been told to expect a platoon of enemy home guard troops in the area. Sentries from the NVA security platoon were undoubtedly keeping watch on the bridge, four hundred meters away.

The toughest part of the patrol was crossing Route 1. The tracks were on the western side of the highway, so the team had to cross to gain access to the switching equipment. Conrad definitely didn't like that part. He would have felt a lot better if they'd been able to stay to the east of the main road. Setting security to the north and south, the team crossed quickly. But it was obvious from the truck traffic that the NVA were moving a lot of equipment south toward the demilitarized zone. The highway wouldn't be nearly so easy to cross on the way out after their strike, especially if things got loud and messy.

On the other side of the highway crossing, the frogmen set up a position four hundred meters northeast of the switch house. Conrad took three commandos and moved forward to conduct a leader's reconnaissance of the target. He wanted to make sure they could pinpoint the switchhouse. He also wanted to make sure they hadn't been compromised; walking into an ambush wasn't his idea of a good time. If they were undetected, they might be able to determine the location of the outside sentries.

It took nearly an hour before he returned to the main group with one of the LDNN. The other two were left to keep their eyes on the target and make sure nothing changed while Conrad picked up the team and edged them cautiously forward to their assault and security positions.

One security team had readied a Chinese Communist RPK light machine gun and an M79. They would block any reinforcements from responding to the impending attack from Xom Phuong and prevent enemy survivors from escaping the objective. The men assigned to assault the target all carried silenced British Sten 9-mm submachine guns. The other security team would block the south with another ChiCom light machinegun and claymore mines. This team fully expected NVA reinforcements once the action started, and they planned to stop them cold.

Each of the blocking forces planned to fire a volley at approaching NVA and wait for the enemy to seek cover and reorganize. In the confusion, the security teams would quickly and quietly fall back to another position fifty meters closer to the target. If the enemy regained composure and counterattacked again, the blocking force would loose another volley and fall back again. The process could be repeated, buying precious time for the assault team. It would also keep the Nung security teams from being pinpointed by the signature of their weapons fire. With such a small team, mobility was their greatest strength, and their fallback positions would bolster their courage and make them feel they were drawing closer to the main force, and security. No one wants to feel as if they've been left behind in a firefight.

As the commandos organized into subunits and prepared to move into their positions, the Frenchman readied the explosive charge. The specially designed device was considerably more potent and sensitive than standard military explosives, but the booster and initiator were really the keys. The entire package had been carefully divided and packaged to provide redundancy and ensure its survival during the surf passage and land patrol.

Conrad had never seen such a device in all his years of experience in underwater demolitions. He'd privately questioned the necessity of special demolitions, but after seeing the rehearsal shots at Coral Beach, where SOG had firearms and demolitions ranges near Da Nang, he became convinced. This target would have required a substantial amount of conventional military explosives, even if Conrad's years of demolitions work had massaged the charge. But even he wasn't allowed to be trained on the secret Agency device. Only a handful of company specialists performed such work after careful training and years of successful, loyal operational employment. Conrad crossed paths with such men only occasionally. The operational skills of the two professionals complemented each other nicely on this mission.

The entire team would have to remain close to

the target because of the number of civilians and NVA in the area. The terrain wouldn't allow a clandestine setup prior to the initiation of fire. The rest of the enemy platoon not on duty was encamped somewhere nearby, but their exact location was unknown. Conrad was unable to locate them during the leader's recon, but he guessed it would be somewhere between the bridge and the switchhouse, since the NVA was required to guard both. Conrad didn't want multiple commando elements moving around independently without knowing the precise location of other enemy forces. He feared detection at this critical point when they were penetrating the target. The Nungs were good, but they were lightly armed and deep in enemy territory. And they were afraid. The SEAL didn't want his men stumbling into each other and producing their own casualties.

He elected not to split the commandos at a release point to avoid compromise. The security teams wouldn't be able to set up in their flanking positions until the first shots were fired, but Conrad made sure they were in a position to cover their directions of security. He'd keep the team together, then immediately split up the groups after the sentries were eliminated.

The target approach was slow. The group picked its path carefully for maximum stealth. Conrad led a two-man stalking team twenty meters ahead of the main body. The two Nungs were dressed in uniforms similar to those of the NVA. Their job was to remove the guards on duty. As they slipped silently forward, they could hear four North Vietnamese guards talking in low tones. They seemed young. Conrad guessed the hard, experienced troops were being used to advise and supplement the Vietcong in the South. That was fine with him right now. He hoped the guards' youth meant that they were bored and inexperienced under fire. The stalking team moved to within twenty meters of the guards and held their position without taking their eyes off them.

Conrad slipped between the two Nung stalkers and squeezed each man on the leg simultaneously. They rose swiftly to their feet and openly ambled toward the guards. And the guards, seeing the pair emerge from nowhere, became uncertain. They stopped talking and turned toward the Nungs without raising their weapons. For all they knew, the stalkers were fellow NVA passing through the area or sent by an officer with a message. Such ruses had worked well enough during other target penetrations. When the commandos were ten meters away, one of the guards grunted a challenge which was answered by a hollow, false laugh from one of the Nungs. The reply only added to the guards' confusion. Every step the Nungs took toward them reduced the distance they would have to fire and helped ensure more effective shot placement. With multiple targets it would also be quicker to shift their fire at point-blank range.

Conrad had taught them well, and they'd used the ruse numerous times in the past. It had never failed to work. The stalkers closed another three meters, then suddenly raised their silenced submachine guns. They cut loose with short bursts of subsonic 9-mm automatic fire, starting on opposite ends and meeting in the middle. If the guards had a chance to react, they would most likely dive to the outside and try to escape. By firing outside to inside, the Nungs stood a better chance of getting them all cleanly the first time. They continued to walk forward as they fired, never breaking stride.

All four guards were down before they could react, but the stalkers weren't done yet. Moving on top of the North Vietnamese, they finished the job with a short burst into the head of each one. The stalkers had performed perfectly. Conrad was a firm believer in using silenced weapons instead of knives whenever they were available. Silenced weapons were quick and deadly and provided more flexibility. If things went wrong, and they often did at close range with the enemy, you didn't have to shift from a blade to a firearm. Just start with a gun and end it early.

Before the stalkers were finished, Conrad signaled the main body to spring into action. They immediately picked up and moved swiftly and quietly into position. The security teams split and moved a hundred and thirty meters to each side of the switchhouse. Four Nungs began moving the bodies of the guards into the brush nearby. The stalkers raised their attention from the last rounds they had pumped into the guards and immediately covered the door to the switchhouse. A separate four-man team moved toward the door to clear the interior of the switchhouse.

Before the interior clearance team was in position, the door to the switchhouse suddenly burst open and an NVA guard appeared, apparently having heard movement outside. The guard was quickly cut down by a silenced Sten, but he screamed as he was hit. He kept screaming until they filled him with a second burst of automatic fire.

That's the problem with silenced weapons, Conrad realized, as the team rushed into action. *The gunfire may be silenced, but people who get shot often aren't.* He'd seen it several times before. He'd seen confusion on the faces of those who'd been hit, the gunshot wounds often not registering on their brains and nervous systems. He'd even seen men run away after clean multiple hits.

The four-man switchhouse clearance team heard the scrambling and shouting of other NVA from outside. As they reached the door, enemy weapons fire erupted from within, and the two Nungs nearest the door dropped. The third immediately tossed in a hand grenade after cooking it off for two seconds from a prone position to one side of the doorframe. It exploded, further shattering the silence. The grenade thrower and one other Nung burst into the switchhouse and cleared the interior, signaling to Conrad when they'd finished.

Conrad swore under his breath. Now they were in *deep* trouble. Surprise was lost. NVA for miles around would be on them any minute. Time to shift gears. Slow and silent was out. Their only hope now was to plant the demolitions fast and run for their lives. Conrad bolted into the switchhouse with the Frenchman. No words needed to be spoken. The Frenchman went to work immediately. As the charges were laid, the SEAL glanced around to make sure the Nungs on the target were deployed for security, then checked the two Nung casualties. One was dead, the other wounded in the right leg and left shoulder. There was no way he could walk. Conrad swore again, very quietly.

Carrying two bodies would really slow them down, but he'd trained the Nungs for that. Leaving their dead and wounded behind would destroy their morale. MACV-SOG could never pay anyone enough money to carry out high-risk missions with those rules. So Conrad had trained them to carry casualties. If they were being overrun, then and only then would they leave the dead. The wounded were never left.

The Frenchman proved his skill; he was ready in just over a minute. He set the explosives for a five-minute detonation delay and signaled Conrad. Just after he activated the initiator, shouts came from the direction of the bridge. The SEAL instructed the Nungs to pick up the casualties and move out fast. They turned toward the east and moved out as if their lives depended on it. Not a man among them had any doubts about that.

They moved at a run, alternating carrying the dead and wounded every hundred yards. On the route in, they'd carefully navigated four different compass legs. Now they cut the most direct and easiest path to the sea. They'd gotten about fifty meters past the railroad tracks when the claymores on the flank security closest to the bridge shattered, followed by screams and automatic fire. The firefight was short and to the point, lasting less than fifteen seconds.

The security team had been instructed to move back to the beach landing site on their own if the operation were compromised. They were to use their fallback positions to give the assault team time to get out, but they were not to return to the target site. There was too great a chance they'd be shot by their own comrades, and they might arrive as the charges exploded. The security team knew the charges would go in five minutes, and they were to keep all reinforcements away until they heard the explosions. That way, they could be sure no one was able to remove the charges once they were set, and the mission would be accomplished. After a few minutes they heard the explosives blow the switching mechanisms in a thunderous eruption. That much, at least, had been successful.

The assault team continued their push to the sea. At Route 1 they kept flank security close and sat panting like dogs as quietly as they could manage, eyes shifting from the road to Conrad and back. They waited just long enough to get a good head count and to be sure they could slip across. Movement and shouting could be heard on the road to the north, sounds of the NVA reacting to the explosions near the tracks. While their attention was turned toward the railway, the assault team bolted across the highway on Conrad's signal. It was nothing more than a race to the ocean from there on.

Fatigue swept the group after the first half-mile, but fear kept them running. They stumbled over the white sand, gasping for breath. Conrad kept two men out front, leaving them out of the rotation of carrying the bodies. They would provide what little point security they could. The best security the team had now was speed.

As they heard the NVA massing to search and surround them, it truly sank in that they might not make it out alive. Any piece of equipment that wasn't essential or sensitive was stripped and dropped on the run. The stalkers who'd been dressed as North Vietnamese stripped off most of their uniforms. If they got separated, they didn't want to be mistaken by their teammates for NVA.

Sporadic fire and dogs could be heard now from two different directions. Conrad was sure that at least some of those dogs would be used to track his commandos. Not good. The dogs would be able to follow them faster than average men. The dogs needed to be slowed down.

Conrad told the Frenchman to keep the team moving, and he fell back to the rear. They'd started to reach sand dunes, which meant they had to be within a mile of the beach. He found a low, narrow spot between two dunes his men had just passed through, pulled the pin from a CS grenade, planted it, and ran to catch the team. The tear gas would linger in the dunes, and its residue would keep the dogs from tracking them.

The assault force had stopped dead in their tracks by the time Conrad caught up with them. The Nung security team from the north of the target had caught up to the main body and joined them, and they were lucky neither group had fired on the other in the dark. That left only the security team to the south still unaccounted for. Luck was still with them. Conrad got the team up and moving again as fast as he could.

The Hun moved rapidly to a point a hundred meters inland from the last dune line. The SEAL stopped them and they dropped to their knees, exhausted. Fighting for breath enough to speak, he

ordered them to set up a tight perimeter to prepare
for extraction. During the retrograde movement,
they all heard heavy but brief fighting from the
southern team as they tried to keep the NVA at bay
and draw them away from the assault team. All
the commandos had been prepared to run directly
to the east if they became separated. Following instructions, if they found no one, they had a window of time to signal the boats for a pickup.

The last gunfire from their pursuers had stopped
ten minutes ago, and Conrad was beginning to fear
the worst. Either the security teams had broken
contact and were running for their lives, or they'd
been overrun by the North Vietnamese. If they
were still on the run, they'd arrive any minute, and
the NVA would be in hot pursuit. Conrad decided
he'd better get most of the others out now.

The Nasties were contacted and requested to
close on the coast, and the rubber boats were ordered ashore. The radio hadn't yet left his hand
when the SEAL heard gunfire about eight hundred
meters away. The Nung survivors were closing,
and the NVA were right on their tails. There was
no time to wait for the rubber boats. He had to get
the others in the water before they were all discovered and trapped on shore by NVA reinforcements.

Grabbing an M79 and six 40-mm rounds from
one of the commandos, he ordered all but four of
his Nungs into the surf to swim out for pickup. The
Frenchman gladly obliged. Conrad hastily recon-
tacted the Nasties and let them know that the situation was now critical and the commandos were
swimming out. The dead body and wounded
Nung from the assault team were stripped and

dragged to the water's edge as everyone inflated their lifejackets. As soon as they were waist-deep in water, they put on their fins and swam against the plunging surf, towing the bodies and all their gear.

The minute the swimmers were off the beach and moving seaward, Conrad took the last four Nungs and moved swiftly inland. He felt better with the majority of the men now swimming safely out to sea. The men set up a 'V' shaped ambush covering a large area twenty-five meters inland from the last dune. The American watched from the top of a rise as the main body swam into the darkness. There was no sign of the Nasties or rubber boats yet; he could only pray they'd arrive soon.

Sporadic shots closed on their position and Conrad got the Nungs up, frantically repositioning them fifty meters south, to a point where he now estimated the survivors would break out onto the beach.

He centered himself among his men to give himself the best control position. About seventy-five meters inland he could hear a group approaching them, panting and talking frantically among themselves as they ran. It was difficult to catch all the sounds among the dunes, but he thought they were coming almost straight for the ambush. One of the Nungs excitedly identified a voice as a surviving member of the team. Conrad took a calculated risk and pulled out a flashlight. He flashed a quick red light signal when the voices got close. There was a pause, then silence, followed by the sound of men running and stumbling toward his position. The

SEAL stood ready with the M79 in case they were NVA.

Three Nungs burst from around a dune, wild-eyed with stark terror. One was wounded and bloody on his left side, and the other two were helping him along. His weapon was gone. One of the other two had a head wound that was bleeding profusely. None of them had any ammunition left. Conrad jumped forward and ran toward them, asking where their fourth teammate was as soon as he reached them. One of them managed to rasp that he was dead and they'd been forced to leave him.

Conrad steered them and kept them headed for the surf without breaking stride. He told them to strip off any excess equipment in the water and swim. He didn't want to litter the beach with gear, but they'd have to lighten their load to escape, so they'd drop it all into the sea instead. He told them the boats were inbound, and they'd need to signal with a flare if they didn't get picked up after thirty minutes in the water. Without losing a step, they staggered to the open beach. He couldn't be sure they understood anything he told them. They were in pure animal survival mode.

With a last glance at them he turned his attention inland. He and the last four Nungs would have to delay the enemy force for several more minutes to give the survivors and the rest of the team time to be picked up by the Nasties. Voices and shouting could be heard from several directions, all moving toward the beach. Dogs barked and bayed, and suddenly several of them started screeching as if they'd been injured. They must have stumbled across the CS grenade in the commandos' backtrail.

Other dogs continued to come. Conrad loaded a 40-mm round and readied his last five grenades. He touched the Swedish K and made sure he could grab it quickly to fire once his 40-mm ammo was expended. Tense, silent, he watched as lights from lanterns or flashlights danced in the darkness, moving steadily toward them.

Five men suddenly appeared around a dune seventy-five meters away. The SEAL released the safety on the grenade launcher with his thumb and sighted over the barrel. He sensed the Nungs aiming their weapons and knew from training with them that they'd wait until he cut loose to open up. Conrad didn't aim the M79; he wanted to keep both eyes open to retain his entire field of view. It would have been a bad time to be surprised by another group of NVA coming from a different direction. He knew the M79 well, and the group approaching them was close for the range of the weapon. He had them cold.

The 40-mm round wouldn't be as effective in the loose sand, but they didn't have any other options. They waited until their enemies were about forty meters away, and then they spotted the main group of NVA as they rounded a dune close behind. *Got you*, he smiled grimly to himself. Now he had them all pinpointed. They were following the trail of broken vegetation, tracks, and the litter of expended equipment, right into the SEAL's trap.

Conrad popped the first round, then dropped his eyes from the explosion to retain his night vision a little longer, immediately reloading. In a serious firefight it was almost impossible to keep your visual purple for long; you could try to close your shooting eye or look away, but before long, muzzle flashes and explosions wiped it out. But he could try.

As he fired the first 40-mm round, time seemed to slow around him. The roar of the grenade was deafening, making it almost impossible for the team to communicate. The world dissolved into chaos.

The first round obliterated four of the five leading North Vietnamese in a brilliant flash. They'd been too closely packed together; they should have known better. The last survivor screamed and staggered a few paces with his arms outstretched before he collapsed in a smoldering heap. The main body began to scatter as they received the next round, then spread out across the front. As they advanced, the Nungs fired slow bursts from their silenced Stens. The NVA seemed confused, unable to pinpoint their prey. The lack of muzzle flashes and subsonic 9-mm ammunition created a panic. They fired wildly in several directions.

But the Stens wouldn't be accurate enough at that range in the dark, and he and the others were running low on ammunition. Conrad fired all six rounds within the first minute, and before he could organize a withdrawal, an enemy illumination round from a mortar ignited and suddenly flooded the area with light. They were completely visible.

Conrad's heart stopped and the blood drained from his head. He was living a nightmare. They had only one chance now. He immediately turned and screamed at the top of his lungs for the Nungs to hit the water. As they rose and fled, Conrad looked back toward the land.

Two enemy soldiers sprang up out of nowhere and attacked. The first had a ChiCom SKS rifle with a three-pronged spike bayonet, and he lunged at the SEAL with a chilling cry. Conrad barely managed to sweep the bayonet slightly to one side as he shifted in the other direction. Using the same motion he swept the M79 around, slamming the other man on the back of the head as hard as he could.

As the first NVA went down, the second knocked Conrad off his feet. Conrad rolled and got to his knees. He threw the empty grenade launcher at the second soldier and grabbed for the Swedish K slung over his shoulder. The M79 sailed wide of its target, who was pulling himself to his feet when the SEAL pulled the trigger on his Swedish K. The bolt went partially forward and the weapon jammed, fouled by his roll in the sand.

The NVA raised his own SKS. Without hesitating, Conrad whipped out the .45 automatic he always carried in a shoulder holster. The NVA had him cold and would still get the first shot off. He did, with fear wild in his eyes, and missed by inches. The American fired four pistol rounds into the NVA, sending him rolling away down the dune. Then he whirled around and fired two into the first man for good measure. Breathing raggedly, Conrad looked back toward the land.

The hair on the back of his neck bristled as he saw at least three dozen NVA rise to charge out of the dunes.

Already knowing it was too late, the SEAL turned and sprinted as NVA rounds burst all around him. He immediately fell down the dune as he tried to run. Scrabbling to his feet, he ran for the ocean across flat beach, the sands shifting treacherously beneath him with every stride. At some point he'd accidentally dropped the .45. He unslung the Swedish K and threw it down as he ran; in his situation a jammed weapon was nothing but an anchor. He was in a deadly sprint to the sea. If he could make it to the water and get just fifty yards out, the NVA could never catch him. But they could still hit him with gunfire.

The illumination flares overhead still lit the night and he felt naked as he ran, bullets angrily cracking the air around him like a nest of hornets. He zig-zagged slightly to throw off their aim.

Conrad was dead and he knew it. There was no way he was ever going to make it to the waterline. He heard mortar fire impacting to the rear, followed by automatic fire. *This is it*, he thought, his heart pounding. He tensed as he ran, knowing it was useless now, waiting for a bullet to rip into him, certain that another group of NVA had sighted him from up the beach.

Then he realized it was 40-mm and .50-caliber machine gun fire coming from out to sea. As he reached the water, he saw two Nasties in the flash of weapons fire pumping ammo ashore. He saw the last four Nungs swimming ahead of him, and he caught up to them just seaward of the surf zone. Two rubber boats snatched the men from the water as the Nasties continued to light up the shore.

In two minutes, the team had abandoned the small rubber craft and were hauled aboard the gunboats. The Nasties turned seaward and sprinted, unloading several final heavy bursts toward the shoreline.

Conrad fell to the deck for several seconds, soaked and exhausted, trying to catch his breath. Then he slowly rose to check the Nungs. All were accounted for, including the Frenchman, who smiled at him a bit smugly and nodded to him. The SEAL felt a sudden irrational impulse to put both hands around the man's neck and squeeze hard. He still couldn't bring himself to think of the Frenchman by his proper name.

They locked eyes for a moment, and Conrad continued his head count. Two dead, two wounded. They'd been lucky. This type of raid was becoming impossible. The losses weren't worth the results, and the targets weren't worth the risks. This mission was too close. Conrad wondered fleetingly how many gray hairs he'd sprouted on that run down the beach.

It wouldn't be easy to replace the Nungs they'd lost, and he felt sick about the body they'd had to leave behind. But SOG still wanted the tempo of the 34 Alpha raids to remain high.

Conrad had other ideas. The firepower of the Nasties was awesome. Why put commandos ashore for missions of limited value? If it was all hit-and-run, they could accomplish a lot of missions from the boats themselves. For many select targets, they could bombard radar and coastal installations to punish the North Vietnamese for their support of the Vietcong guerrillas in the South, minimizing risks to frogmen and saving them for better or more critical operations. When he returned to DaNang, Conrad planned to forward that recommendation to the head of MACV-SOG in Saigon, Colonel Russell. He only hoped someone would begin to listen. He wasn't sure how much more of this kind of operating he could take before his number was up. And he didn't want any more nights like this one.

But he would have them.

4

Razor Cut

July 1966

"Well, we weren't the only ones using foreign con-
tractors," Jason Bracket reminisced, after Knight
trailed off. He spat a neat stream of tobacco juice
into an empty longneck beer bottle. "You remember the one we found, Dave, the non-indig?"

"In my nightmares," Dave Stone grinned back a
little sourly. "If we hadn't gotten that bunch, they
probably would have nailed us eventually. Not a
pretty thing, finding out you've got a price on your
head."

After he'd left the teams, Stone had gone back to
graduate school and ended up as a lawyer. He and
Bracket were still working together after all these
years; Bracket had gotten his PI license, and the
pair had teamed up in a private law practice in Los
Angeles.

"Well, if there's one thing I learned in Vietnam,
it's that dead assassins can't go after anybody,"
Stone sighed, warming to his tale.

* * *

There was no visible warning given before the debarkation, although the coxswain of the last boat in trail had known when the event would take place. He acted as if nothing out of the ordinary was happening and kept the craft on a steady course as the seven oddly uniformed military men leapt quickly from the stern of the patrol craft. The four boats continued ahead into the darkness and pushed steadily upriver. It took only a second or two for all seven SEALs to jump clear of the craft. Anyone who might have been watching from the shore would have missed the event if they'd blinked, but with the added darkness, the chances of anyone having spotted the team were extremely slim.

The squad was virtually invisible in the moonless mangrove night. The boats had neither glided nor slowed down for the unceremonious departure. Instead they'd kept the same steady 1600 RPM rate, and thus the same noise level, as they continued on course. Any Vietcong in the area or villagers sympathetic to their cause wouldn't be able to detect the insertion due to a change in the pitch of the engines of the riverboats. Normally when men were put ashore by the patrol craft, the engine pitch decreased and revved as the boat maneuvered to nose into the river bank. The Vietcong knew this and keyed on such subtle occurrences in their territory. With luck, surprise would favor the Americans this time by their use of the new "bailout" technique.

The SEALs jumped into the murky water fully clothed, with their gray UDT lifejackets inflated.

They immediately bobbed to the surface but remained in a low profile in the water with only their heads exposed. Each face was painted with green and brown streaks of camouflage, modern warpaint for those who lurked in the jungle and killed at close range.

Each man wore a different basic uniform. Two had dark hair and wore no headgear at all. Three of the others had bush hats with the brims cut down to keep sounds from being distorted. The last two covered their light hair with olive drab green medical cravats, once intended to be used as arm slings. They'd found their way onto the SEALs' heads instead, one as a headband, one as a pirate's headdress.

They all had green camouflage shirts of some sort, but two of them wore a tiger stripe pattern, projecting a more aggressive image. Most of them wore jeans. The jeans held up better in the wet environment and cutting underbrush than camouflage pants did, and it was more difficult for the local mosquitoes to bite through the material. And they all wore military issue jungle boots. The team didn't intend to leave the sanctuary of the river this time, so they weren't worried about leaving tracks inland. The VC tended to watch for the distinctive footprints made by western boots.

Their weaponry was a bit more standard than their uniforms. Five of the men carried M16s with twenty-round magazines. One had a 40-mm M79 grenade launcher with a mixture of illumination, high explosive, and buckshot rounds. The grenadier also carried a 9-mm Smith and Wesson M76 submachine gun with two twenty-round magazines. Though the magazines were taped end-to-end, the open end of the second magazine was covered with a condom to keep mud from fouling it. The last man carried an Ithaca 12-gauge pump-action riot shotgun. The Ithaca was devastating at close range in the open. Only two others also carried handguns, favoring the simplicity of a .357 magnum for more firepower in open-field fighting. Although they swam abreast for the mangroves on the bank, they didn't intend to move inland into the swamp or the jungle beyond. This was a river ambush.

The Rung Sat Special Zone (RSSZ) was a huge mangrove swamp southeast of Saigon. Oceangoing freighters could reach the capital city by traversing the main channels running down to the South China Sea. But all these river channels passed through the RSSZ, and the area was a barren wasteland, the perfect haven for Vietcong as well. Shipping constantly came under rocket and small arms attack as the guerrillas harassed and interdicted shipping and vital commerce. Small boat traffic was often boarded and seized or "taxed" by communists.

It was a wild and foreboding place, thick with mud and strong tidal currents that could sweep soldiers away suddenly and without warning. Large mangrove roots made patrolling extremely difficult. The South Vietnamese Army didn't care to patrol the RSSZ any more than the Americans did. The area was called the "forest of assassins" by the Vietnamese. It was impossible to conceal large troop sweeps through the area; they lumbered under heavy loads and became encumbered by the terrain and mud. Conventional tactics had proved unsuccessful against the small mobile guerrilla forces who slipped through the RSSZ like wraiths.

Finally, in early 1966, the U.S. Navy had offered a solution. Using small, unconventional teams of SEAL commandos, the Navy hoped to strike back at the VC in their own safe havens using hit-and-run tactics to match those of the guerrillas. SEAL Team ONE in San Diego deployed a pilot group of three officers and fifteen enlisted to the area. John Sims, their commanding officer, organized the men into squads for combat missions in the area. Based at Nha Be on the edge of the RSSZ, the seven-man units launched nocturnal operations against the communists.

At first, smaller sections of three and four men set up listening posts throughout the area to gather intelligence on the pattern of VC activity. The more the SEALs studied their enemies, the more they came to respect their cunning. It would take continual intelligence updates, constant modifications to routines, tactics, and techniques, and a lot more cunning to outfox the VC.

So far, the direct action squads of SEALs had been operating in the area for six months, and in that time the VC discovered there was a new, deadly presence in their haven. They weren't sure exactly who these men were, but they began to recognize them by such trademarks as their facial paint. The word was out that the "Green Faces" were hunting them. In July, the SEAL detachment had been expanded to include more SEALs for ambush teams.

The squad on this operation was after a specific prey. Recently the VC had utilized one or more guerrilla teams armed with rockets to attack the Saigon shipping. The guerrilla rocket teams were seriously hampering ship and boat traffic. It was time to hunt the VC teams down and put them out of business. Stone's squad believed they could catch the Vietcong on the move in an ambush of their own design. The operation was dubbed "Razor Cut."

Ambush was a major tactic for the SEAL squads. It adhered to simplicity and the element of surprise, both crucial factors in any successful military operation. It was also a bold and devastatingly effective technique. Nothing struck fear into an enemy more than coming under intense and unexpected attack in an area he believed to be safe. The SEALs knew that the major mode of transportation in the RSSZ was small boats. They intended to lay up along the banks and wait in all-night positions to hit their enemies as they slipped around in the dark.

The VC moved at night to set up their rocket teams for the next day's shipping. The squad had tracked the pattern of guerrilla attacks over the last few months. In the area of the current mission, another platoon had operated until July before rotating back to San Diego, and they'd kept detailed notes on their missions and the patterns of the guerrilla raids. And Stone's squad had added considerably to that intelligence. The bail-out technique used to insert from the patrol craft would, they hoped, give them the added edge they needed.

Lieutenant Junior Grade Dave Stone slowed his kick as he closed on the bank. His men immediately lined up on him as he made for the shore, just as they'd rehearsed. Stone wanted to get out of the main current in the middle of the river as quickly as possible, not wanting to be swept too far downstream. He'd selected the ambush site well, a sharp bend in the river. The SEALs swam for the inside shoreline of the bend. The current wouldn't be as swift on the inside riverbank as it would have been on the outside. And the curve was sharp enough that seven men could cover both upstream and downstream approaches with their own eyes, once in position.

For the moment they were still highly vulnerable, all the more reason to get to shore quickly. The river was a danger area, and the further out they were, the more they'd be exposed to enemy fire. If by some freak chance an enemy force had seen them enter the water, or if the operation had been compromised back at Nha Be, the VC could be waiting ashore. As they closed on the bank, Stone spread the men out abreast of him. They touched down to find cloying mud underfoot, but they steadied themselves enough to hold their weapons chest high, out of the water.

With an ease born of long experience, they cleared the water from their barrels and chambered rounds as quietly as possible. If they needed to fire, water in the small 5.56-mm bores of their M16s would create tremendous instantaneous pressure, blowing the upper receiver apart and almost certainly injuring the firer. Stone didn't want any of his men eating an M16 charging handle. The chambers of all their weapons had to be fully cleared to allow the water to drain out. Within seconds, all the weapons were clear and pointed at the bank a few feet away. They opened their mouths to quiet their labored breathing from the swim.

Stone let his eyes light on each of his men, making sure they were alert and ready for instant action. All eyes but his were scouring the jungle ashore for any sign of the enemy. They lay low in the water as the current swirled around them, listening for any breaks in the natural rhythm of the surroundings. The riverboats were well upstream by then, and their engine noise faded into the night, leaving only the soft swirl of warm river water current. They'd timed their swim well. Any noise they might have made would have been covered by the boats.

After five minutes of watching the shoreline, Stone sent ENC Jason Bracket, the platoon chief, and OSI Jerry Eagle ashore. They slipped forward and moved slowly into the jungle for a swift recon of the immediate area. Ten minutes later they returned and silently slid back into the water. Bracket moved next to Stone and flashed an 'okay' sign with his non-firing hand, letting him know that all was quiet ashore. Gliding back into his position without a moment's hesitation, Bracket pointed his weapon ashore.

Stone turned toward the curve in the river, which was another fifty meters downstream. He signaled the group to drift with the current until they were centered on the ambush site at the bend in the river. No words were spoken; none were needed. The squad had trained and worked to-

gether hundreds of times. Their intricate communications were conveyed by hand signals, brief,
quiet clicks of the tongue, and light snaps of the
fingers. Each had been refined during the predeployment training at the Salton Sea in the southern
California desert east of San Diego.

The squad moved as one in an almost ghostly
manner, each man covering a specific area to the
front, sides, rear and overhead. All movement was
slow and deliberate, almost gentle, with the deadly
grace of a poisonous snake sliding through grass.

Stone finally signaled them to a halt. The team
had been briefed before the mission and had anticipated his directions. Everything was going according to the numbers. No surprises so far, but Stone
knew no mission ever went exactly as planned. He
hated surprises and worked hard to anticipate the
unexpected. Each man instantly held his spot as the
squad halted the second time. Once again Stone
sent Bracket and Eagle ashore to recon the immediate area. This time the result was the same as
before, all clear.

Next Stone gave the signal for the men to move
in and occupy the location. This would be the ambush site, and the river before them would be the
kill zone. Each man moved slowly and easily, backing into the foliage of the riverbank and picking
out locations to wait in ambush. The vegetation
wasn't overly thick, but the men blended in perfectly to the dark shade of black against the shoreline. The river was brown and brackish, but not as
dark as the shore. It was easy from the ambush site
to look out through the foliage and see any river

traffic that night while remaining concealed against the bank.

The squad had deliberately come ashore lightly armed, with five magazines for each of their assault rifles. Each man also had two concussion grenades to be used on any ambush escapees who might try to swim underwater away from the kill zone. They brought a PRC 25 radio for communications with the boats, but for the moment there was no sense in using it. In order to make sure it would work when it had to, it had been tested, then stowed in waterproof plastic bag wrapping. If it were broken out early, there was a good chance the river would make it inoperable.

All the same, it meant they'd be out of touch with the boats, which were waiting for them four kilometers upstream. The boats would wait for the sounds of gunfire and an extraction call. As a backup, visual signals using illumination and flares were devised, as well as a final, absolute, "no-later-than" pickup time, called a "drop dead" time. Stone didn't feel uncomfortable with the radio turned off. It was one less distraction, and he knew the patrol craft would stay alert and ready to support them.

He turned to his left as he heard a faint click. From five meters away Bracket flashed him a grin, his teeth a brilliant white against the dark camouflage paint. He held out a pouch of Redman chewing tobacco even though he was well out of arm's reach. Stone grinned back and gave him a silent "danger area" hand signal by slashing his hand across his throat, indicating what he thought of the nasty habit of his redneck chief. He made a mental note to tell the squad not to smile too much while daydreaming in the ambush sites. Those white teeth were a serious giveaway.

Bracket was a real jewel. Stone winced as he watched him dip in a huge fingerload of tobacco and shove it into his left cheek. With a wink, Bracket tucked the Redman pouch away down the front of his shirt and picked up the Ithaca shotgun with both hands. It didn't seem to matter to Bracket that the tobacco was soaked with rancid brown water. *He's probably enjoying the novel taste*, Stone thought wryly. The duckbill on the end of the shotgun barrel, made to concentrate the buckshot into a horizontal shot pattern, extended out toward the end of the brush menacingly.

Bracket was a tough, ruthless old-timer. Nothing fancy, just hard as nails. Nobody screwed with the Chief, and he was a hell of a good man to have on your side in a firefight. He knew his stuff, and he could be relied on to bolster the squad with the experience Stone lacked. They worked well together, mostly because Stone was smart enough to listen to the Chief's advice. Bracket was one of the first men selected to form SEAL Team ONE, a plankowner. He'd already served a tour in Da Nang, up north, conducting classified operations for the CIA back in 1963. He never talked about his first tour, regardless of how often you asked. Top secret, apparently. But Stone knew he'd seen his share of action.

It was Bracket who'd first come up with the idea of jumping off the back of the patrol craft, and it made a lot of sense. He'd even conceived the design behind a silent shotgun round so that a suppressor wouldn't be required on the end of the scattergun. He didn't have much luck selling the idea until one of his old contacts in the Agency had listened to him. Now his idea, which worked on an enclosed piston arrangement within the shell, was being enthusiastically developed by the CIA.

Not only were shotguns deadly at close range, they were hard to trace ballistically, unlike handguns and rifles. That was why so many organized crime hits involved shotguns. The CIA obviously had its own plans for such a weapon. Stone supposed they wanted to have that type of close range advantage for some of their own wetwork around the world.

Stone had seen the Chief kill two VC at close range who'd stumbled onto another site they'd occupied two weeks earlier. He wielded the Ithaca with lightning speed, turning almost 180 degrees between the two quick blasts. Although he'd been in the middle of the ambush formation, his shots were right on the mark, with no 00 buck missing its target to hit another SEAL. The new guys in the squad, having limited combat experience, had hesitated as the VC had approached them from behind, where they were least expecting contact. They lay still until it was too late, and the Chief jolted into action. Bracket took them both out before they could raise their weapons, then ran down a third in three quick bounds and had him laid out before he could scream. They picked the bodies clean of documents and took their prisoner out of the area within two minutes of the first gunshot.

That was the first blood drawn by the squad. It was Bracket's cool head and speed which had jolted the squad into action. Once electrified, they'd moved out well. And afterward, the Chief had had a long, hard talk with Stone. Stone was furious with himself for his indecision. There would be no more hesitations.

Bracket backed up the officer in the missions that followed, bolstering his confidence and making sure he followed through. Bracket was like all the Chiefs in the SEALs. They either made you a warrior or they ran you out of the Teams to someplace you really belonged.

Jerry Eagle was on the far side of Bracket. A young Native American from Oklahoma, he had a lot of hunting experience, and it made him an excellent bush fighter. He covered their backs by facing the shore, but it would be impossible for someone to approach from land without the squad hearing them. Like Bracket, Eagle had served a classified tour in Da Nang and was steady under fire.

Seamen Will Pickett and Dale McDougal were next on the left flank. They'd been inseparable since basic underwater demolition/SEAL training. A pair of fighters, they'd been in moderate trouble in almost every bar in Imperial Beach before deployment. In the bush they covered each other as if they were Siamese twins.

Off to Stone's right, HM2 John Tindle waited with the M79 grenade launcher, the perfect image of slow, steady patience. He'd served a tour previously as an advisor, training South Vietnamese to become LDNN frogmen. Tindle was quiet and taciturn, but a total team player.

RM3 Bill Martin was just beyond Tindle. His

nickname was "Dog," short for "Junkyard Dog," the essence of his intense loyalty and love of fighting. In a flash he'd turn on anyone who verbally abused the squad from the outside.

Last on the right flank was AO3 Julio Chavez. A short, solidly built Puerto Rican, Chavez was fun and easygoing unless you pushed him. The man had the most volatile temper Stone had ever seen. Without warning he'd jump into the attack, and more than once his officer had had to stop him from using his K-bar knife on other sailors.

They were basically a young, hard team with a mean streak, and at times it took all the toughness Stone could muster to control them. He was lucky to have the experience and respect the Chief wielded to back him up.

They sat in the water and mud up to their waists along the bank, all silently searching for the first sign of sampan traffic on the river. The water was warm by any standard, but as they sat in it for the next few hours, it slowly sapped their body heat. Once their core temperatures lowered a couple of degrees, they sat shivering involuntarily off and on during their vigil. The mosquitoes were no big laugh, either. Funny, how such little insects could make your life so totally miserable.

Finally a branch moved, followed by a small splash on the left flank. Heads turned and bodies strained until a hand signal was sent back up the line. It had been a snake falling into the water near McDougal. McDougal hated snakes. Stone was sure he would be squirming for the rest of the night. In the distance, a flight of Hueys could be heard flying low to the south. The SEALs settled back and waited. It was the wait that was always hardest on an ambush. You had to remain alert, ready for instant action, and you couldn't allow your mind to drift too far. And you could never allow anyone to fall asleep. But waist-deep in foul water, with mosquitoes, snakes and leeches to keep you company, it was never too hard to stay awake.

Stone hadn't set up claymore mines for the ambush. The small green rectangular devices could be command-detonated at the exact moment you desired, or rigged with a tripwire. They could also be detonated using time fuse and a blasting cap, similar to lighting dynamite. With one and a half pounds of the plastic explosive known as C-4, it blasted 750 steel pellets the size of 00 buckshot in a specified direction, like a huge shotgun blast. Their usefulness was questionable in a river ambush; the team would have had to get well into the brush ashore to avoid the deadly backblast behind the mines. The water would also create a problem for the electrical blasting caps used for command detonation. Stone had thought about putting them in the trees. Maybe sometime they would leave one or two rigged as booby traps in the trees of one of their sites after a contact. Any investigating VC would get a nasty surprise. He wondered if he could tape white phosphorous grenades to the front of the mines to add to their effectiveness. Maybe another time, but not tonight.

Slight movement and a signal from the left flank. Someone else was on the river. A single boat, according to the hand signal passed down. Hearts pounded instantly. More signals. Six occupants. The boat was blacked out and being poled quietly for propulsion. With the curfew after dark and the way they were traveling, they could only be VC. The squad quietly sprang into action, switching the safeties off on their weapons. Stocks into the shoulders, barrels up. All eyes out front strained over the weapons for the first glimpse of the enemy.

Stone saw it only after the Chief had slowly shifted his shotgun. The small craft was being paddled slowly along the inside bank rather than out in the middle of the river. They were a hell of a lot closer to the bank than Stone had expected.

It was Stone who was supposed to initiate the firefight with his own weapon, but there was an exception to that. If any enemy soldier spotted another member of the squad and recognized the danger, that SEAL was immediately to shoot to kill. This looked like it might turn into one of those instances. The sampan was within six yards of the bank. Stone's heart pounded as he waited for the first shots from the left flank, certain the squad would be seen. His mind raced as he considered the possibilities if the boat were attacked outside the kill zone. This could get ugly. A single AK47 firing back at close range could stitch the whole left flank. The only cover the SEALs had was the water.

The sampan came into view. They were now inside McDougal's position on the left flank. A little closer. The Chief had a bead on the poleman at the rear of the craft who controlled the boat's movement. Closer. The boat passed next to Pickett and was approaching the Chief when Stone finally had a clear shot. If he fired now, they would have four weapons to bear immediately, and probably two others in the next few seconds as the boat drifted downstream.

Stone cut loose with a long burst of automatic fire from his M16, moving from bow to stern, hugging the weapon tightly to control the slight muzzle climb. He hadn't aimed perfectly, only looked over the top of the barrel. The muzzle flash blinded him enough that he lost sight of his intended targets for the moment. Before the first two rounds had left his M16, Bracket began pumping 00 buckshot at the vessel as fast as he could fire and work the action. His first round blew the poleman completely out of the boat, while the others took rounds from point-blank range from McDougal and Pickett. One of the bodies fired two rounds from an SKS skyward as he tumbled from the boat. Within five seconds it was over. Tindle had already pumped an illumination round overhead.

"Cease fire! Cease fire!" Stone screamed. The command was repeated by each man and all firing ceased. The Chief had already fully reloaded his shotgun. The sound of others changing magazines was crisp and brief. It was time to act quickly.

"Pickett, call the PBRs for extraction," the officer snapped. "Dog, get the boat! McDougal, watch the left flank in case there are other boats!" Adrenaline made the men a little louder than they needed to be as they rushed to recover the craft.

"Close the left flank," Chief called to McDougal and Pickett. They adjusted their positions to cover the team in the center. Dog, with a rope around his waist, hastily slung his weapon and stroked out into the current, intercepting the craft as the others covered from shore. Tindle watched the far shore with his M79 in case any fire came from the other side.

Once he grabbed the boat, Dog swam on his back with one hand on the craft and the other holding a Smith and Wesson .357 magnum trained on the gunnel. If anyone was still alive inside, he would have the drop on them.

Once against the bank, the flank security men stayed in position to cover the team while Chief and two others searched the boat. It had filled up quickly with water, with a dozen new bulletholes peppering the sides. Only three bodies were inside, facing down. Bracket trained his Ithaca in the middle of their backs while another SEAL turned them over one at a time to make sure they were dead, pulling them up by their far shoulders. If any of them had been alive, they might have held a live grenade in a last-ditch effort to kill some of their attackers. The investigating SEAL could immediately roll the man back onto the grenade so that his body would absorb the blast. Chief was ready to finish the job, if needed. It wasn't.

"Only got three here, boss," Chief immediately called to Stone.

"Chavez, use your grenades in the water, now!" Stone shot toward the right flank.

"Grenade!" Chavez called out after a couple of seconds. The team ducked down. The splash of the grenade hitting the water was answered a few seconds later by a blast and a powerful spray. The process was immediately repeated toward the right flank, where the current was steadily sweeping them.

"Watch the river!" Stone called to his team. They

scanned the water over the barrels of their weapons, but only one additional body was seen floating in the water and snagged by Martin. Bracket continued to search the vessel. Two bodies were Oriental males. One wasn't. Hard to identify; Hispanic, maybe, but definitely not Asian. A single ChiCom SKS carbine and an RPG-2 rocket launcher were discovered in the boat and confiscated, along with a dozen B40 rockets.

Bingo, Stone thought. They'd managed to nail one of the VC RPG teams that had been firing at shipping. There were a few papers which no one stopped to read. All the documents were thrown into a plastic bag. Chief and Stone turned their attention back to the non-Oriental body, stunned into silence. They looked at each other.

It was then that Bracket spoke. "Better look at this, too," he said quietly. Under the red lens flashlight, the two stared down at a few pictures of large American ships in Saigon, including what appeared to be a small aircraft carrier, and a picture of the base at Nha Be. The Nha Be photo was one of several taken from inside the base and included a shot of the SEAL squad's hut and showers. They were being reconned by the VC, some of whom must work for the Americans inside the installation.

"You think they were an assassination team?" Stone asked.

"Probably not," Bracket murmured thoughtfully. "Probably part of a team who would come some night to mortar or rocket the compound. Maybe mine the hootch or roll in a grenade at night. But I can't make the guy that isn't a Viet."

Stone felt his stomach lurch. His eyes met the Chief's.

"We got them first," he muttered.

"Yeah, but there'll be others," Bracket replied, exhaling slowly. "You can bet on it."

The PBRs growled into the area. Tindle fired off more illumination and a star cluster as the near recognition signal.

"Let's move," Stone called out. "Pickett and I have rear security. We take this body with us," he said grimly, pointing to the non-Oriental. "Everyone mount the first boat in."

A PBR nosed into the site and the SEALs clambered aboard while Stone and Pickett covered the shore. The other boats covered up- and downstream as well as the far shore. Stone and Pickett turned and were hoisted aboard seconds later as the boat immediately slipped away. The formation closed and the boats opened up to high RPM.

Stone couldn't keep the intelligence they'd collected from the rest of the squad. They were all in this together. They had a lot of time left to pull in country, and they knew they'd have to watch their backs the entire time. The VC would be waiting for them to make a mistake.

The body and the photos caused a big stir in Saigon. Stone was called to the U.S. Naval headquarters for further debriefing. He was told there that the papers they'd retrieved indicated that they had indeed nailed a VC rocket team. But there was more.

Apparently, the VC in the area had been providing security for a sapper team that specialized in waterborne operations. The carrier in one of the photos was the USS *Card*, a baby flattop which had been pierside in Saigon two years before. VC frogmen had blown a gaping hole in its side in May 1964, and it had settled a few feet to the bottom of the river. The incident had been a big embarrassment to the Americans, who'd downplayed the enemy success.

Stone was told that it had not been VC who'd blown a hole in the *Card*, but he wasn't told who had, nor could he get an answer as to the identity of the non-Oriental. Third-country nationals working for the communists as skilled frogmen would be big news to the press, hardly the stuff that small, manageable guerrilla wars were made of. Finally Stone was told that the captured documents had revealed that the VC teams had been resupplied twice by Soviet submarines off the coast.

Stone's squad had taken out some key players in the enemy force structure harassing the South Vietnamese capital. But he was ordered never to reveal the information. It wouldn't be in U.S. interests to publicize anything about Soviet submarines or foreign advisors running with the VC. Stone left Saigon knowing there was a lot more to this war than he ever cared to know. He wondered if there were many more secrets the top brass in Saigon and the politicians in Washington never bothered to tell the public.

As he became more deeply involved in the war, he found out there were.

5

Lightning Strike

January 1968

"And therein lie some of the roots of modern-day terrorism," Stone concluded. "You really can trace its early developments through a few of the nastier guerrilla tactics we saw in Vietnam."

"And if there was ever any threat special operations forces were tailor-made to handle, it's terrorism," Bracket agreed.

"Tell that to the top brass in Washington," Nick Stine muttered irascibly. Duane Mallon shook his head, and his gray eyes narrowed a fraction.

"The SEALs will be needed again," the older man insisted gruffly. "The call will come down, quickly and unexpectedly, same as it always has. And when it does, no budget cries or policies or attitudes are going to matter."

"True enough," Gary Dennison spoke up from the table he was sharing with Kevin Wright. "Look at the *Pueblo*. There were admirals who wanted to respond to that with conventional tactics, but in the end, they needed frogmen. And they will again."

The Captain looked very tired and very serious, as serious as Gary Dennison had ever seen him. In a flurry of activity, the young UDT platoon officer in charge had been thrown onto a plane and dispatched from Subic Bay. Dennison felt as if he'd been fired out of a 16-inch gun from the battleship *Iowa*. It was the twenty-fourth of January, and he was still hoping he could weasel his way into some operations in the Mekong Delta in South Vietnam. He badly wanted to join SEAL Team ONE; it had been a goal of his ever since he'd heard about the naval commandos. Only the most experienced UDT officers were selected for duty with the SEALs, and he'd worked hard to become the best of the best at underwater combat swimmer operations. Now all his hopes of supporting a SEAL patrol in Vietnam were momentarily out of the question.

He was being sent on another, entirely different mission in another part of Asia. He had no idea what was up, but it wasn't an exercise. His commanding officer had made that perfectly clear. He just hated the thought of being assigned to some staff temporarily during a crisis.

At first he feared it would be another no-notice exercise, the type he so hated to play in. But it soon became apparent that something big had happened, and for once in his life, Dennison was going to be in the right place at the right time. He'd immediately praised his good fortune, but on the long flight to Japan, uncertainty had begun to gnaw at him. He had no idea what to expect, and for the first time in his professional life, he was a little scared.

The trip had caught him totally off guard. Life in the Philippines could be like that; it was easy to sit back and enjoy the local entertainment and tropical setting. But relaxation time was over. Dennison heard the news, and it wasn't good. It wasn't good at all. An American ship had been captured by the North Koreans. Worse, it wasn't a civilian or merchant. It was a U.S. Navy ship.

The flight to Japan was a long one, and once on deck, he was met and whisked off to the headquarters of U.S. naval forces in Japan at Yokosuko. CINCPAC had ordered UDT Detachment Alpha, the administrative headquarters in Subic, to send an experienced officer immediately. Dennison's platoon was in Subic Bay temporarily, and he was readily available. He hadn't slept in over twenty-four hours, and by the time he reached Japan it was the middle of the night.

The activity level at the naval headquarters was frantic. Everyone had been working overtime under tremendous strain. The top-secret briefing was short and to the point, and so were the senior officers receiving the information. The North Koreans had indeed seized an American naval vessel. USS *Pueblo* was a small ship with a huge secret. Commissioned in May 1967 as an ALK-44, it was later redesignated AGER-2. The designation meant it was an auxiliary general environmental research ship, but that was all a facade.

Pueblo was packed with electronics, sonar, and other equipment for signals intelligence collection, or SIGINT. Besides listening to the airways, it monitored underwater information via hydrophones and other gear. Sensors charted the temperature and salinity of the water off the communist coast, all vital information if there was a need to attack or spy on a country using submarines. *Pueblo* had been caught in the act of spying on the surface, although every major country did the same and worse. As long as they remained in international waters, most countries turned their heads. It was an unwritten rule. In January 1968, the North Koreans abruptly decided to change the rules.

This wasn't the first time an American spy ship had been attacked; CINCPAC's surprise was hard for Dennison to totally understand at first. He became more incredulous as the whole story unfolded. *Pueblo*'s sister vessel, USS *Liberty*, was attacked for collecting traffic on the Israelis during the Six-Day War the summer before, in 1967. The Israelis, while trying to hide their intention to attack the Syrians in the Golan Heights, assaulted the American ship in international waters but failed to sink it. The ship survived, although a lot of the crew were killed or wounded. It was an example of how vulnerable the vessels were to a hostile country who failed to appreciate international law in relation to their own political objectives.

The fact of the matter was that the ships could collect a lot of important information through SIGINT, but against an angry and determined opponent, they were armed with nothing more effective than a butter knife. The intelligence ships were

slow and virtually unarmed; their only shield was
deception. In the cases of *Liberty* and *Pueblo*, that
shield had been a transparent veil.

Two destroyers had previously accompanied
ships like *Pueblo* in their work along the Soviet,
Chinese, and North Korean coasts, but they were
dropped because it was felt that the warships
added an aggressive tone to the missions. The risk
was considered low, and the vessels made sure
they stayed in international waters.

But there were also more recent reasons to be
alert to the Korean communist threat. USS *Banner*
had preceded *Pueblo* in operations off North Korea
several months before. The ship had been surrounded and harassed by eleven P-4 patrol boats
at one point, but the North Koreans had finally
fallen away. Repeated warnings by Pyongyang had
cautioned the Americans to halt the surveillance
operations, but those were standard and routine
threats the KorCom transmitted at regular intervals.

Two days before the seizure, *Pueblo* had been circled by two North Korean high-speed gunboats.
The crew had been unable to get through to their
operational commander in Japan for fourteen hours
to report the details of the event. The situation was
an international incident waiting for a place to happen, and now the U.S. Navy's worst nightmare had
come true. One of their ships had been captured by
a hostile country and taken into a foreign port.

There were eighty-three men in *Pueblo*'s crew,
but to judge by some of the terse transmissions,
some were believed to have been killed during the
capture. Nearly thirty of the men worked the com-

plex array of electronic collection equipment aboard. Two were civilians, and by the way everyone danced around their identities at the briefing, Dennison was sure they were either NSA or CIA. He was told not to worry about who they were working for. The crew had been removed from the ship and taken to an undisclosed location. Any possible rescue attempt would be someone else's responsibility. CINCPAC had called Dennison out to formulate a possible solution to another problem.

During the entire briefing, Dennison was sick at heart for the captives. He knew the Koreans could be vicious and brutal. Dennison had befriended several Korean UDT during exercises in South Korea. They were hard, toughened from a lifestyle and training policies alien to Americans. One had told him the story of a South Korean agent captured in the North. The man was slowly, savagely tortured and dismembered. He lasted nearly two weeks while the KorComs kept him alive for more. It made Dennison's blood run cold just to think of it.

Pueblo had left in early January from Saesabo, Japan, less than two weeks before it had been attacked. At the time of seizure it had been seventeen miles offshore, well outside KorCom waters. Now it was in one of the most heavily defended harbors in the Pacific Theater. When they finally got to the UDT mission, Dennison sat mutely and listened to the concept.

What they wanted to know from him was beyond belief. He blinked several times, uncertain how to respond. The senior officers wanted to

know if a small team of UDT could clandestinely
board *Pueblo* in the North Korean harbor and blow
up the remaining electronic spy equipment before
the KorComs and Soviets had a chance to disman-
tle it and take it off the ship.

Soviet KGB and GRU were about to get the intelligence bonanza of the decade. Once it had been
taken from the ship, there would be no way to stop
the exploitation of that equipment. A sabotage operation might render the gear inoperable, but it
could still be dismantled and studied. What was
needed, quite frankly, he was told, was to blow the
instruments to smithereens. Dennison could see by
the tone of the briefing that the Defense Department and intelligence community were desperate.
There were a lot of intelligence secrets the Soviets
would be able to unfold with that gear in their pos-
session. The admirals didn't just want the equipment destroyed, they wanted it blown sky high
and scattered into thousands of pieces.

What CINCPAC wanted specifically was a way
to destroy the gear on the ship as quickly and effectively as possible. There were ways to destroy
the vessel, but the actual target was the SIGINT
gear onboard. An airstrike wouldn't be reliable
enough. First of all, the North Koreans had prepared significant air defenses in the area to prevent
just such an attack. And a vast array of fighter aircraft had moved into the Wonsan area where the
ship was taken to. It looked like the perfect aerial
ambush to Dennison. Second, even the best results
from an airstrike would only put the ship on the
bottom of the harbor. There was still no guarantee
that the electronic gear would be destroyed. It

could easily be salvaged from the sunken ship. Third, there was no way to conceal an air attack. The government had no deniability, if they desired to have it, in order to protect the captive crew.

Dennison had a headline for the men briefing him. There was nothing on earth that would protect the prisoners now. If the KorComs wanted to hurt them, they would know the meaning of pain.

Discussions continued. A submarine could get into the harbor. Dennison was shocked. He'd thought it would have been way too shallow for such a venture. The fleet guarded its subs jealously and never advertised coming so close to a coastline. Dennison raised his eyebrows and guessed they routinely did. A sub was the best way to sneak in. But using torpedoes, the submarine itself couldn't accomplish the guaranteed destruction of the electronic gear either. At best, all they could do was sink the vessel.

What a submarine *could* do was put a team of frogmen into the harbor with pinpoint precision. It could provide a good base for a demolitions operation. Dennison looked at the faces of some of the men in the room and easily put two and two together. A submarine had already been selected, obviously, and several of its officers were present at the briefing. Their confidence led him to believe that this crew and many others like it had been in communist territory already. There were a lot of rumors about U.S. subs having penetrated the Black Sea and Vladivostok, among other places. Wonsan Harbor would probably be a walk in the park by comparison.

Okay, that was the ride in and out, and Dennison

believed they just might be able to do that part. That was a big portion of any military operation. But that wasn't the only way to skin a cat. He found out his wasn't the only feasibility mission being discussed. He was told there was another option using a swimmer delivery vehicle, or SDV. The small free-flooding submersibles were designed to carry UDT further than they could swim. He wasn't sure what the other plan involved, besides a lot of explosives. An SDV could get a handful of men right under the ship. They'd be able to hand-plant explosives on the outer hull and reliably put the ship on the bottom of the harbor. Their ability to destroy the electronic gear onboard was probably better than any strike from a distance could accomplish. But again, how could the United States be sure the gear onboard was definitely destroyed and unrecoverable?

That left only one other plan. A team of frogmen would have to sneak aboard and destroy the gear with hand-placed explosives, a lot of them, packed right on the gear itself. But the admirals made it even more clear. There was enough hot water to scald everyone right now, and the last thing CINC-PAC wanted was a harebrained scheme from some junior officer from UDT. Dennison was told in no uncertain terms that whatever plan he hatched in the next twelve hours had better be workable. Because if they received the Execute Order from Washington, Dennison himself would be leading the frogmen.

The admirals weren't asking for volunteers, and Dennison was not to mistake the briefing for an invitation to participate. All the time and money

Uncle Sam had spent training him and his UDT platoon hadn't been invested so they could run around Olongapo with tanned, tattooed arms, telling outrageous frogmen tales. He had better be able to live with the results of the feasibility plan. As the admirals saw it, the only sure way to complete this job was to put men aboard and plant explosives right on the gear itself. That would be the toughest option of all to accomplish . . . unless recovery of the team wasn't part of the definition of mission success.

Dennison was smart enough to think of that one right away, and he watched the senior officers' eyes, trying to detect a hint of a kamikaze raid. Frogmen don't do suicide missions, and these guys were obviously desperate under the current national embarrassment. He couldn't detect a betrayal, and they had managed to convince him that if the mission was launched, CINCPAC would do everything possible to get his men out. Caucasian bodies killed on *Pueblo*, outfitted in wetsuits with American weapons, could only work in favor of the KorComs in their propaganda war.

Dennison was given twelve hours to come up with a feasibility plan. If the plan was approved, the men would rehearse that night in Japan and conduct the operation the following night. Time was their enemy, and the clock was ticking. If it could be done, they had to launch quickly, before the equipment was stripped from the ship. The frogman felt as if they were on a suicide pact. Everything was happening too quickly. This was the biggest crisis the United States had faced in years. And Dennison had never felt so utterly alone.

The basic plan was already laid out. The option was to close on Wonsan Harbor, insert the combat swimmers into the bay, and allow them to scuba dive to *Pueblo*'s berth. Once located, the frogmen were somehow to clandestinely board the ship, quickly move to plant the explosives on key equipment, and get back into the water before it all went up in smoke.

The operation, codenamed "Lightning Strike," was incredibly high-risk for the frogmen. The chances of clandestinely getting into the harbor and onboard were actually pretty good, as Dennison saw it, even though the KorCom defenses were first-rate. But once onboard, he knew the UDT men had no chance of sneaking around without bumping into the guard forces. The North Koreans were too good for that. In fact, the Korean communists had a highly active frogman detachment of their own who frequently conducted commando operations into the South. The Koreans would probably expect the Americans to attack from the air with a secondary by water, and they would be reasonably ready for combat swimmers.

The frogman believed he and his men could get to the ship and get onboard, but there was no way in the end to avoid tangling with the KorComs. They could try to go in hard with guns blazing from the start, or they could try to go soft, sneaking around with silenced weapons, trying to retain the element of surprise for as long as possible. Everything he looked at indicated an alert enemy expecting an attack. It would take timing and skill to get his men aboard, and then the real danger would begin. He would never have actually said it, but he couldn't help thinking that CINCPAC needed the Invisible Man, Aquaman, Spiderman and Superman for this team.

It would have to be a fast job if they were going to live to tell about it. Surprise wouldn't last, but they needed surprise for as long as they could keep it. Then speed was the key, sprinkled with a little distraction. If they succeeded in reaching the equipment and planting the charges, they could initiate them with time fuse. That meant they would have time to get off the vessel, but it would also give the Koreans time to discover the charges and pull them off.

No, time fuse just wouldn't cut it for the charges. That meant he would have to command-detonate the explosives with the new Radio Firing Device. The UDT men would have to blow the charges while they were still onboard to ensure positive detonation and minimize the time the KorComs had to find those charges. They might be able to pull that off, but they would have to be very fast and unbelievably lucky. They needed much more of an edge.

Dennison finally came up with a rough plan. The team would have to be small. He would take five men with him. That was too many for an SDV, so they would have to scuba on their own from the sub. Six men meant three dive pairs, enough to take the required amount of explosives. Yet the team would be small enough to dive together.

Normally it would be a big enough team to carry out the wounded if they took casualties, but this time Dennison wasn't holding out any hopes of that. Anyone seriously wounded would be almost impossible to get out under the circumstances. There was little chance of them getting a wounded man back underwater on dive status.

Having studied the most recent SR-71 spy plane photos, Dennison knew that one of the forward anchors on *Pueblo*'s bow had been dropped by the North Koreans. That was their ticket to getting aboard. The UDT men would use Emerson closed-circuit scuba dive rigs, which didn't give off any bubbles. No one would see them approach on the dive. The UDT men had rehearsed this type of clandestine attack repeatedly against alert defenders and had always succeeded; you can't catch what you can't see.

The down side was that they would have to wear the dive rigs onboard the ship, since they'd need them after the strike. He expected they'd have to literally jump off the ship, go underwater and dive away quickly. It meant they'd be heavy climbing the anchor chain, and their reaction times on deck would be slowed a bit.

Each man would carry half a haversack on his back, ten pounds of C-4 plastic explosives. Sixty pounds in an enclosed space would scramble the electronics. Once onboard, they would move as quickly and quietly as possible to set the charges. Since Dennison expected to have to kill several of the guards on the way in, he expected to lose the element of surprise completely. The contacts would probably be at close range, so submachine guns were the weapon of choice, all with suppressors.

At first contact, and Dennison knew it wouldn't

take long for that to happen, fhe frogmen would switch out of stealth mode and capitalize on confusion and speed. They would fight their way to the compartment holding the gear. He charted two routes to the area from the point where he expected to gain access to the weather deck from the anchor chain. It would take only seconds to lay the charges, so long as they had a few good rehearsals. Then they would fight their way back to the bow, blow the charges, and dive back into the water. As confusion spread throughout the ship, they would swim away underwater and make for the submarine. Timing would be the key, but the frogman knew they still needed more.

CINCPAC helped add one big surprise. The KorComs really expected an air strike, so they would stage one, but only as part of a diversion. While American planes were lighting up the communist radars and turning all eyes to the sky, the frogmen might get the four minutes Dennison figured they'd need onboard the ship. It was all starting to come together, but the risks remained high. CINCPAC and the White House must have wanted this one *badly*.

Back at Subic Bay, Dennison's UDT detachment was assembled and dispatched with open-and closed-circuit scuba equipment while he planned in Japan. The entire platoon came with him, though the team would consist of only six of them. The extra people provided backups, just as each NASA space shot had a backup astronaut crew in the event that someone got sick or injured during rehearsals at the last minute. And the others would be needed to assist with preparations and the sub-

marine lockout and lock-in that would be required
to launch and recover the frogmen while the sub
remained in Wonsan Harbor.

Weapons for the team were flown in from Subic
Bay and Okinawa. The UDT detachment had no
real silenced weapons that were any good. All
those were given to SEAL Teams ONE and TWO
for Vietnam operations. Dennison told the staff that
silenced weapons were the only way they would
be able to make the mission work. The CIA had a
few flown in from a cache in the Western Pacific.
The frogman heard later that they'd come from a
secret Agency training base on the Isle of Tinian,
where certain Oriental agents were prepared for
high-risk missions deep into denied communist
countries in the Far East.

Dennison asked for 9 mm Swedish K sub-
machineguns, and he got eight of them. The weapons seemed to be in perfect condition, with perfo-
rated suppressor sleeves just aft of the front sight.
They were the best around, quiet and reliable. Six
would go on the operation, while the other two
were backups and would go on the sub. He also
asked for silenced Smith and Wesson model 39
handguns, but he was told none were available on
such short notice. There were only a few of the
S&W 9-mm automatics, and the SEALs had them
in Vietnam. Dennison knew that but asked because
his platoon was familiar with the weapon.

Instead they received eight Browning Hi-Powers
for handguns. They were all silenced, a version
Dennison hadn't even known existed. Serial numbers were absent; these must have come from the
Agency as well. He guessed that the sterile weap-

ons were provided for deniability in case things went sour. All the ammunition was of European manufacture and fired reliably even after being submerged to one atmosphere, the same conditions the frogmen would put it through.

Dennison didn't like the thought of all this deniability, but he was enough of a realist that he was prepared to accept it. His men had no trouble adjusting to the new weapons, since their function was similar to weapons they trained with regularly. The silenced weapons *might* let them do this without drawing every Korean within four hundred yards of the ship. The odds were slowly being minimized.

He decided not to take any grenades or pyro except for a few CS tear gas grenades. If they had to fight, they wanted to capitalize on confusion. Explosions other than the charges would only pinpoint their location. All the stops were being pulled out, but CINCPAC was leaving UDT Detachment Charlie, the platoon that specialized in submarine operations in the Western Pacific, onboard the U.S.S. *Tunny*, the special operations submarine, in the Gulf of Tonkin. They were needed to support operations in Vietnam, and they couldn't add anything to the operation as it was presently planned. To move them now would only delay the operation, and CINCPAC knew that time was the second enemy.

Dennison and the most experienced men from his platoon were selected for the mission. They were the best his UDT command had at combat swimmer and submarine operations, outside Det Charlie. But while the young officer had become emotionally attached to the feasibility plan, he figured the chances of it being given an execute order were slim.

Within thirty-six hours, the entire operation had been planned and rehearsed. Dennison was on the verge of getting sick. The stress and lack of sleep were tearing at his immune system. Then the unexpected happened. They were ordered to go. The mission was on.

A shocked Dennison went into high gear. He was running on pure adrenaline now. One of the most important cornerstones of UDT/SEAL training held them all together once again: Be ready anytime for a mission. The frogmen were in absolute top condition. They trained for it daily. Now, when they needed it, they were sharp and could go on less sleep.

The members of his platoon not involved in preparations and rehearsals were placed aboard the submarine and sent to sea. The sub began the transit to Korea. Twelve hours later, Dennison and his men parachuted from a C-130 at last light in the Sea of Japan. Awaiting them on the surface was the submarine with the rest of the UDT detachment alongside it in a rubber boat. Dennison and seven of his men, the primary team and two backups who'd rehearsed with them, all jumped into the ocean using static line parachutes. Once in the ocean the parachutes were sunk, and the men were picked up and brought to the sub. They clambered aboard and the hatch was secured. The submarine sank quickly below the surface and continued to close on the coast of North Korea.

Dennison and his men were on the verge of exhaustion. They were lucky to have several members of the platoon aboard to assist. All the required gear was laid out and cleaned, including the weapons they'd carried on the rehearsals. The weapons and dive gear had all been tested, then packaged and parachuted together in a bundle from the C-130 with the frogmen and recovered by the platoon members in the rubber boat. Each piece was now meticulously inspected while the first team and backup men were finally allowed to sleep. The RFDs and electronics were waterproofed and the charges were carefully constructed.

That sleep was the only thing that saved the primary team from the effects of exhaustion. They slept nearly twelve hours, although they refused the sleeping pills the doctor onboard offered them. Dennison didn't want traces of barbiturates in their systems for the mission. They would have to kill at close range, and reflexes would determine whether they lived or died. The odds were bad enough. They needed every edge they could get.

As the submarine silently penetrated North Korean territorial waters, the UDT men assembled at the forward escape trunk and staged all their gear. They couldn't afford to bang around with diving gear once the sub was near the harbor. The final closure had to be made in absolute silence, and the submarine crew would be limited in their movements during the time they penetrated the coast. It was obvious this crew had been in such a position before. They were experts at quieting the boat to the most minute detail.

A final brief was held, and the UDT men positioned themselves. ENC Kevin Wright was the platoon chief and the best shot they had. He would be Dennison's second in command and walk point on the ship. Steve Horn and Ray Bradley were the best demolitions men in the platoon, and Dick Anderson and Jose Chavez were good with their guns as well as expert combat swimmers. Anderson and Chavez were the best underwater navigators Dennison had, and Chavez had picked up a lot of tactical tips from his brother Julio, who was in SEAL Team ONE and had served a tour in Vietnam.

The Captain slowed the submarine to a crawl inside the harbor a little over two miles from *Pueblo*'s berth. They were very vulnerable at this point. He could come no closer. He showed Dennison the captured vessel using telescopics in the periscope and gave him a glance around the harbor. Dennison appreciated the gesture. It helped; seeing the lights of the harbor at night let him note terrain features and positive navigational aids in the dark.

The sub couldn't bottom out due to its design; it had to remain at slow speed for the lockout. It would circle the area of the final dropoff at the same two-mile point.

The lockout was a delicate operation. It took a seasoned crew to maintain depth as seawater was pumped in and out of tanks to offset that taken in and out of the escape trunk. To execute the lockout in the shallow depths of the harbor required a miracle. But this crew was top of the line.

The captain came forward to the escape trunk to wish Dennison and his men a final good luck. He shook the UDT officer's hand and assured him they would be there when Dennison and his men returned. Then he turned and rushed back to the control room.

The lockout went better than Dennison had anticipated. Because of the size of the trunk and the number of men on the team, the lockout was crammed into three cycles. The water in Wonsan Harbor would be a major enemy in the dead of winter, and Dennison feared what it might do to the operation. The cycles took a lot of time, but he had a good diving crew. He hated having so many cycles in cold water, but there was no other way. It was tight each cycle, and the men were cramped and uncomfortable. They accepted the almost unbearable and claustrophobic conditions because their UDT training had been so severe. After basic underwater demolition/SEAL training, you could do almost anything.

The first cycle put out two support divers, deck riggers from the platoon with extra open circuit air tanks. HT2 Dan Bateman and HM3 Larry Mason lay on the outer deck and waited for the frogmen to lock out. The next two cycles brought the primary six-man team out of the sub. The first three lay out on the deck with the two deck riggers and breathed air from the open circuit tanks they carried. In the middle of the harbor at night, the open circuit bubbles would have been almost invisible as the harbor surface was whipped by a chilling, brutal wind.

The cold was another deadly enemy to be faced. Each man was forced to wear a full quarter-inch wetsuit to stay warm. They'd been tired even after twelve hours of sleep, but that instantly passed as the harbor's frigid waters flooded the trunk and engulfed them. The wetsuits made it bearable, especially if they could keep moving. While they worked, their bodies burned calories and produced internal heat. At rest, their core temperatures slowly but steadily slipped away like the spirit from a dying man.

Their training let them eat just before a swim with no serious ill effects. They had eaten a final large meal just before suiting up for the dive to give them additional calories to burn and hold them for the long hours of stress ahead.

Wright, Horn and Bradley were the first to lock out. Dennison kept Anderson and Chavez, the primary and secondary underwater navigators, inside the sub for the last cycle. That would keep them warmer longer, and with luck keep them a little sharper for navigating the dive. Dennison also stayed onboard until the last cycle, remaining in a position to receive final updates from the captain and crew until the last possible moment.

As the men from the first cycle lay on the outer deck, they became dangerously cold. The darkness was overwhelming, and they had to struggle to relax and stay alert. It took only thirty-one minutes for the last of the team to lock out, but it seemed like hours. As they linked up, the two support divers shook their hands and gave a thumbs-up, then reentered the trunk to lock in and await the team's return.

The UDT men all swam slowly and steadily to the surface on Dennison's signal, exhaling out of their mouths to prevent embolizing from the compressed air of the open circuit tanks they breathed from. They were saving the gas in their Emersons for the dive near the target ship. Once on the surface, Dennison saw that the weather conditions were going to be rough. A cold north wind was blowing, and there were snow flurries streaking the air. It was black and hellishly cold. That was good. It might make them work harder, but it would help against the Koreans.

"Thought you guys would never come out!" Chief Wright said in a low tone, as they bobbed in the water.

"Let's get moving," Dennison said. "We need to warm up and we have to be on time."

"I'm all for that. Let's hit it!" Horn muttered, shivering.

The lockout had gone as planned, but they had to move out immediately. The cold water would quickly sap their strength. They were now in a slack tide, that time between an incoming tide and an outgoing tide when the currents were negligible. In this area, the tides ran over six feet, and that meant the currents were killers, harder than any man could possibly swim against. Even Dennison's strongest combat swimmers wouldn't be able to match the strong tide, so the mission had been planned around it. The tide had gone in, and soon it would come out. If they made it to the target quickly and got delayed, the outgoing tide would help them return back out to sea at the end of the mission, when they would be at their weakest, when they would need it the most.

The wind was brisk, creating swells just large enough to hide the men well on the surface. That would allow them to wait until they were half a mile from the ship before they dived for the final leg. Swimming carefully on the surface allowed them to navigate accurately, conserving their pure oxygen rigs and cutting down valuable time when underwater navigation mistakes might be made due to longer distances. The cold water cut down the amount of time the carbon dioxide absorbent functioned inside the Emerson rebreathing dive rigs.

But while it had its discomforts and disadvantages, Dennison still welcomed the biting cold. While his team swam hard and generated heat, they could keep themselves reasonably warm. The KorCom soldiers guarding the ship and piers would be miserable under the same conditions. A light snow blew in the wind. It was perfect. It would lower the Koreans' attention spans, and cut the odds more in favor of the UDT. The wind and hoods on the Korean parkas would mask any noise the frogmen made while boarding.

As the frogmen closed on the ship and penetrated deeper into the harbor, the surface swells lessened. The inner harbor was more sheltered from the wind. Twice, patrol craft passed within two hundred yards of the team, but they remained unseen. Finally, a little over a thousand yards from the *Pueblo*, when Dennison was certain of the location from the silhouette of the ship, he gave the silent signal to dive.

The frogmen inserted their mouthpieces and inhaled from their rigs. Twice they exhaled through their noses into their masks, allowing air from their lungs to seep out the sides of the masks. This purged their lungs of nearly all the open air and put pure oxygen into their systems. From that point on, they carefully kept their mask seals unbroken. If bubbles escaped, they could potentially alert a guard on the pier once the frogmen reached the ship. And the gas was their lifeblood underwater. The more they had, the further they could dive. Once it ran out, they had to surface or die. If they surfaced near a pier or ship, the KorComs could spot them. When gas escaped the system, it bled down faster than necessary. Hundreds of dives had taught the UDT men how to relax and retain every precious molecule of oxygen efficiently.

The Emerson closed circuit rig had been adopted by the U.S. Navy in 1963 and had been in use for several years in the UDTs. Each of Dennison's men had over two hundred dives on the rigs. Chief had nearly seven hundred. The rig contained gas and recirculating bags incorporated in a vest that the diver slipped into and zipped up the front of the torso. At a moderate work tempo, a trained man could use the rig for up to four hours, but in these cold conditions Dennison figured they'd be lucky to get away with half that. On land, the rig weighed thirty-five pounds, and Dennison had to figure that weight into what they carried on the ship climb. They could have tried to stash the rigs under the ship, but they were sure to be compromised once onboard. There wouldn't be time to search for the rigs while they were being shot at. Once they jumped off the ship, they would have to go back on bag and stay under, diving quickly away from the vessel. That meant they had to keep them on during the assault.

Anderson and Chavez carried attack boards. On them were compasses and depth gauges to allow the frogmen to navigate underwater. The men were all linked together by five separate lengths of line, each several feet long and clipped into their belts. These "buddy lines" kept the men together in the dark, while the second attack board that Chavez carried served as backup to Anderson, the primary navigator. If Anderson lost his mask or became disoriented, Chavez would immediately take over. They would surface only in a life-threatening situation. Losing a mask didn't fall into that category.

If you lost a mask, you continued along for the ride, holding on as if you were blind. In fact, you were. Each man had the attack boards attached to his rig with a lanyard. This would save time and prevent loss of gear in the darkness.

As they swam steadily toward the well-lit pier, the water around them became lighter, eerily brilliant. Dennison looked around him at the formation of combat swimmers, suddenly seeing them as suspended, translucent. The bioluminescence in the water was nearly blinding, showing as thousands of tiny green sparks streaking from the divers' bodies as they moved. The faster and more sweeping the movement of a hand or fin, the more brilliant the color.

The men dived shallow at twelve feet, stopping twice to peer out of the water. Each peek sent one man, the primary navigator, to the surface to confirm their bearing. Anderson would pop his head out of the water, exposing to just below his eyes, then immediately resubmerge, minimizing the chance that anyone would see and recognize him as a diver. The navigation was right on the money.

It was a single leg shot, the easiest dive they

could have constructed. The plan had been to offset to one end of the ship rather than shooting straight for it. The team would swim past the stern and travel the length of the ship to the bow under the pier. That would allow Dennison a leader's reconnaissance of the target, a final look at the ship before they attempted to board it, alert to any unknown conditions up to that time and confirming their final plan of action. The dive continued, and the team made good time.

As they neared the vessel, the floodlights on the pier illuminated the water more. Dennison had been considering this, and in the final hundred and fifty yards, he had the team dive deep to twenty-five feet. The water overhead covered the bioluminescence, and the frogmen slowed their pace to stir the water less. As the team approached, they suddenly slipped into nearly complete darkness, as if a huge thundercloud had eclipsed the moon. They immediately ran into a piling. The darkness was the shadow created by the pier. They stopped and sent Anderson to the surface. As he came up to peek, he hugged the piling for added concealment. They were right where they wanted to be, beneath the pier, adjacent to the ship and just off the stern.

The team swam piling to piling toward the bow of the vessel. They remained underwater and made their way carefully. Dennison went shallow with his head only two feet under the water. Although he never broke the surface, he could clearly make out the distorted outline of the ship as he looked up. He was able to count at least half a dozen guards as he moved slowly along with the team.

The pier was well lit, but he was concealed in the deep shadow, and nothing seemed out of the ordinary. The light rays were bent considerably and the ship appeared curved into a great crescent, but Dennison had learned to take such shallow water peeks long ago. It was the best leader's recon he could conduct.

Across from the bow, they stopped and waited about ten minutes. They were ahead of schedule and had to start their climb at a specific time. The diversionary air strike wasn't due quite yet. Timing was everything. During the wait, their bodies cooled quickly, and before long they were shivering. Dennison moved two minutes early, trying to warm the men up. He knew they couldn't be shaking once they were on the ship. It would be hard enough to fight at close quarters without that. With all the weight they carried, the climb would definitely warm them up.

The team swam the few yards from the pier to the bow of the ship underwater, then contoured around to the seaward side. Dennison saw Anderson measure several arm lengths from the bow along the farside hull. By crudely measuring, he now knew that the anchor chain was just beyond their reach from the hull, and they quickly found it in the dark.

On Dennison's signal, the frogmen detached their buddy lines and stowed them. They held the anchor chair lightly and took off their fins, clipping them to their sides. The attack boards were stowed the same way. Then they helped each other re-sling their Swedish Ks and waited. When the okay signal was passed, Dennison looked at his watch and

counted down the final minute. It was time. He
turned to Chief Wright, nodded, and squeezed his
arm three times. They rose gracefully, and silently
broke the surface of the water. Dennison's heart
was pounding. He no longer felt the cold.

The ship was much darker on the seaward side,
away from the lighted pier. Dennison had hoped
as much and was glad to be working in the shadows. The area was very quiet except for the low
dirge of the wind. Ambient noise of men moving
and working on the dock drifted around. The frogmen pulled their face masks down around their
necks immediately upon surfacing to prevent any
glare off the lenses.

Dennison briefly scouted the rail of the ship
overhead and then silently nodded to the Chief,
who immediately started to climb the chain.
Chavez and Anderson fell in to the end of the line.
Each covered the ship's rail with their silenced submachine guns in case a KorCom soldier happened
to look over the rail at this most vulnerable moment. The men moved quietly up the chain, slowly,
allowing the water to drain off their bodies. The
last man up, Chavez, stayed directly below the others, allowing most of the drops falling off them to
hit him before striking the water, helping quiet the
noise of the climb. It was nearly silent.

At the top, the chain entered the hull below the
weather deck. Dennison knew from the photos that
a handling line was tied off to the anchor and ran
up the chain to the deck. The frogmen used the line
for the final few feet to the deck. The line and chain
were freezing, and the climb was harder than Dennison had imagined, but the men made it to the

deck undetected, the entire climb taking less than two minutes.

The climb had warmed them well. As each man slipped over the rail, he kept a low profile and moved to the shadows behind deck equipment. Their open-bolt firing weapons were out and cocked. Dennison didn't hesitate. The four-minute clock was ticking. He signaled Chief Wright to move out.

Before the entire group stood up, two KorCom soldiers came up the ladder well to the bow, talking low. The frogmen froze in place, and two seconds later, as the guards looked up in shock at the unexpected sight of wetsuited men, Chief dropped them both with two quick, silent bursts at five feet. One lay still while the other continued to move. Another short burst and he was still. The empty shell casings from the 9-mm hit the deck like loose pocket change.

Dennison sprang into action. He signaled Horn and Bradley to move the bodies into the shadows while everyone else dropped to one knee and covered in all directions. Dennison's mind screamed at him to abort the operation right now, but his training and discipline wouldn't let him. There was no time to hide the bodies completely. The team wouldn't be aboard that long. The others held their positions and brandished their weapons for security. Ten seconds later, they were ready to move.

This time, Chief moved quickly. They would have to rely more on speed than stealth now. First blood had been drawn. The men slipped from shadow to shadow. At every turn, Dennison expected to meet more soldiers. They saw two more, but the team managed to remain undetected. Dennison was stunned. He'd expected a much heavier guard force. The cold weather might have kept them inside. One minute down, three to go.

The UDT men moved along their primary route. They gathered at the hatch to the ship's innards, and Dennison signaled again. The hatch was opened normally, without haste. A guard inside looked up casually, and saw the hatch was opened the same way one of his fellow guards would have done it. Chief and Dennison both shot the guard several times. He hit the bulkhead noisily and slid down to the deck, dropping his AK47 in the process.

Dennison covered forward as Chief loaded a new magazine into his Swedish K. The rest of the team pulled out the shoulder stocks to their submachine guns and locked them into position. Moving fast, they dragged the guard into a storage space. It was locked. They couldn't afford to wait. Dennison told the others to leave the body, and they moved swiftly toward the target space. Something felt very wrong. Even with the contacts, it was too easy. Dennison hadn't really expected to get this far.

As they moved inside, they lifted their feet carefully. Water dripping from their wetsuits made their steps squeak slightly if they moved too fast or changed direction abruptly. They sounded like a basketball team on a highly waxed court. Dennison had noted this and other fine points in his final brief from the lessons they'd learned during their rehearsals.

They made it to the target space and stopped

briefly outside. Chief covered the steel door, which opened toward the inside, while the others stacked up behind Dennison. Chief lined himself up on the side of the door with the lock.

They'd rehearsed this part over and over. While Wright focused on the door, the others prepared to enter the space. Everyone couldn't fit inside, so Dennison would lead Horn and Bradley initially. That left Anderson and Chavez to cover down the passageways to secure the team's back. They hesitated at the door only a few seconds. Chief never took his eyes off it. He waited for the quiet "open it" command that Dennison would give him once the group was ready to go. Their hearts were pounding, and they opened their mouths to eliminate the slight added noise of their labored breathing.

The men could hear talk inside, seemingly casual. Three sudden steps very close to the door instantly alarmed Chief and Dennison, and the door swung open before they had a chance to take action. A uniformed North Korean soldier came halfway out the door before he ran into Chief, and the close quarters and the possibility of bullets going through the soldier's body and hitting his teammates made Chief hesitate.

He grabbed the front of the man's shirt and rammed the barrel of his Swedish K into his stomach. The soldier grunted and went down hard, and Chief dragged him out of the doorway and into the corridor. He couldn't have made a smarter move.

Dennison knew immediately what he had to do. He pushed at the door with his non-firing hand; in his excitement he threw it too hard, and it banged against the bulkhead as he entered the room. He burst into the room and dropped to one knee, bringing up his Swedish K and shouldering. His mind was racing and searching out targets as his body automatically handled the weapon. He spotted two uniformed men, one seated and one standing, who looked in total bewilderment at the door. They never knew what hit them.

Dennison sighted over the top of his weapon and put a quick burst of automatic fire into each man. Across the doorway from him, Horn had entered and mirrored his movements. He too put a burst into each man. It was over in less than five seconds. The empty brass from the expended rounds sounded like pennies hitting the bulkhead and the deck. A haze of smoke from the muzzles of the weapons floated in the air.

Dennison forced himself out of the semi-trance he'd fallen into when he'd crossed the threshold and entered the room. He called out to the passageway and let the rest of the team know the room was under control. Instantly he realized he'd spoken too loudly, but it was too late to call the words back. They had to remain as quiet as possible and move fast.

Horn checked the Korean soldiers; both were dead. Dennison checked the time. Three minutes had passed. They were taking too long. Chief stuck his head in the door and told the officer that the one enemy soldier in the passageway was dead as well. Dennison hadn't heard Chief put a burst into the soldier once he had him on the deck. He reloaded without thinking while Chief scanned the space for anyone hiding. The area was clean. Too clean.

Dennison and Chief saw it almost at the same time. The target space had been totally ransacked. There were stripped wires and electronic garbage all over. Dennison dropped his weapon and let it hang by the sling around his neck as he stood in shock. The communists had beaten them to the punch. They'd already taken out every electronic component in the room. They must have feared an American attack would destroy their prize.

No wonder they'd met so few soldiers onboard. There was nothing left to guard.

Chief's eyes locked with Dennison's for a tense moment. Horn and Bradley wanted to plant the charges and get out quickly. Dennison couldn't think clearly. He was angry and frustrated. This wasn't supposed to happen.

He'd anticipated that some of the gear might already be gone, but not all of it. If they planted the charges, they would accomplish nothing, and the Koreans would take able to prove that the Americans had been there. The commando operation would be taunted as a huge failure as the North Koreans paraded the electronic equipment in front of the international press. The United States would suffer another humiliation. And planting the charges would take more time, now a worse enemy than it had been.

Dennison knew he had no choice. There was no reason to waste further time planting charges for no reason. The smartest thing to do was get off the ship immediately, before they got caught.

"Get ready to move out!" he ordered quietly,

grimly. He faced looks of shock and disbelief. "We have to move out *now!*" the officer hissed angrily. "Get ready! Stack up! There's no need to plant the charges! The gear's gone!"

If they got out now, all the North Koreans had were several dead soldiers. They wouldn't embarrass themselves by admitting the incident. But they had to leave right away. The operation was deniable only if they escaped. Dennison started getting arguments from the group.

"There's no time to argue!" he snapped, cutting them off. "Line up! *Now!*"

Wright immediately realized the urgency of the order and took point. Everyone lined up and Dennison gave the word to move out quickly.

They shut the door to the ELINT space after pulling the Korean from the passageway into the room. They took a different route out. At the second passageway intersections, they nearly ran into two Korean soldiers who passed by, preoccupied with their conversation.

They made it out to the weather deck but were blinded by the darkness. Their visual purple had been robbed while they'd been inside, and now they were at their most vulnerable. They hugged the bulkhead and proceeded toward the bow, moving slowly and cautiously, alert and charged with fear. Before they'd gone twenty feet, Chief Wright stopped.

"Why go to the bow? We can get off right here, Lieutenant," he whispered.

Since they weren't going to blow charges, they could leave. Dennison felt stupid.

"You're right! Everyone rig for dive."

The frogmen detached their fins from their gear and prepared their Emersons. Chief and Anderson watched for guards as the men prepared to get over the side and underwater.

Suddenly an alarm was sounded. Shouts were heard from the bow of the vessel. Dennison turned his head toward the bow and realized how lucky they'd been not to have kept going in that direction. The alarm spread quickly as men from the pier scrambled. The diversionary air raid was on.

Two men came running from the bow and were engaged by Chief at ten feet. Chief unloaded nearly his entire magazine before they both went down. One of the Koreans was able to fire two shots from his AK47 before he went down. The element of surprise was gone.

The UDT men scrambled to get their fins on their wrists and their mouthpieces and regulators ready. Dennison ordered them over the side immediately. They had no time to waste. They would have to find their mouthpieces in the underwater darkness. It was more important to disappear immediately. Chief and Dennison covered the others as they leaped off the vessel and plunged noisily into the bay. As they turned to depart, a Korean soldier shot a pistol at them from above, sounding an alarm. Dennison whirled around and put a burst into his torso, then turned and jumped.

The icy water was a shock. The men sank and groped for each other blindly. Three of them had their mouthpieces and three didn't. They forced themselves to relax and took a few breaths off the working rigs. In a matter of seconds they were all secured and breathing off their own equipment.

There was no time to attach the buddy line or don fins. Chavez had his compass out and fins on. The others linked arms, and they all kicked hard away from the vessel. Chavez took a general bearing and kicked with all the power he could muster, an underwater sprint. They were swimming for their lives. Wright and Horn were on the ends and were barely, awkwardly able to slip on a single fin each. The others donned their masks as they moved.

An explosion rocked the team with a brilliant flash. The KorComs were tossing grenades into the water near the pier and ship. The UDT men found strength they never knew they had. They kicked hard, desperation putting distance between them and the ship. Before long they'd all managed to don their fins, and the pace became blistering. The explosions decreased steadily in intensity as they moved on.

They kept up the pace on the dive until they were in danger of overbreathing their rigs, and Dennison finally slowed them down. Chavez surfaced twice to find a reference he was looking for. A single buoy in the harbor marked them at a specific spot. Once they had an exact reference point, they adjusted their navigation. Anderson then assumed the lead; Chavez had exhausted himself getting the team away from the ship. The men made it to the general area of the submarine and surfaced. There was a lot of small boat activity in the harbor, but it would take a miracle for the KorComs to find them now. The men drifted along easily.

As they floated on the surface, Dennison directed the men to attach the submarine recovery line. The single line was placed between Anderson and Chavez in the middle, and they spread out nearly forty yards apart. At each end they turned on a strobe light hooded by an infrared lens. Then they drifted and waited.

The cold quickly sapped them. The close quarter combat and the strain of a narrow escape had drained them to a critical point. They wouldn't survive until dawn in the water. If the submarine couldn't find them soon, they would die. The tide was beginning to go out and was picking up speed. Once it was in full swing, they would be swept out to sea and would never be able to make shore again.

At five minute intervals, men at each end of the line clacked two metal sticks together underwater. The sub would sense all the sounds and activity in the water and single out the sticks to home in on. The strobes would be picked up by the periscope.

After an hour in the water, they were in deep, deep trouble. The frigid night would kill them before they could be found. Dawn was only two hours away. The men shivered uncontrollably as they bobbed in the swells. The cold numbed their limbs, making every movement sluggish hell. Dennison was on the verge of giving up hope.

Finally, out of the darkness, the periscope closed slowly from about fifty yards and snagged the line. They fumbled to get their regulators into their mouths and clung to the lines as they were swept away. They hung shaking at the ends of the snag and buddy lines.

Their platoon was ready for them; they knew the

team would be in bad shape. Diving open circuit rigs, Bateman and Mason quickly ascended a tangent line attached to a point forward of the escape trunk and up to the top of the submarine's sail. The divers took one man at a time off the buddy and snag lines and dived him to the escape trunk. The team survived one more hour in the water as they were locked into the trunk in two cycles. Bateman and Mason recovered the tangent line and came in on a third cycle.

Inside, each man in the team was nearly hypothermic, barely able to move. They were stripped of their gear and helped to a hot shower, and coffee was pumped into them. Within thirty minutes, their core temperatures were nearly normal. The submarine slipped out to sea as North Korean coastal patrol craft scoured the harbor.

Dennison took the debriefing in stride. He'd expected to be roasted for the failure, but he was told he'd done the right thing. The debriefing was over in less than two hours. What was there to say, really? The UDT men were put on a flight back to Subic before the next night.

In the aftermath, it all felt like a dream. In the months that followed, Dennison watched with the rest of the world as the *Pueblo* crew became the point of international media focus. He hoped they could be rescued; he had a better idea than most of the severe treatment and torture they were being subjected to. Finally, in December 1968, they were released after an admission of spying. They returned to America as heroes, until the inquiries that fried the skipper and senior officers. The episode was an embarrassment to the Navy and the nation.

The Koreans passed the most important captured electronic and cipher equipment to their Soviet comrades. Coupled with other captured American equipment from a top-secret site on a mountaintop in Laos in March of that same year, and with the help of a spy ring in America headed by a man named Walker who had passed American codes on to Moscow, the Kremlin was able to exploit a tremendous number of U.S. secrets. Unfortunately, the full extent of the damage wouldn't be discovered by the United States until years later.

Dennison believed the political embarrassment was the reason none of the awards were ever approved. He'd put the team in for a variety of medals. They had risked their lives. They deserved recognition, but he never heard anything about them. He even heard at one point that he'd been put in for a Silver Star, but he could not have cared less. Nothing ever surfaced, and after two years he finally dropped his discreet inquiries about awards for his men. He was told he could never talk about it. They could never wear medals for that operation. It had never taken place. It was top-secret.

Shortly after the mission, Dennison lost his desire to get into SEAL Team ONE in Vietnam. Before the mission he'd felt that UDT was less than any SEAL Team. Operation Lightning Strike changed his mind completely. He was proud to be in UDT, and to serve wherever he was needed. And before his six-month cruise was over, he pulled three dozen cache and bunker demolition missions in Vietnam.

And a SEAL squad accompanied most of those missions as security for his platoon.

6

Cambodia

August 1968

"Weren't Jose Chavez and Larry Mason both involved in that accident on *Grayback* a few years ago?" Stine frowned thoughtfully. Dennison nodded, his expression grim.

"Nineteen-eighty," he confirmed, his mouth a hard, thin line. "A valve was misaligned during a lock-in sequence, creating a near-vacuum in the chamber. They both passed out and drowned in a few feet of water before anyone could get to them." The company fell silent for a moment.

Ray Bradley hadn't fared any better. He'd become a PRU advisor and had died when one of his men had tripped a boobytrapped 105 Howitzer round back in 1969. The rest of the team were all still alive, though. Dan Bateman had joined the LAPD SWAT and occasionally found himself working with Dave Stone and Jason Bracket. Dick Anderson transferred to the East Coast and became a member of SEAL Team TWO, and Steve Horn had also stayed in the teams. Kevin Wright left in the mid-seventies and became an FBI agent, one of the first members of their hostage rescue team. And his shipboarding experience in North Korea helped the FBI develop a maritime counterterrorist capability.

"To Jose Chavez and Larry Mason," Dennison said after a moment, raising his beer mug in a toast and draining it dry. "And to other teammates and friends no longer with us."

"Speaking of friends no longer with us," Tony Franco piped up in an attempt to lighten the moment, "where in the hell is John Tindle? Not like him to miss one of these reunions."

"He's in Australia on the SAS exchange, probably arguing tactics with Troy Duncan in a bar in Perth," Dennison grinned.

"Troy Duncan?"

"SAS color sergeant. He worked a few missions with the SEALs in Vietnam as part of another exchange. There was even a mission in Cambodia that almost did the lot of them in."

They were a long way from water, too long, and it was making Dick Gilbert profoundly edgy. He felt way too dry. None of the five SEALs felt like settling back and putting their feet up, but they were in the bush and committed now. Although the entire platoon had received jungle warfare training in Panama and Puerto Rico before deploying to Vietnam, they really felt comfortable only around water.

It wasn't the jungle or the terrain that made them uneasy, though; it was the sense that there were a lot more NVA in the area than in the normal swampy areas they worked around the delta. This was the enemy's base of operations, and the SEALs were unwelcome intruders.

The area was absolutely unlike anything the SEALs had gotten used to. Most of the tour had been spent slopping around the swamps and mangroves further south of Cau Mau Peninsula or along the muddy Mekong. Up here on the Cambodian border, the terrain was high and dry, and the hills were owned by the VC and NVA. Since the Tet Offensive earlier in the year, the activity attributed to the Vietcong had dropped off considerably. But the North Vietnamese had picked up the slack. They were solidly in control now, and they let everyone know it. The VC had been chewed up during Tet, and the NVA weren't a bunch of ragtag country bumpkins. The war was shifting more from guerilla to conventional confrontation every day. The SEALs felt Tet 68 had been a turning point, probably for the worse as far as the United States was concerned.

They were looking for armor. BT2 Dick Gilbert never thought he would see the day. This was a mission better suited to the Army, but he didn't care. All he wanted was a fight.

Julius Conrad's death had changed him, hardened him. After Gilbert had gone through training he'd been assigned to SEAL Team ONE, and Conrad had become a second father to him. He was the senior man who'd taken Gilbert under his wing and taken care of him, and Gilbert had worshipped him. They'd been in the same platoon and spent many a southern California night on liberty from

Camp Pendleton to Tijuana. Conrad had pulled classified operations out of Da Nang during two earlier tours, one with the Agency and one with MACV-SOG. He wasn't just a combat vet, he was one of the best SEALs alive.

Or had been. A Vietnamese LDNN attached to the platoon had tripped a boobytrap during a riverine insertion earlier in the year. Conrad had been behind him. The Viet had been blown apart instantly, and Conrad had been seriously wounded. He'd bled to death in Gilbert's arms as the platoon had tried desperately to extract their critical teammate.

Now all Gilbert wanted was to get a piece of Charlie, or Nathaniel Victor, as they called the North Vietnamese. He'd snapped—and worse, he knew it. He was out in the field for all the wrong reasons, but he no longer cared. Before he had to rotate home, all he wanted to do was rack up a huge body count. He was in the feverish grip of an ugly, dangerous emotion, one that could risk the whole squad, but Gilbert no longer thought logically or rationally. He'd seen too much of the war ever to make it back to the real world. With Conrad dead, it was no longer a job to Gilbert. It was personal.

There were five SEALs in the squad, and because they were near the end of their tour, casualties wouldn't be replaced. Instead, they used a Kit Carson scout for double duty, on point, and as an interpreter. The ex-VC had turned from fighting for the Vietcong in the bush after his village had been ravaged by the communists. Now he gladly paid his old comrades back and made plenty of money to boot. The team appreciated his substantial skill in the jungle. He knew the enemy and he knew where to look. Kiet was worth his weight in gold on an operation like this.

There was one extra man on the mission. Sergeant Troy Duncan was an Australian soldier from the Special Air Service, the famed SAS. He'd spent a prior tour as an advisor to the South Vietnamese Army in II Corps. Duncan had seen a lot of action and knew how to move in the jungle. He had told the group about SAS selection, a grueling month-long process where men were driven to the breaking point in murderous hikes through mountainous terrain with backbreaking gear strapped on. They were forced to carry straining combat loads.

Of the hundred and twenty-four men who'd started the course in Duncan's class, only thirteen had made it and were "badged." Then the new men were trained for nearly a year in specialties before being integrated into the SAS unit. Duncan said the New Zealand SAS selection and training was similar to theirs, and it was rumored that the NZSAS would send a troop of men later in the year to work with the Australians, who operated mostly in Phouc Tuy Province, southeast of Saigon. Duncan was one of several SAS men who ran with a SEAL platoon as a change of pace. It was an informal exchange arranged by in-country SEAL platoons and the SAS. In return, a few SEALs had run recon and ambush missions with small SAS teams in III Corps.

The Australian SAS had come to Vietnam in 1966 with solid experience of jungle fighting in Malaysia and Borneo. Based out of Nui Dat, the small SAS patrols conducted mainly recon and ambush missions in Vietcong territory. With all their experience, the SAS, like the SEALs, also used small teams to move, but had increased the size of their groups from four-man to five-and six-man teams. When casualties hit, it was easier to carry the wounded and still return fire and provide security with a few more men. And it was easier to handle prisoners when you had more than four men in a patrol. Just like the SEALs, the SAS felt the perfect tour in Vietnam was six months vice twelve. In their recon environment, the longer tours made the men less effective from cumulative fatigue.

They learned a good trick or two from the SAS. One was to use a shotgun to hit a prospective prisoner's legs on a "snatch" mission. The wound produced usually wasn't too bad, but it would temporarily shock the victim so that he could be seized. Duncan knew recon, and he knew the border area they were in right now. He was another big addition to the squad.

According to the latest intelligence, the NVA had started moving armored vehicles south on the Ho Chi Minh Trail to use against the Americans. That would be a significant threat, especially to the isolated border posts used in the counter-insurgency fighting. Armor could topple them one at a time, like dominoes, leaving the country stripped of a defensive shield. The SEALs were part of a series of small recon teams looking to confirm the rumors.

It was known that the NVA had used armor to overrun the Special Forces camp at Lang Vei in I

Corps that February. Lang Vei had been a launch site for MACV-SOG operations into Laos, though that wasn't generally known. The NVA decimated it on their way to lay siege to the Marines at Khe Sanh, as if it were second base on the way to home plate. All that had happened far to the north. Now it looked as if the NVA might have brought armor south, and if so, they could well have been in a position to cut South Vietnam in half and threaten Saigon. Not good. So now Special Forces teams and Australian SAS recon teams were ordered out to try to cover the vast green expanse, looking for enemy armor.

Gilbert's platoon was nearing the end of its six-month tour, and they'd gone upcountry, away from the swamps, looking to diversify their operations. They spent a lot of time overflying the border area in helos looking for likely areas for missions, but no one was fooled by the jungle below. The NVA clearly staged in huge base camps inside Cambodia, where the Americans weren't allowed to go. Officially, that is.

There was plenty of evidence that the Air Force had been conducting B-52 strikes into the sanctuaries for some time, despite U.S. denials. The earth bore huge, ugly scars from carpet bombing missions. There was no doubt that those bombing missions hurt the VC and NVA. Most of the captured prisoners and defectors claimed that it was those B-52 operations that struck the deepest fear in the enemy. The bombings were hard to predict, although the enemy did get good intelligence from their foreign communist advisors and had a superb network of agents in the South. The air strikes also caused the enemy forces to remain on the move a great deal. But since the President had halted the bombings in March, more supplies had spilled down the trail. And the VC and NVA were steadily recovering, licking their wounds, and getting stronger once again. Every day that it was allowed to continue lengthened the war by weeks.

Enemy armor hadn't been much of a presence in the war up to that point. Everyone back home in the States believed this was just a small guerrilla fight. Now they were talking armor. Gilbert believed the intelligence. He'd heard from a friend in MACV-SOG that the NVA had begun running a fuel pipeline from North Vietnam through southern Laos to support such heavy equipment. One thing was for sure: he wouldn't mind the mission so long as they made contact.

This was definitely no place for a SEAL squad to get into a firefight. You could feel the enemy presence, thick as coastal fog. But all Gilbert wanted was a bigger body count.

He wished they'd been able to bring doctored ammunition with them. The classified program was a perfect tool to be used against the enemy. Under the code names "Bean Pole" and "Italian Green," teams of special operations units introduced ammunition that had been altered by the CIA to explode in rifles and mortar tubes of the enemy forces. The American units would infiltrate VC and NVA sanctuaries and leave the doctored rounds.

Gilbert didn't think that was enough. He'd tried to convince some of the SEAL officers that they should also doctor items to be left behind. A few assault rifle magazines, canteens, cameras . . . items that would blow up when the enemy picked them up and used them. That would return the terror to the enemy who had used worse tactics for years on their own people.

HT3 Ron Tuttle turned toward Gilbert and slowly moved next to him. Tuttle was second-to-last in the patrol, with Duncan just before Tuttle. Gilbert kept his eyes on the backtrail, ever vigilant for the enemy. He was rear security, the eyes in the back of the patrol's head. He made sure no one was tracking them or would stumble on them from the rear as they moved slowly and carefully through the bush.

Because they had a Kit Carson on point, they moved more quickly than they would have ordinarily. The most probable contact would likely come from behind them as enemy soldiers in their own base camp area roamed about, talking and smoking. Each time they moved ahead, Gilbert also made sure the squad didn't leave any obvious signs of their presence on the backtrail. When you get tired, you make mistakes, and if anyone so much as dropped a pencil it could give away their presence. The SEAL made sure they didn't make those kinds of mistakes.

He had a full-size M-16 with a new 40-mm grenade launcher beneath the barrel. It was experimental, but he'd heard the grenade launcher was being modified and would be issued as a regular weapon in the Army and Marine Corps the next year. The device he had was dubbed the XM-148. It was a single-shot weapon that fired the projectile from the barrel at a velocity of two hundred and fifty feet per second. In the bush, he never loaded high explosives rounds. The HE had to spin for several meters out of the barrel before the explosive head was armed, and the bush was normally too thick to ensure good impact where you wanted it to go. He'd missed a few NVA because of it and had learned his lesson. He hated missing NVA.

There were also flechette rounds filled with small steel darts, but they were too light in the thick brush. Gilbert preferred the buckshot rounds. If there was a chance encounter at close range by one or two enemy soldiers, he was confident of his ability to draw first blood with buckshot and get the team moving before the enemy could counter. And when Gilbert had to fire, he wanted to make sure he hit someone.

The squad halted for a moment, and Tuttle squatted down next to Gilbert facing the opposite way, watching Duncan to his front. Tuttle carried a Stoner 63 assault rifle. The Stoner could be configured in many ways. Tuttle carried his with a 150-round drum magazine attached. With a cyclic rate of fire at about a thousand rounds a minute, the weapon worked well to mass firepower for breaking contact. Tuttle cradled it as if it were his only child. He'd even used rifle grenades from the end of the weapon for a few operations, and a special noise suppressor twice. The weapon was frequently used by SEALs but virtually unknown in other military units. Tuttle leaned over until his mouth was only a few inches from Gilbert's ear. He was passing word to him from the front of the patrol.

"Welcome to Cambodia," he whispered, barely perceptibly.

Gilbert grinned slightly and glanced at Tuttle. They weren't supposed to be in Cambodia. He knew they would be moving along the border, but the officer in charge, Lieutenant Morasco, hadn't told them they would be slipping *across* the border. Gilbert liked the OIC; he was refreshingly unorthodox, a rare combination of charisma and competence.

On this mission, Morasco carried an odd-looking M-16 fitted with a noise suppressor on the end of the barrel. The suppressor eliminated the muzzle flash without slowing the velocity of the assault rifle round. Although the round made a ballistic crack downrange because it broke the sound barrier, it would be hard for anyone near the victim to determine the direction the shot had come from. The suppressor was a MAW-A1 made by SIONICS Corporation. The name stood for studies in operational negation of insurgency and countersubversion. SIONICS was founded in 1967 by a former OSS officer and based in Georgia. Their silencers and suppressors were first-rate. Gilbert had seen Morasco's weapon used, many times. It was highly effective.

They had now crossed the border, and Gilbert knew they would make contact. Payback time, once again. He was starting to feel a lot better.

The patrol had inserted by helo earlier in the day. At first light they had executed a series of false insertions, finally getting out almost a mile from the border. They laid up for half an hour two hundred meters from the landing zone, quietly listening for enemy activity. They established radio contact with the helos right away, in case the LZ was hot, so that they could immediately get gunship support and a couple of birds to extract them. They didn't hear any enemy activity initially, and they gave the birds clearance to depart. The squad moved deeper into the jungle toward the border.

Ten minutes before they found the trail, they heard a strange sound. In the distance they heard sticks being struck together. It sounded like bamboo to Gilbert. He stopped often to make sure no one was trailing them and twice moved rearward almost out of sight of the team to listen closely on the backtrail. He heard nothing there. But the sticks worried him.

Duncan had told them the story of an SAS patrol that had been discovered and tracked by a large force in III Corps near the Parrot's Beak on the border. The VC had used gunfire and banging stick signals to coordinate search teams in the area and unnerve the patrol. The SAS men had avoided a fight and slipped away, but it had been unnervingly close. At one point, one of the SAS troopers had had his hand stepped on by a VC searcher who'd failed to discover them. The VC had been lucky. The SAS men had three weapons trained on him, and the slightest twitch of a finger would have doomed him.

Gilbert and the others wondered if they'd been discovered, but the stick signals had only been brief and then had stopped. There wasn't the frenzy of signals from all directions that would have indicated a dragnet.

Within a few minutes of the signals, the patrol

found a large trail near a stream. The trail was
hard-packed dirt, except for the slick mud on either
side of the stream. The stream overran the trail and
produced mud on either side for about fifteen meters. There was no overgrowth of plants on the
trail. It looked like it was used regularly. The scout
and one SEAL, Damon, were sent down to the
stream area and returned after five minutes.

The SEAL informed the OIC that there had been
more than fifteen enemy soldiers on the trail that
day. He'd made the estimate by drawing a mental
line across the trail. Next he moved forward about
thirty-six inches and drew another imaginary line
across the trail, using his thirty-nine inch M16 as a
measuring stick. He counted the boot and sandal
prints in the box and divided by two to get fifteen.
It was a good estimate and indicated even further
that the trail was well used. Nearby, the pointman
had discovered two sets of sticks clustered together
as a visual signal to other VC and NVA on the trail.
The markings indicated a well-used footpath. Morasco quickly pulled the team off the trail.

"Where'd you learn the boot trick?" Morasco
asked Damon quietly, after they were settled about
fifteen yards away from the trail.

"MACV RECONDO course," Damon whispered
back with a lopsided grin.

Not bad, the OIC thought. He'd heard a lot of
good things about the course, run by 5th Special
Forces in Nha Trang. Graduates went to MACV-
SOG recon teams, long-range recon patrols, Rang-
ers, Special Forces Project Delta, and others.
Duncan had been there and given it high marks,

telling the SEALs that only the Malaysian Tracking School had surpassed it.

They continued until it was nearly dark, hearing a generator in the distance at one point that had run for nearly forty-five minutes. By the time darkness fell, they'd buttonhooked into a lay-up point and remained on ambush, waiting for any NVA trackers who might be on their trail. The team established communications with base through a forward air controller who was airborne. And when the blackness was absolute, the group crawled silently for an hour out of their last position. There they stopped in a tight perimeter so that each man could touch the man next to him. They lay still and took turns staying on watch. But none of the men slept well.

No one snored or talked in his sleep; predeployment training let the SEALs screen out those traits. Only one claymore mine was laid out in the direction from which they had crawled. They weren't taking any chances on being discovered.

The next morning, as first light crept into the jungle, the men noticed an increase in flies. That could indicate the presence of an enemy base camp, with open food containers or latrines, in the immediate area. Fast hand signals were passed between the team members. They were suddenly wide awake.

Shortly after, they heard the noise. It was a strong rumble, heavy machinery. The entire team sat up. Definitely not a convoy of trucks. This was different. This was tracked vehicles. They'd found armor, and it was close. Sweat beaded the SEALs' foreheads.

The team had unknowingly laid up just a hundred and fifty meters from a main road. This was no foot trail. This was a hard-packed dirt road capable of handling regular vehicular traffic. The OIC let it become light enough to move and took two SEALs and the scout in the direction of the road with a camera. They were determined to get the proof they'd been sent in for.

Within ten minutes there was a gunshot, followed by three more. The group in the lay-up position froze. Everyone knew what was next. The four men scrambled to make sure they were ready to move. This was going to turn out to be a run-for-your-life exfiltration. They rose to one knee, two men covering the area toward the road and the other shifting his gaze to the side and rear. If the others didn't make it back from the road in another thirty seconds, the three would get to them as quickly as possible and try to beat the NVA before their teammates could be captured.

The emergency action wasn't necessary. Within seconds they came crashing through the dense jungle growth, not caring for once about the noise they were making. Rifles in the lay-up position came up to meet them as they finally broke through to the team, verifying that they were SEALs and not NVA. The scout was the third of four to come through, ensuring that a misidentification wouldn't occur. He hastily pulled a red scarf from around his neck to let the Allied men identify him through foliage if they were separated. The four men didn't stop, but slowed long enough to rally the group and start east at a breakneck pace.

"NVA soldiers on the road," Morasco gasped, "just as we snapped a few pictures of the armor.

One stepped off the trail to piss and tripped right over me. I shot him and then we hit three of his buddies waiting on the road for him. Two more got away, but they'll be right back, no doubt. We've gotta roll! Fast!" The scout took point and everyone reversed direction as they folded and collapsed in harmony. They'd moved less than a hundred meters when they heard shouting and gunfire to the rear. The NVA were officially in pursuit.

Gilbert moved as fast as he could while trying to cover the rear. His job was the toughest. There would be no way to hide their tracks at this pace. The NVA would be on them in a matter of minutes. They had to shoot and move. Gilbert took out another magazine of 5.56 mm and held it with two fingers of his non-firing hand. He knew he was going to need a quick reload.

"Tuttle, get the claymore ready!" Gilbert called as quietly as he could manage to the SEAL in front of him.

Sounds to the front and left, sharp staccato of snapping twigs, and the rustle of brush. Shouts, signals. The team stopped. They would have to change course. Zigzagging would do only limited good; it would be obvious to the NVA that the SEALs were headed back to the border and across to South Vietnam. Just as the group was about to pick up and move again, Gilbert caught noise to the right. Two NVA soldiers popped up out of nowhere and leveled AK47s at Duncan and Tuttle, inexplicably not seeing Gilbert.

"Contact right!" Gilbert screamed, as he cut loose with a full magazine. The shout and fire caught the NVA by surprise, making them miss their original marks. Duncan and Tuttle dived down as AK fire stitched the air above them. They swung their weapons hard and began to fire at their assailants. By this time, Gilbert had finished his magazine and shot off the buckshot load from the 40-mm. The NVA disappeared, either hit or scrambling for cover.

"Break contact! Let's move! Go! Go!" Gilbert hollered as Tuttle planted the claymore dead in their trail, pointing rearward. Their position was now pinpointed, and the NVA would focus on the area of the contact and come in force. Gilbert swung his weapon to the rear and dropped his empty magazine just as another NVA came running up the backtrail.

Gilbert's weapon was empty. He had to stop the enemy soldier from getting by and into the group where a crossfire could happen. Standing up, he took one gigantic step forward and met the shocked NVA in full stride with a front kick to the chest. The soldier went down hard, both feet flying out from under him. The SEAL slammed the full magazine into the weapon, drove the bolt home, leveled the gun, and fired five quick rounds into the other man.

He turned to run with the patrol and watched Tuttle pull the time fuse initiator on the claymore with Duncan covering him and Gilbert from a kneeling position. The rest of the team had taken off, leaving them to catch up as soon as the claymore was planted. Duncan's L1A1 assault rifle pointed menacingly into the brush, searching for targets.

Gilbert took off past Tuttle and Duncan, and they

picked up and recovered. The patrol was on the run. Duncan and Tuttle passed Gilbert on the fly, resuming their original squad positions. Thirty seconds later the claymore erupted, followed by screams that faded off into silence. The patrol shifted their direction to the northeast and continued to move out hard. Sporadic fire broke out all around them. The NVA were shooting at some of their own in the confusion. *Good*, Gilbert thought savagely. *Rack 'em up!*

They could hear their pursuers coming in hard from the rear and right. They had a long way to run yet, and they would have to produce some more casualties to get the NVA off their backs. The team crossed a deep ravine with at least one group of enemy soldiers in tight pursuit. Fighting for breath, they pushed hard up the opposite side of the ravine. As they neared the top, Gilbert paused and turned toward the sounds of the enemy behind them.

"Come on, then, mate!" yelled Duncan, as he turned and waved frantically to Gilbert. "What are you doing?"

"I'll be right behind you," Gilbert called back. "I want to give them something to think about."

"We can't take them all out!" Tuttle protested, his voice hoarse with desperation and exhaustion. "Let's go!"

"If we don't take a few of them out, they'll never slow down!" Gilbert snapped. Everything Conrad had taught him was erupting in his mind, blossoming into tactics. Conrad's blood rushed madly through his veins. "We need to dump some of this ordnance so we can lighten our load and move faster! Don't argue with me! Cover me from fifty meters up the trail! I'll be right behind you! Go!"

Tuttle and Duncan exchanged a dubious look and took off after a few seconds' hesitation. They'd already paused too long. Gilbert turned and faced downhill.

"Payback's a medevac," he hissed. He pulled two fragmentation grenades and the only two white phosphorus grenades he had from his web gear. Grenades weren't too deadly in the thick jungle unless they landed in your lap. "Willy Peter," white phosphorus, was a different matter. It had a thirty-five meter bursting radius, but you could throw it only about thirty meters on any given day. A deadly gift, but almost as dangerous to the giver. But Gilbert knew if he threw it down the slope he could get it farther away. Perfect position for a Willy Peter throw. *Time to warm the Chucks up.*

As he heard the NVA approach, he waited until he guessed they were within range, then heaved the two frags one right after the other. The explosions ripped the silence to shreds and punctuated it with the screams of the dying. The ravine erupted with return fire, but it went high; they didn't know where he was. It was the reason Gilbert hadn't used his M16. He didn't intend to give his position away.

The NVA knew the Americans were within hand grenade range, and several rushed forward, firing and yelling. Gilbert let the spoons fly on both white phosphorus grenades and hurled them downhill, then turned and ran for all he was worth.

The grenades burst into two brilliant plumes of white smoke. At least half a dozen NVA screamed and scattered. Their assault was dispersed. The Willy Peter would burn until the fuel was consumed or the flames were smothered. It was a terrifying weapon, perfect for discouraging pursuit.

Duncan and Tuttle let Gilbert pass, then collapsed in behind him as they raced to link up with the rest of the squad. They made it and pushed on for another two kilometers. As they moved, Gilbert fell back to his rear security position. They were dangerously exhausted by the time they finally stopped and sat down for a quick rest. There was still a lot of movement around them. The helos had been called for extraction as soon as first contact was made, but the team still had to make it across the border for the pickup. The birds were still inbound, and the SEALs were told there was no close air support available.

The sharp crack of a bullet shattered the silence, hitting Tuttle in the left arm. The team returned fire and Gilbert crawled over and pulled Tuttle back. In seconds they realized they had contact on three sides. Trapped. And the NVA was tightening the noose. The OIC made a gutsy call as each man realized he had only one chance of escape. This was a drill they'd never had to execute for real, though they'd rehearsed it dozens of times.

"Break out! Break out! Break out!" Morasco screamed. It was a last-ditch, desperate move. Gilbert's heart leapt into his throat. The others repeated the command to each other to ensure all hands knew what was happening in the chaos of the battle. They pulled out all the ordnance they could hold in hand. Damon and Duncan extended light anti-armor weapons with self-propelled rockets. Extra rounds for the assault rifles and grenade launchers were hastily readied. Morasco and Gilbert prepped tear gas grenades, and the word raced down the line that the team was set to move.

"Break out, twelve o'clock!" Morasco shouted, repeating it twice to make sure everyone got the direction. The men spread out abreast on their hands and knees as the direction was called relative to their last movement. They lobbed gas grenades to the sides and rear, and clouds of white smoke started to form a curtain around them.

"Stand by," the SEAL officer ordered, waiting for the smoke to conceal them completely. "Stand by! Stand by! FIRE!"

The men came to a kneeling position and unleashed a heavy volume of fire before them. The LAWs exploded forward. The SEALs got to their feet and ran ahead, firing and changing magazines as they moved. Tuttle stumbled ahead beside them, able to run but not to fire.

The team broke out of the noose and continued to move. Gilbert set up the head count and Duncan took Tuttle forward. Everyone had made it out. They moved hard at a dead run. Gilbert decided to delay the NVA as long as he could. He stopped long enough to drop two M14 "toe popper" antipersonnel mines in their backtrail. He looked up when he heard a noise close by. As two NVA tried to move in on the group, Gilbert picked them off with a burst of fire at close range.

Suddenly he was bowled over by an NVA soldier who jumped on his back flashing a knife. Gilbert rolled and pinned the smaller man, headbutted him in the face, and used both hands to twist and break his wrist. Then he picked up the dropped knife and drove it into the NVA's chest, stood and kicked him like a punter in the ribs, and turned to run for his life.

A second man screamed out of the foliage and charged him. The SEAL only had time to grab him by the front of his shirt and pull him down, rolling onto his back. He continued the roll, using his feet to throw the soldier over his head, but instead of letting him go, Gilbert held on tightly. The momentum put the NVA on his back and pulled Gilbert over on top of him. The SEAL straddled him and drove a fist into his throat several times with all his strength, crushing the man's windpipe. It was over in seconds, and Gilbert rose to run after the rest of the team. He located the fleeing patrol and fell back in with the others.

Gilbert heard the small explosions from the mines he dropped as he ran, heard the screams of the NVA who'd found them the hard way. The NVA were taking heavy casualties to capture the squad. Gilbert knew it was the only way to win. They had to make it too expensive for the NVA to continue.

The sound of approaching helos could be heard above the trees. Suddenly they broke out into the landing zone. Gilbert hadn't realized they'd made it back across the border. The first helo touched down, and Tuttle and three SEALs boarded. As it pulled out, a second helo touched down and swept up the rest of the team. Sensing their prey was about to escape, the NVA unloaded everything they had at the aircraft. The helo pulled pitch and took fire all the way out of the LZ while the squad emptied their last magazines into the sources of tracer fire below. The helo took several hits, but it still flew, and the doorgunners unloaded hundreds of rounds all the way out of the area.

Gilbert's mind reeled. He was crazy with elation. They'd nearly been captured and killed. A lot of NVA had died by his hand today. By his hand. The danger was electrifying, intoxicating; it flooded his limbs like liquid fire, lured him like a whore. *It feels so good to be alive*, he thought, stretching lazily in his corner of the helo, like a cat. *I wish Conrad could have seen me. I wish Conrad was alive.* He felt sanity slipping away like water off glass. He didn't care.

Tuttle died on the way to the hospital; he'd sustained a second wound during extraction that had lodged in the base of his neck. No one else on either extraction helo was touched, though each bird had over a dozen bulletholes. Gilbert lost the last shreds of his sanity. Nothing made sense to him anymore. He lost all interest or concern in anything outside the field. All he wanted was blood.

And he got it.

7

Neptune's Trident

June 1969

"What finally happened to Gilbert?" Nick Stine asked, the characteristic tilt of his head making Mallon smile in spite of himself. "Did he survive Vietnam?"

"Surprisingly enough, yes, he did," Franco nodded. "He tried life in the States for a while, but couldn't hack it. He ended up as a SEAL trainer in El Salvador. As a matter of fact, I bumped into him once in the middle of the night, in the Gulf of Fonseca. I was on my way to Nicaragua with a small armada of fast, heavily armed boats filled with Nicaraguan guerrillas. Gilbert and I came too close to engaging each other in the dark before we figured out we were all friendlies. Then we laughed and hollered and carried on, breaking all the rules of noise and light discipline. We were lucky we didn't get our fool heads blown off. And all Gilbert wanted to know was how he could come with me and get a piece of the action. Far as I can tell, he still hasn't stopped looking for a body count. Last rumor I heard, he was contracting in the Middle East."

Stine whistled low in appreciation.

"How do guys like that become frogmen?" he wondered aloud.

"Well, how does anyone become a frogman, really? I mean, it's not exactly your standard run-of-the-mill occupation, is it?" Franco drawled.

"I dunno," Bob Braddock murmured thoughtfully, his quiet voice somehow carrying across the room. "I can't remember a time when I *didn't* want to be one. When I was a kid I had this neighbor, an ex-Marine who'd served in the Pacific in World War II. I used to sit spellbound for hours and listen to his stories. And there was one he told about a little-known group of men who preceded the Marines ashore, armed only with knives and dragging along haversacks of explosives. What made the biggest impression on me was the awe with which this huge, hardened leatherneck spoke of them."

"There was actually a Marine out there who had something good to say about us?" Franco teased. "I may pass out and die of shock."

"Well, I guess it had to happen sometime," Stine smirked, shrugging laconically. He started whistling the Marine Corps hymn, and then they all joined him as he burst into their particular takeoff on the song: *"From the Halls of Montezuma to the shores of Tripoli, we are proud to be the first ashore, right behind the UDT!"*

They laughed, cheered, and pounded on the tables, and there was a general refilling of beer mugs.

"So you joined the frogmen and ended up in my

platoon in Det Charlie, naturally," Stine teased Braddock. "Between you and Rick Raydon, I don't know how I ever survived it. I remember your sea daddy, larger than life and twice as ugly, and capable of clearing the decks when he bellowed. You remember the time he killed the NVA sapper under that ship in Cam Ranh Bay? Took a knife in his side and still snapped the enemy diver's neck! Now, *that* was hardcore. And he taught you well. Came in handy on the Neptune's Trident operation . . ."

On the day of the rescue operation, their submarine, USS *Tunny*, lay clandestinely offshore. The platoon was staged for a rescue, as they had been numerous times before. Braddock was one of the surface swimmers, and he carried an M3 Greasegun for security. After so many drills, he'd have thought they were as ready as they could be, but when the call came in, they'd been caught flatfooted.

"We have a Mayday call . . . A-6 Intruder . . . hit by an SA-2 SAM . . . outbound and climbing for altitude . . ." The call came from somewhere in Radio and was directed toward the Conn, the submarine's control center. Braddock's heart started to pound. He remembered Raydon telling him not too long ago that the plane would try to gain altitude in case they had to shut down engines and glide. Altitude meant distance, and it was now a race to get over water.

"They're on one engine . . . losing altitude . . . two minutes to Feet Wet . . ."

The submarine raced closer to the coast. This one

didn't look good. The crew probably wasn't going to make it to the sea. Braddock said a silent prayer as the seconds ticked by.

"Fire . . . they're on fire . . . loss of control . . . they're out! They're out! Ejection at about nine thousand feet. Wingman says they're right near the coast, but over water. Stand by for a fix!"

Come on, Braddock thought. *Make it!*

The fix showed the pair to be about two miles over water. The wind was blowing them out to sea, but surface traffic in the area was thick, and every small boat for miles around would be racing in to collect the bounty Hanoi had on any American crewman. The sub altered course and sprinted to a position projected by the indicated wind aloft by the covering wingman. Braddock felt like a center-fielder running with his eyes on a fly ball, desperately trying to get his glove under it before it touched the ground.

"Two good chutes reported. One crewman on SAR radio . . . condition good. His raft is deployed. Nothing heard from the second crewman . . ."

The submarine raced on, and it was going to be close. The crewman hit the water four miles offshore, and two North Vietnamese boats were right on top of them. And the standing orders were to stay clear and remain out of the area if there appeared to be no hope for the downed crew.

"One of the crewmen has radioed that he is about to be captured; a small boat several hundred yards away is closing fast. The other crewman never came up on his radio and can't be spotted, although the first one stated that he'd seen him land about half a mile away."

This would be the third and closest rescue effort the captain, Bannon Alexander, had been involved in on this cruise. He wasn't ready to throw in the towel yet, but he knew they were probably going to miss this one. The sub closed to less than a mile, and it looked like they were already too late. The Captain tightened all the muscles in his jaw and started to pace angrily back and forth as the officer of the deck gave him a running report on the closing NVA boats as he watched them through the periscope.

They weren't going to make it. Those pilots were as good as dead.

He pounded his fist down on the back of his chair and thought hard for a moment. *Not again*, he thought. *Not this time. No way.* Spinning around quickly, he bellowed down the narrow passageway.

"UDT, stand by! Stand by!" He didn't even stop to listen as his crew relayed his command to the frogmen staged by the outer hatch. "Blow all ballast! Surface! Surface the boat!"

Horns blasted and the sub shot upward. Her crew clung desperately to any point of stability to keep from falling over.

"Two thousand yards and closing, Captain!" the officer of the deck announced sharply. Steve Justin, the OIC of the UDT platoon, stumbled into the Conn to try to figure out what the Captain was doing. The two men locked eyes for the barest of moments.

"We're continuing to close on the nearest enemy vessel, Lieutenant," the Captain informed him before he could even get the question out. "It's a fishing trawler with another only a short distance away. We have to keep the American pilot off that boat, so we have to give the V something else to think about. We don't have enough time to man the deck guns, and the crewman's raft is too close for us to risk firing them anyway. Don't let them get that pilot, Lieutenant. I don't care what you have to do. Don't let them get either man. Now, open the hatch and go!"

"We'll need some sort of cover or we'll be sitting ducks in our rubber boats, Captain."

"Don't worry about the first boat; I'm going to run it down. But if we slow down we'll never make it in time, so we're going to blow by the aircrew men in the raft!"

"Fifteen hundred yards and closing," the officer of the deck called out.

"You won't be able to launch your rubber boats until we slow down! We'll man the guns then and keep the second boat away!"

"Got it!" The Lieutenant nodded sharply and started to move off.

"One thousand yards and closing."

"Tell your men to hang on to anything they can on deck!" Alexander called after him. "I'm not about to let the NVA get those men. We're not slowing down. Now go!"

Justin scrambled up the hatch of the now-surfaced sub and met his men, who were frantically trying to inflate two boats while they prepared their gear on deck. Their job was made that much more difficult by the speed of the sub, normally nearly at rest for such a launch. They weren't going to have everything ready in time, but the sub was right on course for a collision with the trawler. Surfacing from out of nowhere, the sub got the sudden and complete attention of the North Vietnamese. Within seconds, small arms fire was cracking over the deck.

"We're not going to make it in time!" Nick Stine yelled to the officer.

"Stine, you and Raydon strip down and get your fins on!" Justin called back. "Get ready to jump as we pass the pilot's raft! Dive out and swim hard to get out of the way of the sub's screw! Get to that pilot and don't let the V touch him! Braddock, you and Anderson shoot at that nearest trawler and anyone else in the water as we pass! Don't miss any of them!"

Raydon hastily tugged off his gear, throwing his M79 grenade launcher into a partially inflated rubber boat on deck. Braddock wielded his .45-caliber submachine gun, but he knew it wasn't powerful enough in the open. At two hundred yards he watched the sampan begin to move and slow. He didn't want the NVA to get behind the sub and get into a position where they'd be able to shoot the pilot, Stine, or Raydon. As the sub passed between the pilot's raft and the sampan, the two senior frogmen dove into the water and swam hard to the pilot. The man was screaming with joy and waving his arms as wildly as any fan whose home team had just won the championship.

The sub began an emergency slowdown, and it was everything the UDT men could do to hold on for dear life. As they sped past the sampan, Braddock kept his eyes glued to it. The sub would miss it by seventy-five yards, and the M3 Greasegun wouldn't do much from that distance. There had to be something else he could do to stop them cold.

Looking around frantically, Braddock spotted Raydon's grenade launcher in the rubber boat. He turned and grabbed it.

"Jake, hang on to me!" he screamed to the frogman next to him. He had to turn precariously to follow the trawler as he aimed the barrel of the weapon. He was well off balance. The sub was moving, the sampan was moving, and Braddock wasn't stable. There would only be a chance for one shot, and he couldn't afford to miss. Ignoring the leaf sight on the barrel, he sighted over the top and followed the boat with both eyes open, maximizing his parallax vision for depth perception. The world narrowed to the sight just over the barrel. He cut loose. The sampan took the round in the stern and came dead in the water as two men were blown overboard.

"Yeah!" the OIC screamed. The sub was slowing rapidly. "Get those boats inflated and over the sides!"

The frogmen scrambled to get the boats fully ready. As the submarine came to full stop, the boats went over the side, and all eyes were glued to the pilot and UDT men in the raft nearby. The second enemy vessel was hastily departing the area. Braddock and two other frogmen remained on the deck of the sub to cover the action. Suddenly a cry came from the conning tower. An officer with binoculars yelled and pointed in the opposite direction.

"There! Over there!"

Braddock picked it out immediately after he

shielded his eyes from the glare of the sun off the surface. It was a parachute in the water. The other crewman!

Glancing off the port side, Braddock realized that it would take several minutes for any of the rubber boats to get to the other man in the water. He immediately dropped his gear and donned his fins. There wasn't time to wait for an order. Diving off the sub, he stroked as hard as he could toward the parachute. The chute was over two hundred yards away, and there was no sign of the downed crewman. Suddenly Braddock realized what must have happened. It had almost happened to him on a couple of water jumps. The parachute had come down directly on top of the pilot. As the material soaked with water, it sank and would slowly close on anyone underneath.

There was a bulge under the soaked material. Braddock reached the canopy and flailed toward the object. It was the crewman. Braddock hastily whipped out his K-bar knife and cut the material away. The pilot was unconscious and limp, but face-up. Braddock gave him mouth-to-mouth resuscitation as he floated in his lifejacket.

The seconds ticked by as the frogman tried to force a response out of him. Nothing. Almost a minute; still nothing. Time was running out.

"Come on!" he yelled. "Breathe!" He tried a few more exhalations. No response. "Breathe! You're not gonna die on me! Breathe!"

Suddenly the crewman coughed violently and vomited water and blood. He gasped for air.

*   *   *

Braddock lay back in his bunk, feeling justifiably smug. They'd saved the crew and taken out a few North Vietnamese in the process. And now, finally given a chance to rest and reflect on it all, he was as content and complacent as a snake sunning itself on a rock.

The second pilot's arms had flailed during the ejection, and both had been broken. He was unable to talk on his radio while descending in his parachute or get into his raft once in the water. As the parachute soaked up sea, it collapsed on him and nearly drowned him. He was powerless to prevent it. If it hadn't been for Braddock's fast action, he would never have survived.

That operation, like all of Det Charlie's operations, was top secret. As a result, they never received any sort of special recognition for their actions. They never advertised their tactics and techniques, so that they could use them again successfully.

And they did.

8

Unauthorized Brightlight

December 1968

Joshua Marco finally looked up from his beer.

"Gentlemen," Marco said gravely, "I think the next toast ought to go to Colonel Nick Rowe. He was a legendary Green Beret, a VC POW a few of us managed to rescue during an unauthorized Brightlight mission into the U Minh Forest in 1968. He went on to build a fantastic survival and POW training course at Fort Bragg. Then he was killed in the line of duty while advising on another battlefield a couple of years ago."

"What?" Tom Dickerson was stunned. He'd gone on to civilian work for the Defense Intelligence Agency, but he'd started out as the idealistic, wet-behind-the-ears NILO who'd talked Marco into commanding that Brightlight. Woody Woodruff and Dutch Tash both froze for a moment before they could bring themselves to respond. They'd been on that mission as well.

"How in the hell did it happen?" Woody asked

quietly, tracing patterns in his beer mug's condensation with a finger.

"It was a total waste," Marco said bitterly. "A Philippine communist Sparrow assassination team shot and murdered him the day before I was finally supposed to meet him. Five years in the hell of a VC prison, only to die like that. He deserved a quiet retirement, but instead he chose to serve wherever he was needed, for as long as they let him. Nick Rowe was one hell of a Green Beret."

"A toast," Dickerson said tersely after a moment's silence, his blue eyes flashing cold fire. "To Colonel Nick Rowe, one of the greatest heroes of our time."

As one man, they raised their glasses and drained them dry.

"We know that the VC have moved the POWs all over the southern Cau Mau Peninsula. It's been extremely difficult to try to track them," he said dryly, tonelessly, his voice as crisp as his uniform. Lieutenant Tom Dickerson, the Navy intelligence liaison officer, paused for a moment to let his words sink in. He drummed a finger on the smooth, cold green metal of his desk, studying the man across from him.

Lieutenant Joshua Marco was trying to remain as detached and analytical as Dickerson. It wasn't quite working. A slight furrow in the brow betrayed the SEAL's concern for the American captives. Marco rubbed his square chin pensively and his dark eyes clouded as he lapsed into unpleasant thought. He could imagine too well the hell they must be going through.

"Three of the POWs were released by the communists to an American peace group last fall in the Cambodian capitol," the NILO picked up where he'd left off. That cool, dry, usually toneless voice actually soured a bit on the words "peace group." "During their debriefs, they said they'd been held way down south in South Vietnam's IV Corps and it had taken the VC a long time to get them to the sanctuaries across the border. Once they made it across, though, the communists took them in a sedan to the capitol. The peace activists wanted to use them for propaganda purposes as badly as the VC did, but they were thwarted by Uncle Sam. The POWs didn't have a chance to stay out of the limelight, so they did their best to remain as quiet as possible in front of the cameras and international press. No U.S. officials were going to be allowed near the three until they were back in the States. During the plane ride home, the group stopped for a refueling in Beirut, Lebanon."

"I know where Beirut is, Lieutenant," Marco drawled with a smirk.

"Sorry." Dickerson shrugged with what might have been the faint ghost of an amused smile. "Anyway, some of the Agency's people boarded the plane and surprised their hosts. Holding everyone at gunpoint, they took the POWs off. It was a slick, quiet move directed by the top brass in Washington. Some former Special Forces guys working contract for the Company did the deed. Those POWs really went through hell and were glad their addition to a liberal sideshow circus had been cut short. They arrived home quietly, a lot happier than they had been in a long time."

"Good! So where does that leave the others?" the SEAL asked with a raised eyebrow.

"We think they're still in the U Minh Forest," the NILO replied. "The 'Forest of Darkness' itself."

"You've got to be kidding me. There's no way we're going to stroll into the U Minh and make a hit on a camp. The place is *owned* by the VC, day and night!"

"Look, Marco, I can't do a lot more than try to pinpoint their location." Dickerson sighed with exasperation. "Pitzer, Jackson, and Johnson were lucky to have been released last year. Pitzer had been in there with Nick Rowe since October 1963. That was before John Kennedy was killed. Think about it. The POWs in North Vietnam have it really bad, but think about the guys being held in the U Minh. Those three guys last year took the release. Johnson was so sick he probably wouldn't have lasted another month in captivity." The intelligence officer paused for a moment. He was letting his emotions do his talking for him, not a habit he generally permitted himself.

"We know a lot of guys are dead," he continued more quietly. "Most down here in IV Corps die from malnutrition and disease. Three other Americans held with Pitzer, Jackson, and Johnson died that way. The VC don't have to beat them when they can tie them up in a cage in the swamp overnight with no insect net and let the Mekong mosquitoes feast on them. You've been out there on ambush, you know how it is. It takes a lot of care just to keep the regular troops from getting sick from leeches, jungle rot, and malaria. The POWs have it a lot worse. And the Vietcong beat on them anyway. Most of those who die just give up. You should read the debriefs from Pitzer and the others. You can only hack that much abuse for so long."

They lapsed into silence for a long moment. Dickerson's dreadfully quiet, controlled voice only made the mental images worse, somehow. Marco narrowly suppressed a shudder of revulsion.

"We also believe the VC have executed a few of the hardcore American POW resistors," Dickerson muttered tersely. "One was a Special Forces NCO named Roraback who was captured in III Corps in 1963. Another was an Army advisor, an NCO named Bennett, who was held in the same area and gave the 'Cong fits. The third was an officer named Versace, also captured with Rowe and Pitzer. He was the toughest. He gave the VC a real hard time. After the Saigon government executed a few guerrillas in 1965 for terrorist attacks against civilians, the VC offed a few POWs like Versace and the others, or so they claimed. Maybe they never executed them. Maybe they were just isolated and died of malnutrition, and the VC later claimed to have killed them. It doesn't matter. Either way, the guys are dead. That did the trick. The South Vietnamese quit executing captured guerrillas, with a lot of pressure from us."

Marco picked up two grainy black-and-white photos from the top of the small pile. Leaning forward, he rested both elbows on the desk and stared at the photos. One was of Nick Rowe in a tiger striped uniform. His hands were on top of his head and he was walking in a field of tall grass. Obviously a staged capture photo.

"That was taken from the body of a dead VC guerrilla. This," the intelligence officer said calmly, tapping the second photo, "is Rowe and Pitzer in a cage they were held in at the southern tip of the peninsula. That's Rowe again on the left, eating rice from a cup. They looked pretty healthy because they'd only been in captivity for a month. We pulled a Brightlight rescue operation on the camp about a year after it was finally pinpointed, but the POWs had been moved." "Brightlight" was the code name of recovery operations launched after conventional SAR efforts had been terminated.

"That seems to be the story behind all the intelligence about these guys," Marco pointed out. He looked the NILO in the eyes. "What's the problem?"

"We have the best technical intelligence money can buy, but the VC have much better HUMINT. They always get the word when we're going to make a move. We end up losing every time."

"What makes you think my men and I can make a difference?" Marco asked, impaling the other man with a penetrating gaze. The NILO cleared his throat and paused before he spoke.

"No one knows I'm here," he said quietly.

"So?"

The NILO just stared at him, waiting for it to click. It clicked.

"You mean this proposal isn't sanctioned?" the SEAL asked. It wasn't really a question.

"Bingo," said the spook. Marco looked at him for a few seconds, then shook his head in disbelief.

Dickerson leaned forward, a new emotional edge to his clipped speech.

"Listen, Marco, I can get you the best intel we have. No one has to know. I've seen the way these operations have been running. Every time the South Vietnamese are cut in at all, we end up in a dry hole. I can get you intel on any of the enemy force strengths and where the major camps are."

"That's not the point, Dickerson. I have to have a confirmed target to make a strike." Marco leaned back and jabbed a finger at the maps irritably. "And even if you had the intel, we're a small group. We'll need a lot of backup for an area like that. We always do. I just don't see that we can penetrate the U Minh. There's a hell of a lot of details to iron out."

The intelligence officer looked desperate. He leaned even closer, lowered his voice more. "Listen to me, Marco. I've seen the screw-ups down here. We've come close so many times and failed . . . but you guys are SEALs. You're different. I see the post operations reports. When you guys go trolling, you always bring in a body count. You clean the VC's clocks every time you have a chance to plan and execute a deliberate strike your way. Nobody in the Delta can touch you guys. The 'Cong know about the Green Faces, and it scares the ever-loving crap out of them." He paused for a moment, gathering his thoughts before he continued.

"Those POWs right now have only three fates, Marco. They can try to escape. If they fail, they'll be lucky to live after the VC get through with them. They can take an early release and get used for propaganda against their country, something directly opposed to the Code of Conduct. Or they can rot and die in a jungle camp. I can't see a lot of things in this country that are worth dying for," he said, jamming his finger down on a photo, "but getting these guys out is one. I can't sit back if I think I can narrow down the area they're in. I can't let them die if I think I can make a difference. Most of the men who walk into those camps don't leave them alive. Marco, we owe them a shot. I think I can get you closer than any team has ever been. But I can't go get them. I'm only an intel weenie. Only teams like yours have a chance in there. A big force could never infiltrate the AO."

Marco held up a hand and lowered his gaze. At the very least, he was starting to like Dickerson a bit more than he'd thought he would.

"Okay, I get your message," he said after a moment. "But that doesn't give me or my men a target. I don't need a lecture, I need an objective. And the only promise I'll give you is that I'll look at it and tell you if we can do it or not."

"My friend," the NILO beamed, "I have something right up your alley. I've studied everything I can get my hands on. Fact one is that all the POWs in the South are going to be held near major VC camps and concentrations. All the intel and debriefs from escaped or released POWs have confirmed that. I agree that hitting a major camp may be remotely possible, but it would also be suicide. A small team might be able to get in, but once the hornet's nest is stirred, they'll never get out alive.

"Fact two is that there are a lot of ways the VC travel, but down here in IV Corps, they travel almost exclusively by small boat. You know it's all rivers, canals, and streams. Those few POWs who have gotten out of the Delta alive confirm that every time they were moved, they were moved by boat."

"Great," Marco muttered irascibly. "That narrows it down to several thousand streams, rivers, and canals laced throughout the region."

"No, I can do better," Dickerson said evenly, his mask of cool efficiency firmly back in place. "First, we know that Rowe and probably several other American POWs are still being held in the U Minh. I've looked at everything I can possibly find, and I think they're in the northern part, west of Tan Phu. I have three recent HUMINT reports and they all jibe with VC troop concentrations."

"Go on," the SEAL murmured, becoming interested in spite of himself.

"I think the VC would move the POWs if they thought they were threatened with a rescue attempt or raid. From what we know, they either throw them in a boat and book, or they drag them into the swamps. Our teams have tried to track them, but they've always lost the scent or gotten popped at by snipers until it just wasn't worth the effort. There are only a finite number of canals they can use in the area I believe the POWs are being held in. If you could lead a small team into the site, you could conduct a reconnaissance of the area and possibly locate them when they move."

They lapsed into silence for a few moments while Marco pursed his lips in thought. He finally looked up, slowly, his expression unfathomable.

"I don't think we can pull it off. Even if we *could* locate them, and that's a big if, we'd be overwhelmed by the 'Cong in the area within minutes of making contact."

"Before the Tet Offensive, I might have agreed with you," Dickerson countered smoothly. "But it's different now. The VC were used as the vanguard for the NVA and were decimated by Tet. Their ranks were thinned considerably, and their leadership has fallen under heavier control by Hanoi. I've been watching the intel reports, and I think Hanoi is making a subtle power play. They're going to take more control of the field leadership in the war. They're even going to want control of all the political cards, and that includes their main bargaining chips, the POWs."

"Go on," Marco nodded, frankly intrigued. The boy was pretty bright, for an intel weenie.

"I think the POWs are going to be consolidated into areas of strong NVA control. The POWs down south will probably be moved north, possibly even to Hanoi eventually. In the meantime, I think they're going to be taken into the NVA strongholds across the borders in Cambodia and Laos. And if you think the U Minh is tough to crack, try the area where COSVN is located," the NILO muttered, referring to the insidious communist headquarters in the South.

"I still don't think it will work," Marco shrugged apologetically. "We don't stay in the field for long periods and we don't patrol aimlessly if we don't have a spot marked on the map. The U Minh is huge. I just don't see how you're ever going to be able to narrow it down and tell us when they might be on the move. It's too hit-or-miss. I'm sorry, I really am, but I don't think we can help you."

The other man sat for a while, then rubbed both hands across his face vigorously. Marco tried not to look at the photos on the desk. Dickerson tried desperately to summon an argument, but couldn't think of anything to say.

"Okay," the NILO sighed at last. "Well, it was worth a try." He began to collect the pictures and the maps.

Marco hated it, but he knew it couldn't be helped. He remembered a mission from his last tour. He'd watched from an ambush site as an Army company had heloed into a village. Later he'd found out they'd been after a village chief who was a VC cadre. The VC easily scrambled out of the village, alerted by the noise of the helos. He knew they did the same thing when it came to the POWs. There would never be a way to get them out unless a team went in quietly on the ground first. *That's it!* he thought suddenly, almost bolting out of his chair.

"Wait just a minute," the SEAL whispered excitedly. Dickerson stopped and looked at him. "Let me see the map near Tan Phu again." The intelligence officer hastily laid it out. He had no idea what Marco might be thinking, but he wanted to try anything that might have a chance of success. Marco looked at the map for nearly a minute before fingering the canals around the red area west of Tan Phu.

"You think they're there, right?" he asked, jabbing at the spot that seemed most likely.

"Better than that, I think they're in this area that covers two or three grid squares right here." Dickerson pointed, excited. "There's been heavy bombing in the last few weeks, especially here and here, and the VC will take a pounding for only so long. We had Mohawk aircraft in the area yesterday, and they detected a major troop concentration in these three grid squares. If the United States sends a sweep of ground troops through the area, they'll be gone in a flash and we'll be left with nothing. We're too predictable. I'm sure the Army is planning to do just that. I want to beat them to the punch and get a small team in quietly on the ground before they send in a few battalions."

Marco looked closely at the map.

"I counted a lot of small canals and streams," he said thoughtfully, "but only four major waterways I think they'd use if they were in this area and wanted to escape an attack. I don't think we can penetrate those grid squares, especially if there's a major VC base camp in there. But I do think we can cover the major canals around the perimeter. If I take the entire platoon, that's fourteen men, we can get in there quietly on the ground and split up into four small groups. Each team moves in slowly and carefully around the perimeter of this area you've marked until we have each of the four major routes covered by a group."

Dickerson's heart raced, and he took a deep breath to steady himself.

"What type of access do you have to a large heliborne reaction force?" Marco asked him.

"That's easy. I can get a company or two easily from the 1st Air Cavalry Division."

"Here's how we work it, then. Once we're in place, you call in the helo force. That should cause the VC to move. As soon as they hear the helos inbound, they'll bolt. They can't stay in a large force and evade. They'll split into dozens of small groups. I've seen it happen a lot. Once they split up and start moving, my team should see them on the ground, especially if they use the canals we think they will. If we can hit them quickly, we may have a chance. In a riverine ambush, everyone always goes into the water immediately. So we look for a boat with a POW in it, jump it, and throw everyone in the water where they can't fight back. We might be able to snatch a POW from the water before they can regroup. And even if we can't hit the VC ourselves, we can stay hidden and vector the helo force right on top of them. Hell, one of the captives may even be able to break loose in all the confusion and simply escape. Either way, it would pay to have a handful of us there on the ground to try to grab one."

It was a desperate concept. It was also just crazy enough to work.

"Marco, I could kiss you right now," Dickerson said, grinning. "It might work. It just might work!"

Two days and a dozen long hours of planning later, Marco and his platoon were on the ground. The SEALs had split into two groups for insertion. Each had used small dug-out indigenous craft that they poled and paddled up the streams and canals. When they got close to the rear, they sank the boats and abandoned them, closing slowly on the target area by wading up the waterways along the banks with thick brush. The insertion was slow and deliberate; they had a lot of obstacles to dodge. Several times the SEALs couldn't afford to move until the VC sentries they spotted had finally been distracted or waited out. Some of the canals were heavily boobytrapped with grenades and other improvised VC devices. The closer they got, the more devices they were going to find. A good indicator, if a potentially deadly one. But the two squads finally made it to the grid squares in question.

Marco had decided in the end to conduct movement in two seven-man squad teams. Smaller groups had a better chance of moving undetected, and since they'd first started working in country, the seven-man squads were the natural fighting and patrolling element that they normally operated in. If one squad was compromised and had to be extracted, the other might be able to lie low on the ground and still complete the mission by breaking into pairs. Once in the area, the two groups had a prearranged time movement schedule they would keep, with each SEAL group slipping to a specific canal to set up and wait. Two of the groups would have four men, and the other two would only have three. This minimized radio communications, which Marco didn't trust and didn't want to initiate if they could be avoided. The VC could easily pick up their transmissions with captured radios.

Most of the movement into the area was covered by an elaborate series of overflights by high performance aircraft intermixed with continued bombing. Some of the aircraft were fast movers and others were cargo aircraft, but all made noise and drew attention, which got Marco and his men past the worst danger areas. Dickerson helped coordinate the flights and made sure none were conducted by helos or forward air controller aircraft.

They wanted to make the VC uneasy, but helos and FAC aircraft would have signalled a potential ground assault before the SEALs were in position. Dickerson had a hard time covering the fact that the SEALs were on the ground. He was able to pull it off and still coordinate the distraction flights by telling anyone who asked that the SEALs were after an important visiting COSVN-level cadre.

Within thirty-six hours of insertion, all the SEAL groups were in place and ready to recon or conduct a snatch. The VC owned the area, but they were still forced to travel at night. The heliborne assault would be made the next day, at first light. That would flush the VC out when they felt naked in the daylight and give them another reason to run and hide rather than stand and fight. If there was one thing the SEALs had learned, it was that if you could complete your mission and never have to engage the enemy, you almost always brought all your guys out in one piece. All these factors had been carefully weighed by the Americans before the launch of the operation.

Dickerson concocted the story about the COSVN-level cadre making a visit into the area, and thus he was able to get the support he needed without spilling the POW story to the Army helo troops. The less people who knew about the real objective, the better.

Marco's three-man team bumped into a lot of VC during their final penetration into the target area. The men carried silenced handguns for just such a contingency. Marco carried a .22-caliber Colt Woodsman with a suppressor. It fired a small round but was extremely quiet. At close range, anyone hit in the right spot would go down. And OS1 Pat Woodruff and RM2 Joe "Dutch" Tash each carried a 9-mm Smith and Wesson M39 with a threaded five-inch barrel.

In the last six hours, Marco and his group had had to kill one VC and had come close to shooting three more in their penetration of the area. That was the tricky part. They had to avoid contact at all costs. If the VC showed up missing at the end of their guard duty time, the mission might be compromised. The one they'd had to kill was buried in thick mud, and with luck, hidden forever. They had to deceive the VC only until after the airmobile assault at dawn. Desertions were up within the VC ranks since the Tet Offensive, so there was actually a fair chance the missing man would be considered a deserter for the time being.

When first light was just a few minutes away, Marco gently shook the two men who'd rotated watch with him. They'd taken the opportunity to sleep for a few hours in their final concealed position as they'd waited for daylight and the air raid. Marco truly didn't know if the operation would go as planned, and as each hour crawled by and they watched a lot of VC come and go, he only hoped all his men would be picked up by the helos if the situation went bad.

The Army knew the SEALs were out there. Dickerson had had to tell them that much to make sure they knew it wasn't a free-fire zone. If the Army had to identify their targets with care, they would also be careful in engaging potential POWs. But there was going to be a lot of movement once the action started. The SEALs would use radios, signal mirrors, and orange VS-17 panels to get the attention of one of the extraction birds when they were needed.

It was deathly still when Marco, Woody, and Dutch heard the frantic screech of a monkey and a bird about five hundred meters to the east. They were on the western edge of the grid squares; those cries had to be coming from a VC encampment. Then, in the distance, the first faint hum of the helicopters became audible.

"It's an alert system," Marco hissed, impressed. "It's a damned alert system! Those animals can sense aircraft at a further distance than a human. They sound an alarm and the V get a bigger head start into the bush!"

"Brilliant." Woody nodded calmly, unflappable, as always. "That's one for the Barndance Cards," he barely breathed in reply, referring to the code name for SEAL post-operation reports.

Within seconds, the VC could be heard noisily sounding the alarm and scurrying to abandon their camp. Someone repeatedly struck a gong, and a bugle sounded in the distance. The helos continued to close from the east. They were coming low and fast and would be over the area in another two minutes, plenty of time for the communist soldiers to vacate the camp. No wonder the Americans had never succeeded in rescuing a POW . . .

Marco heard the radio come alive as two of the SEAL groups reported movement of dozens of enemy soldiers. No POWs were identified among the enemy groups yet. Then one team on the far side of the grid squares had to initiate contact and was forced to move and hide. The VC wouldn't pursue them, instead running for their own lives as the helos attacked.

Marco had chosen the westernmost side for himself, hoping the VC would try to move any POWs they had deeper into the U Minh. Only the SEAL groups stood between freedom and another POW camp in the swamp.

"Movement," Dutch hissed sharply, his eyes glued to the east, up the canal. The sounds of a large group moving quickly toward the SEALs' position became audible. Then, as Marco lifted up slowly to get a first glimpse, he saw them. There was a small footpath on the far canal bank, and several VC appeared on it, moving rapidly. They were dragging along a lighter-skinned man with a full dark beard and dark hair. He wore black pajamas, like the VC, but there was no mistaking him for one of them.

Marco's heart raced. A POW! An American captive! Before he could react, several small craft came into view directly in line with the group on the far canal bank.

Helos broke overhead and split into hunter-killer teams which zipped around in patterns covering different sectors in the grids. The VC were scrambling and breaking into small groups of five and less, dispersing into the swamp like smoke. Marco, Woody, and Dutch would have only one chance to act.

"Hit the boats!" he yelled at the other SEALs, as he rose up on his knees and opened up in short bursts at the craft. Woody immediately did the same, and their fire caught the communists flat-footed. Dutch cooked off two grenades and threw them in a high arch to explode in the air above the boats. The soldiers jumped into the water, immediately negating their ability to fight. Marco did this deliberately to cut the odds severely and looked toward the far bank as he reloaded another magazine.

"Cease fire!" he said twice. He and Woody both knew they had to watch where they fired to avoid hitting the POW, but they also knew they had to take the risk. Marco had trained repeatedly to be able to change magazines by feel so that he could keep his eyes on developments downrange. As he watched now, he saw the soldiers on the far side scatter and pull the POW into the bush.

"We can't go after them and keep the radio up and dry," Woody said aloud, their noise discipline broken with the contact.

"I know," Marco answered him with a hint of frustration. "We've got time for one call before we need to get out. Give me the handset."

As Marco called in his information, he watched the helos dance in the sky. Woody reloaded while Dutch covered them. Several small gunships were making runs on isolated packets of resistance which were foolish enough to fire at the aircraft. Sporadic gunfire in all directions laced the area. In all the excited radio chatter, Marco could break in only long enough to get a pickup call about a hundred meters to their rear. He hadn't imagined the conventional troops would tie up the radio for so long. Valuable minutes were being lost. The helos were having a field day. There were targets everywhere. Marco couldn't get the information about the POW out on the airwaves yet, but if he and the other two SEALs could get airborne, they could quickly lead a team to the far side of the canal, cordon off the area, and try to locate the American before the VC escaped.

The SEALs picked up to move, Marco on point to cut down the amount of time it would take. They stopped once to flash an orange panel at a helo when Dutch opened up at something behind them. Four VC had stumbled onto their position, and he'd hit three of them at point-blank range as they'd come through the bush. As Dutch went prone and rolled to the left, Woody swung his muzzle around and caught the last communist soldier in the back as he tried to flee.

A few minutes later a Huey swept in and picked up the SEALs. Marco knew how easily the situation could fall apart even now, so he stayed quiet about the POW for the moment. If they failed this time, they might be able to try the same tactic another day. Immediately the SEAL officer ordered the crew to get a couple of helos in trail with troops aboard, vectoring the aircraft to the area across the canal. The area was laced with a few trees and a lot of high grass. No groups of VC were visible from the air, and Marco frantically scanned the ground for any signs of them.

With no immediate enemy groups to target, Marco had to revise his plans quickly. He wanted to avoid cordoning off the area now unless it was a last resort. First, if the VC were cornered, they might kill the POW and find a way to melt into the swamp. Marco remembered what Dickerson had said about the standing orders of the VC guards to kill their prisoners if rescue was imminent. They'd be less mobile. He had to make sure that once they were back on the ground, they definitely had the area the POW was in cordoned off. He couldn't let the VC slip away with the captive as they had so many times before. They were too damned close for that.

"We need to take a VC prisoner," Marco called to the pilot. "Drop down on the first soldier you find scrambling around by himself. We'll jump out and grab him. We can find out from him where our COSVN VIP went," he explained above the din of the helo, sticking to their cover story.

"You got it!" the pilot called back over the intercom, immediately relaying to the other helos and banking sharply.

Thirty seconds later they got the message that a gunship was lining up on a lone suspect at that moment. The lone enemy soldier, clad in black, was in the middle of a field waving a large light-colored piece of cloth. It could be a lure into a trap; it had happened on other raids. A trap . . . or a defector with critical intelligence . . . or an escaped POW . . .

Marco grabbed the pilot's arm and bellowed over the noise of the engine.

"Tell them not to fire! Pick him up! We need the intel! Tell them to pick the guy up!"

"They already got the message from a Command and Control Bird. A helo is going in to get him. We won't be needed for it," the pilot shouted back in reply.

Marco's helo circled with two other Hueys close behind. All eyes were glued to the ground for a tense moment. Then the transmission came over the radio.

"He's an American," the pilot gasped in pure amazement. "They just picked up an American POW!"

Marco and the other SEALs exploded, screamed with clenched fists, pounding each other on the back and yelling. The pilot came up on the intercom again.

"The guy was a POW! They're flying him out now! I can't believe it! Okay, okay, settle down in back. He might not be the only one. Keep your eyes peeled; look for more."

The helos continued to circle and weave as they took sporadic gunfire from pockets of resistance. Before long, Marco began to coordinate pickups of the SEALs still scattered throughout the area. It took an hour and a half before they were all accounted for, but they finally made it out safe and got involved in mop-up from the air.

The Vietcong didn't stand and fight; they broke into small groups and faded into the swamp. The air assault was largely ineffective in destroying the guerrillas, but it would be weeks before they could regroup and reorganize. The Americans would have a month's breathing space. That, and the fact that an American POW had actually been brought out alive, made it all worth the effort.

The SEALs returned to base, downstaged, and debriefed. They volunteered to go back in if the POW could pinpoint more prisoner locations. He tried, but he ended up leading another force into a camp that had been emptied during the raid. They were met by empty POW cages. If there had been other American prisoners, they were now long gone.

Seven days later, Dickerson finally visited the platoon. He filled in the gaps about the end of the operation. But first he wanted to get all the information he could from the SEALs: how they'd penetrated the area, where they'd set up, what they'd seen, how the VC had reacted to the helo assault. The day after the raid, Marco had read in the Defense Department's overseas newspaper, *Stars and Stripes*, that it had been Major Nick Rowe who'd escaped captivity.

"That ambush you launched started the chain of events." Dickerson grinned, running a hand through his pale blond hair. "At the sound of the first alarm, Rowe was being dragged out of the camp by a small group of guards who were his dedicated cadre. When you hit the group as they moved, they split up even more and went into the bush. Rowe said every time they changed direction they found themselves being pursued, and the V were really shook. He managed to convince one of the guards that they'd be killed by the aircraft unless he listened to him, and they slipped away from the rest of the squad. Rowe promised the soldier he'd keep him alive. Said they'd all surely die if they followed the squad leader, who was apparently determined to make a stand against the attacking force. He knew if the VC were cornered, they'd shoot him and run for their lives. Like I told you before the op, those are their standing orders. We knew that from Pitzer and the others."

They exchanged a look at that, and Dickerson sighed, shook his head, and continued.

"Rowe finally convinced the soldier, and they struck out on their own. The VC took point after a while to speed them up. They were surrounded by thick brush, and the VC slung his submachine gun behind his back to free up his hands. Rowe found the right moment to dump the magazine out of the weapon and push it into the mud. All that left the guard with was a couple of grenades. The 'Cong noticed the missing magazine a few minutes later and was really going into shock. Just wasn't his day, I guess. Rowe got him moving again and whacked him over the head with a huge stick as soon as his back was turned. Then he headed into a field and stomped down the grass. With a small LZ out there, he began to wave a white mosquito net he'd been carrying with him, and he managed to draw the attention of one of the helos. That's when one of the Cobra gunships started lining up for a gunrun on him."

Marco whistled and picked up the story.

"I got airborne about that time and told them we needed to pick up a VC prisoner for information to help locate our VIP. I hoped they'd think I was talking about that fictitious COSVN cadre."

"Well," Dickerson chimed in cheerfully, "just before the gunship rolled in hot, the word came through to pick up a prisoner, so the gunship was waved off. A Slick swept in, Rowe ran to the bird and dived in, and they powered out of the swamp."

"Man, we were *that close* to blowing him away," Marco breathed.

"That's not the half of it. Only days before, Rowe had found out he was being transferred to 'higher headquarters.' "

"Just as you predicted they'd start doing with

the prisoners," Marco nodded, almost a salute.

"The cover story he'd been using for years in captivity had been blown by information provided to the communists by peace activists back in the United States. The V were furious with him; they'd lost a lot of face. Rowe thought he was going to be executed. He got out just in time. And the rest is history," the NILO concluded, leaning back in his chair and grinning like the Cheshire cat. "But the story doesn't end there. Rowe was hustled back to regional headquarters in Camau, and insisted on immediately leading a commando force back into the camps."

"That's insane!" Marco murmured admiringly. "He ought to get the Distinguished Service Cross."

"Tell me about it!" the NILO agreed. "He believed there were other Americans out there, though he'd been held separately after Pitzer, Jackson, and Johnson had been released. Last January they took him to see a propaganda film one of the traveling VC propaganda teams was showing. He was sure he'd seen at least three other American captives in the crowd, but he wasn't allowed anywhere near them. Anyway, Rowe led a rescue team back into the U Minh, and they hit the site of his last camp. Sure as hell, there were other POW cages a few hundred meters away in another branch camp, but no POWs. Plenty of physical evidence that they'd been there, but the V got away with them."

He was somber for a moment, and then he glanced up at Marco and held out his hand. They'd gotten Rowe out, and it was a start. "It worked, you dirty swamp hog," Dickerson laughed. "You and your team did it!"

Marco took his hand, joining him in the laugh. "*We* did it, you little intel weenie! We all did it."

The two men savored the moment, then slapped each other on the back.

"I'm going to write your team up," Dickerson grinned. "You guys deserve a lot of credit."

Marco's smile faded. "You can't do that," he muttered grimly.

"What do you mean? Why the hell not? You've got to be out of your mind, Marco! You guys should be recognized!"

"Listen, Slim, it worked," the SEAL sighed. "We got a man out. Alive. One man. It really worked. And it could work again. We both know there's other guys out there." Marco looked him in the eye, pausing for a brief moment. "Give the credit to the 1st Air Cav Division. That's the only way we might pull it off again."

The NILO slowly nodded in total understanding. It was the only way. If the story of the SEAL operation got out, it would make *Stars and Stripes* and be in every VC headquarters overnight. They'd never get another man out using the same technique. If they kept their mouths shut, it might work again sometime. It was worth a shot.

"Okay," Dickerson said quietly. "Okay. I understand. But it sucks. You guys deserve a lot better."

"Maybe someday I'll meet Rowe. That would make it all worthwhile."

Marco and his men worked closely with Dickerson the rest of the tour. They hit several other possible POW camps in the next few months, but they never managed to find another American. Still, they saved a total of twenty-three South Vietnamese who'd been captured and held in the swamps. At the end of the tour, Dickerson asked them if it had been worth the effort.

To a man they believed it had.

9

The Other Vietnam Vets

November 1969

"I remember a CIA planning session not too unlike that one." Tony Franco nodded solemnly, gesturing with his beer mug. "That mission was a disaster, though, as far as I'm concerned. I'd love to blame it on the spook who talked me into it, but it wasn't his fault."

Franco had always been outspoken in his low opinion of the Agency, but it hadn't stopped him from eventually joining them when he left the teams, after Vietnam. It was a love-hate relationship that began during his first advisory role in Da Nang in 1962. This was one of the stories he hated to tell but always found himself telling at these gatherings. In a way he was punishing himself, but he couldn't help that.

Franco couldn't rely on the Agency to give a SEAL all the information he needed, as hard experience and three other Vietnam tours had taught him. This time he wasn't buying. He had a lot of contacts in country, and he'd managed to surround himself with a personal intelligence network. It beat settling for whatever scraps of information he could wrangle out of the CIA.

This tour, he'd been assigned as an advisor to a provincial reconnaissance unit in the Kien Giang Province. They saw some tough fighting and got missions so rotten no one else would touch them. Some of his men were criminals who decided that fighting and being paid good money for it was better than rotting in a South Vietnamese jail. Most of them were just ethnic Vietnamese who never fit in anywhere else. The rest were VC defectors. It took someone hard to handle them.

If you paid the PRU for weapons they captured from kills, they could deceive you by killing any poor schmuck for his gun, whether he was a VC or not. The same went for ears. Those things just never worked. The only thing that did was fear. The SEAL worked hard to foster the belief that he was crazier and deadlier than any three of them. His team had to be made to fear him more than any VC cadre.

But under Franco's unorthodox methods, they fared far better than most units. At least they could live it up until they caught a bullet.

Franco and his PRU operated all over the province. They launched commando operations into the VC's backyard. Missions ranged from raids to snatches of VC cadre to ambushes. They collected captured documents for intelligence exploitation, hit supply routes, and knocked off VC tax collectors. The tax collectors were the best. They never turned in all the loot from those missions. Franco supplemented rewards to his men with that money and used some of it to enhance his personal intelligence network.

The VC and NVA had sunk their own agents deep into the South Vietnamese infrastructure. One of them even wormed his way into Franco's PRU team. Franco used him to turn intelligence against the VC which ended in the deaths of two female assassins posing as prostitutes in Cholon. It was no accident that the double agent in Franco's team didn't survive that operation either.

No, Franco definitely couldn't trust the Agency. He was never more keenly aware of that fact than at moments like this, when they were trying a little too hard to talk him into something.

He studied the faces around the dark, polished conference table, then swirled the water in his glass. Too many CIA brass present, which unfailingly aroused his suspicions. *I don't like this*, he thought, setting the glass down and battling the urge to drum his fingers on the table. *They're trying too hard to sell me on the mission. And I wouldn't buy a used car from any of them.*

Once the initial briefs were finished, the room cleared out, leaving him with the key CIA players. That was when the meat of the story came out.

"We really need the guy alive," his case officer wheezed. "He does us no good dead. He has critical intelligence we need to exploit. It could make a big difference." Bill Jason was a short, balding man in his mid-forties, and he did more to inspire distrust than the rest of the room put together. His small dark eyes darted around nervously, and he licked his narrow lips a lot as he talked. There was a vaguely rodent cast to his jaundiced features. *No, I'm definitely not buying a used car from this one.*

"Listen, Jason," the SEAL sighed, after a moment's thought, "you know I can't guarantee we can snatch a guy like that in that area." Franco jabbed a finger at the map on the wall for emphasis. "He'll have his own bodyguard detail and travel only with larger units of VC and NVA."

"Yeah, we know that," Jason nodded in fawning acquiescence, mopping the sweat off his brow with a stained handkerchief. "We also know there are a lot of other teams who could attempt a snatch. It's gonna be a tough one, very hot. There are going to be casualties. We really need this guy, but we don't want to risk an all-Anglo SEAL or Special Forces team."

There it was again. The dirtiest missions, given to the "more expendable" non-whites. Franco glared at his controller.

"My men are not expendable," he said slowly, quietly, emphasizing every word. Jason swallowed nervously and licked his lips again. "They're not afraid to take it to the V, and they're not afraid to die. They'll follow me regardless of the target. But I've built them up and invested a lot of time and effort to get them this far. They're effective and they bring in results. I won't be a part of throwing all that away! Find yourself some other expendables," he snapped acridly, rising from his seat to leave.

"Franco, wait! Clear out, everyone. Leave me alone with him." The speed with which the other CIA men obeyed him forced him to grudgingly revise his estimation of the man upward. Slightly. Jason plunged into a different approach.

"Look, there are elements of this operation that even I can't reveal," he began, glancing around nervously, as if he didn't want the walls to hear him.

"Cut the crap!" Franco snarled, cutting him off. "I don't do suicide missions, and I sure as hell don't care if one more Soviet advisor is bumping around in the night out there when I patrol. If we meet in the dark, there's going to be a firefight, and I intend to go home alive. I don't care if he lives or dies, any more than I care about any of the hundreds of other foreign advisors out there who don't officially exist. I'm not risking my neck or the lives of my men, who trust me completely, on trying to creep into an enemy regimental headquarters with a handful of guns to try to capture some Ivan cowboy on a mission impossible. I've been in that area before," he muttered, whipping out his K-bar knife and pointing it at the map for emphasis. "There's a VC for every blade of grass."

The CIA man sat down and sighed heavily. When he spoke again, his voice was quiet and controlled, but with a vicious edge Franco had never heard him use before.

"Okay, Franco. You want the truth, I'll give it to you. Just make sure you really want to hear it." Jason fired up a cigarette and inhaled deeply. "This guy isn't just another Soviet *Spetznaz* officer providing guidance on commando operations to the

VC. Oh, he's doing that, all right, but we also know he has a substantial intelligence background. He specializes in American electronic warfare equipment."

Franco sheathed his knife and sat down. *Damn*, he thought. *He's got my attention.*

"This isn't about capturing a prisoner. It's about saving some of our own." The Agency man rose and paused as he walked toward the window. He stopped with his back to Franco and gazed out as he continued. "For years now, the VC and NVA have picked up a lot of Americans, including a few from the Agency. They have POW camps spread out all over. The system in the North holds mostly aircrew, while the jungle camps hold mostly ground troops and helicopter crewmen. The system is fragmented, but controlled effectively by Hanoi. The NVA get a hell of a lot of assistance from other communist governments for all that."

The CIA agent finally turned and looked at the SEAL.

"For some time now, we have accumulated intelligence information that suggests that at least some of the American POWs have been taken into other countries."

"It doesn't take a brain surgeon to figure that out, Jason," Franco said coldly. "They're taking them into their sanctuaries in Cambodia and Laos where we can't get to them easily."

"No, no, that's not what I mean." Jason cut him off, holding up a hand impatiently and shaking his head. "I'm talking about China, the Soviet Union, possibly even North Korea. Eastern Europe. They're handing over POWs as partial repayment of their debts to their communist buddies for assisting them in the war."

Franco looked at him with mild shock. After a long pause he blinked and said, "You know what that means, don't you?"

"Yeah, I know what that means."

"We're never going to see those guys alive again."

"Maybe not," the case officer sighed, settling into the chair on the other side of the table. "Maybe not, but if we don't find out the exact routing and why and where they're being taken, they are definitely history."

Franco leaned back and exhaled slowly. "So what's that got to do with this guy you want snatched?"

"He's part of the routing. He's been identified as a KGB officer, and we believe he's one of a very few men responsible for touring the communist sanctuaries and selecting a handful of Americans to disappear from the POW camp system. Most of the ones he chooses will have technical knowledge, while others may just be the hardest resisters, the ones they want to experiment with over long periods of time. They may want to refine their methods of breaking men. This way they have a supply of real live American military men and no time restrictions. They have all the time in the world to find the best methods of taking men's brains apart piece by piece."

Jason finished his cigarette and threw it on the floor, stamping it out. "It could take ten or twenty years," he said coolly. "Maybe even longer. There's no pressure. Those subjects are never going home."

He rose and returned to the window, leaned against the glass, looked out at nothing. "This is all just a theory. So far, I can't prove squat. The few of us who believe this is taking place can't seem to agree on what it means. To me, it doesn't matter. If they're hiding some of our men, we have to find out where they are and do something to stop it and get them back. Too many of the men who should be showing up in the prison camps we know of aren't showing up. We can't account for them. Either there's another system we haven't identified, or they're being taken away . . . or both. But if we don't pin this one down, a lot of good men who think their country will get them out are going to wind up wondering years from now why no one ever came for them. All this seems to jibe with what we believe has happened to other aircrews downed across or near communist borders as they flew intelligence missions in the fifties and sixties. Maybe they're taking men from Vietnam to join others they already have behind the Iron and Bamboo Curtains.

"This guy we want you to go after may hold the key. He's one of the few we've identified that can reveal the whole scam. We try to keep track worldwide of all the key KGB and GRU players in this, but most are beyond our reach. This one is not only in Vietnam, he's in the South. He's close. We have a confirmed sighting. We've looked at the mission and the difficulty. It's a tough one. We think we can get a team in, but getting out will be almost impossible without causalties. This guy does us no good dead. Just going in to kill him won't give us a thing. But we may be able to fake the V into be-

lieving he was killed in the action. That's where we
need you. Making it look like an assassination is
right up the PRU's alley. The VC would believe
that if they knew PRUs were involved."

Franco got the picture, maybe a little more
clearly than the Agency man had intended him to.
PRUs were the action arm of the Agency's Phoenix
Program. They targeted infrastructure cadre and either captured or killed them. That was their trademark. The Company *wanted* a few of his PRUs to
get themselves killed. Their bodies, left behind,
would make the cover believable. That was why
they didn't want to sacrifice an American SEAL or
Special Forces team. All the worst jobs . . . Franco
didn't like it, but he'd accepted it a long time ago.
He held his temper and kept listening.

"If the VC and NVA think he's dead but the
body is lost, when in fact we have him alive . . .
well, that would be the best of all possible worlds,"
Jason concluded with a shrug and an oily reptilian
grin. Franco sighed mentally. He might consider
working with him on this one, but bosom friend-
ship was clearly going to be out of the question.

"What makes you believe he'll talk if we can pull
this off?" the SEAL asked him with a level stare.
"I've seen torture, and it's unreliable. The subject
will tell you what he thinks you want to hear just
to make you stop the pain you're inflicting."

"Leave that to us. Chemical interrogation can do
wonders. We'll have him talking in a matter of
days. But we need him alive. We *have* to have him
alive. You know the area. You have the best team
available. You're it, the best chance we have at
this."

Franco stared at the map on the wall, weighing the prospect of quick deaths for his men against the possibility that American POWs could be used for that kind of prolonged experimentation. *I hate this*, he thought. Without turning, he finally spoke.

"All right, Jason," he said quietly. "All right. But we do this my way. I don't want any of your Agency buddies screwing this up."

"You got it, Franco. Anything you need."

And the Case Officer meant it.

The plan was simple. Franco knew they would never be able to slip a force large enough for the job into the regimental headquarters. That would be suicide. They had to recon the area and determine the primary and alternate escape routes the VC had mapped out in case of an attack. Those same small recon teams would then cover the escape routes while a massive strike was called in. In the confusion, as the VC fought rear guard actions and allowed their leaders to slip into the jungle, Franco hoped to be able to snag the Soviet.

His plan was to match the snatch site up to a nearby waterway and make it appear to be a drowning. But once the teams on the ground were detected and the snatch attempted, Franco wouldn't be able to guarantee the success of the deception. The situation wouldn't be predictable until they got there and reconned. It wouldn't be easy, but if they got their hands on the Soviet, he'd find a way to get them out. And if he couldn't, he would personally make sure it was the last firefight the Soviet would ever be in.

Franco handpicked two five-man teams. He

would lead them in. They planned and rehearsed for two days. On the third, the Agency controller told Franco they'd intercepted SIGINT, which indicated that the VC regimental headquarters would be moving in a few days. It was time to insert the team.

The men used sampans to arrive on station. They inserted by swimming ashore at night, maximizing stealth, low visibility, and quiet. Once on land, they moved carefully to a base camp and set up shop in an austere field setting. Franco knew they'd be out there for several days, the kind of operations he hated most. But there was no getting around the fact that this one was going to take time. Reconnaissance was a deadly science when you were outnumbered so heavily.

After two days of careful movement and recon, he was sure they had the two most likely escape routes located. Each led away from the headquarters in opposite directions to waterborne indigenous craft which could carry the escapees swiftly downriver. Franco positioned one indig team on the route he suspected would be secondary. He would remain on the primary trail with five others.

From intelligence the Agency had given him, he knew the layout of the regimental headquarters. The Soviet stayed in a hootch on the east side of the camp. Franco decided to lie in wait on the eastern trail. And in the prebriefing he'd let his Case Officer know that he'd be calling in the direction of the air attack from the field once his recons were complete. He called it in from the west. That would help drive the escapees toward the eastern trail, he thought. He hoped.

The recons had been extremely difficult. The indig he'd taken along had been less than thrilled at finding themselves so close to so many VC. But they'd been promised a beautiful bonus, so they had accepted the mission without too much grumbling. For two days they'd listened to the sounds of hundreds of VC working all around them. They'd remained as far out as they could, and their movement was slow and careful. By a miracle, they remained undetected after two days. Their objectives, the two snatch positions on opposite trails, lay outside the big camp, and they gave the VC a wide berth.

Each team set up about four hundred meters outside the camp. That was as close as Franco wanted to get before the strike. Each team was set up in a simple, linear ambush arrangement. Franco set up claymore mines in a daisy chain, connected with detonating cord. Once initiated, the entire string would blow simultaneously. But instead of ensuring that each mine had an interlocking field of fire so that no one could escape, he purposely left gaps between two sets of mines. At those points, he placed a one-pound lump of C-4 explosive linked to the det cord. He then placed himself in a position where he could identify trail runners. When the man he wanted was in one of the C-4 gaps, he would blow the entire minefield. The man in the gap would be knocked down by the blast and stunned, while the others around him would be killed or wounded by the steel pellets of the claymores. Then it was up to speed, firepower, and luck to snatch the Soviet and bolt away into the jungle.

Franco lay along the trail. The trap was set. The final calls had been made to the control officers in the rear. The worst part was always the wait until dawn. The Americans always struck at dawn on their air assaults. Best case, that caught the VC in their hootches and left American ground forces to fight as the sun came up and visibility improved. The problem was that the tactic made the Americans predictable. This time Franco would use that to his advantage.

As first light broke through the trees, the unmistakable sound of a large armada of helicopters rose from the west. Within seconds of the first sounds, the VC could be heard shouting and scurrying for the jungle. The first helos that broke overhead were gunships that raked the western edge of the village. Franco hadn't wanted to use fastmovers for fear of hitting the ambush team to the west of the camp. The helo gunship's fire would be more controlled and precise and would raise the chances that the Soviet wouldn't be killed in his hootch on the eastern edge.

After one intense firing run, the ground force landed on the target and sporadic gunfire ensued. By this time, the majority of the VC had fled the camp and melted into the swamp. The sporadic sniper fire would keep the American unit pinned down to allow the vast majority of the Vietcong force to escape.

Several groups had run through his ambush site, but Franco hadn't laid eyes on his prey. Fear was a tangible scent in the air. The place was crawling with VC. As the fighting increased in the villa, Franco heard the ambush to the west erupt in a blast followed by a heavy volume of fire, then more explosions before the noise died down.

Franco felt his stomach slide slowly into his boots. He must have miscalculated. You could never predict the VC. The Soviet must have fled to the west, and the other team must have found him. Damn! Franco's team couldn't move now for fear of being compromised. He was almost beside himself with self-doubt and fear for the other team. After all the preparation and tough reconning, he had laid the perfect trap. He wanted the Russian so badly he could taste it, but it looked as if he might actually have slipped away.

Suddenly another band of about a dozen enemy soldiers came barreling through the brush. Franco barely had time to get a positive identification before he had to act. It was him! Just like his picture, except for a slight beard. He was easy to spot; he was blond and stood a full head taller than any of the VC he was with. The safety-bale wires were already detracted from the dual clackers Franco had primed the claymores with. Never dropping his eyes from his man, he squeezed the clackers three times, sharply.

The explosive field blew with a tremendous blast. Franco felt searing heat flood over him in a thick, rolling wave that carried smoke and debris along with it. He was up before the blast was fully spent, sprinting into the kill zone. On the side nearest the camp, the three man PRU group erupted in a heavy volume of fire using AK47s and an RPK light machine gun. Their timing and execution were flawless. Trinh stayed to cover the escape route to the north. As Franco moved out, one of his

men, Van-T, stayed glued to his side with a silenced Swedish K submachine gun, covering his
advance so that the American could focus entirely
on his prey. One of the other three had immediately fired canisters of CS tear gas down each end
of the trail outside the kill zone.

As they broke onto the trail, Van-T shot two VC
who were trying to crawl from the site. The Soviet
had been knocked down by the initial blast and
was trying to get up, but he was in mild shock. He
was bleeding from both ears.

As the three PRU continued a heavy volume of
fire toward the village to ward off any attackers,
Franco stepped forward and kicked the Soviet
squarely in the jaw, knocking him cold. He quickly
stripped him of his munitions, threw a set of hand-
cuffs on his wrists, and slung him over his shoulder. They were only thirty seconds into the
ambush, but he knew his team was heavily outnumbered and outgunned. They were in deep trouble. No time to make this look like the Soviet had
drowned or disappeared. The Air Cav was driving
more VC out of the village and toward Franco's
team. It wouldn't take them long to figure out what
had happened. Franco had to get the team out immediately.

He turned and yelled for Van-T and Trinh to
help him move. Franco had Van-T take point while
they fell in behind him. But as Franco and his men
left the site, the blocking force of three to the west
fell under heavy fire. One man was wounded and
the other two were pinned down. Franco, thinking
his men were on his heels, continued to move out
quickly.

The Soviet was heavy, and moving him through the thick brush soon became an act of sheer will. Two hundred meters away from the site, he heard the PRU security team being overrun, and only then did he realize they'd been caught. There was nothing he could do. His heart froze as he heard a lone bugle close behind. The VC knew what had happened to the Soviet, and they'd picked up the trail. It would be easy to track Franco and the last two PRU in this vegetation. They were fighting for their lives. They had to find a landing zone, *now*.

Franco and his men wouldn't be able to hold the VC off by themselves. It was time to call in heavy firepower. The Air Cav had a team of two Hueys and two gunships circling and waiting for the call. Unable to find a clear LZ, Franco found a break in the trees and got on the radio. He'd scouted the area during the recons and knew it was no use looking for an LZ in this thick jungle. There wouldn't be one. Franco knew after he heard the contact to the east that the five-man team there had no chance of survival unless their ambush site was hit by helos. He called in fire on both ambush sites, hoping to scatter and wound or kill some of the VC, with any luck allowing any survivors of his team to bolt into the jungle. It wasn't much of a chance, but it was the only one they had.

The SEAL paused and dropped the Soviet. He had his team prepare for pickup. The Russian began to stir and tried to rise and struggle, so Franco grabbed him by the shoulders and kneed him in the stomach. In the Russian's weakened condition, it was enough to knock him out. Then he gagged him tightly, so that he wouldn't be able to cry out and give their position away.

The helo came in hot and flared after Franco put a pen flare through the trees to mark his position. He hadn't expected to find an easy LZ, so earlier he'd rigged the extraction helos with McGuires. The helo came to a hover and threw out long ropes weighted at the ends with sandbags. There was a harness at the end of each rope as well, and the men scrambled for them. The Soviet was tied in first, and an extra line attached so that he wouldn't be lost on the ride out. Then the others hastily fastened themselves in. They hailed the crew chief with a wave, letting him know they were ready, and Franco noticed that the doorgunners on both sides of the helo were spraying the trees. Only then did he realize that they were taking fire from two sides. The noise of the hovering helo had shut out everything else.

The helo began to lift away, and Franco and the others emptied their weapons into the surrounding terrain. Tracers followed them up through the trees, and Trinh took a round through the chest. All Franco could do was watch him bleed until the helo could set down in a safe area. They did, moments later, and the men were taken aboard for the ride back to base.

Van-T tried to staunch the flow of his teammate's blood while Franco made sure the Soviet was bound and clipped to the deck. Couldn't have him falling out of the helo, not after all this. When he was finished, he wiped the sweat off his brow and turned back to Trinh. The man was ungodly pale, soaked in blood. The wound in his chest was gaping. He wasn't going to make it. Franco sank to his knees beside him, helpless. The harsh sounds of Trinh's ragged breathing, barely audible in the roar of the helo, knifed into him. *This is my fault,* he thought. *My fault. These men were my responsibility.*

The breaths were getting shallower, weaker. Inaudible.

Trinh never regained consciousness.

The SEAL sat there for a long moment, staring at nothing. He wanted to hit something, hard. His prisoner came to mind. As if on cue, the Russian groaned and stirred. Franco looked at the man with hatred. *My team paid the ultimate price for you, you son of a bitch,* he thought. *You'd better be worth it.*

Rousing himself, he got on the headset and asked about the ambush team to the west. Had they been picked up? Had anyone seen any survivors? Were they still out looking for any?

There was no sign of them. They were lost. All of them. *Jesus,* he thought, over and over until he thought he'd go out of his mind, half a silent prayer and half a curse. He sat stunned for the rest of the ride back, holding his head in his hands, occasionally glancing up at the sole surviving indig. Nine of his best men lost for a single foreign advisor. *Jesus.*

They landed the helo at the pad amid a small crowd which had followed the progress of the mission and the fighting. Several South Vietnamese counterparts were among the Agency men, not having been let in on the full extent of the operation for fear of communist infiltrators among them. The operation had been sold to them as an Air Cav raid into another area entirely. Without their usual advance warning, the VC had been caught flat-footed. The South Vietnamese at the helo pad weren't pleased, he could see that from their expressions. And he was too damned tired to care about that or anything at all.

Jason rushed up to Franco as the helo shut down. He was ecstatic.

"You're incredible!" he bellowed over the noise of the turbine, arms outstretched. "I never dreamed you'd be able to pull this one off, amigo!" Franco looked down at him, and a red haze began to cloud his vision.

"Save it," he snapped, backing the other man against the skin of the aircraft, suddenly livid with anger. "It cost us a hell of a lot of lives. I was lucky to make it out myself! This is going to cost you, *plenty*. I want compensation for their families!"

The Agency man swallowed hard and licked his lips nervously.

"I know you paid in s-spades, Franco," he stuttered. "I'll m-make sure it was worth it. You have my word on it."

That from the man I wouldn't have bought a used car from. Franco took a deep breath and dug his nails into his palms, fighting for self-control. He wanted to tear into Jason worse than he'd ever wanted anything in his life. After a moment he managed to turn his glare to the helo.

"What happens to him now?" asked the SEAL, jerking his head in the same direction.

"First stop will be the Farm, back in the States," Jason said more calmly, sensing that the danger had passed. "Then we have a special place for him, nice and secluded. He won't go home until we get our own guys back. And we'll have all the time in the world to bring him around to our way of thinking." He smiled slowly in anticipation.

They stayed and watched as a South Vietnamese security team pulled the prisoner from the helo. The team unfastened his bindings and stood him up to move him to a nearby jeep. His head lolled onto his chest; he was still out of it.

Suddenly and without warning, one of the security men pulled a .45 Colt automatic handgun from his holster, put the barrel to the Russian's head, flipped the safety off, and pulled the trigger. Before anyone could react, the Soviet was sprawled on the ground. The Vietcong spy turned the gun on himself and fired a last fatal round. All in the blink of an eye. Franco just stood there, staring in total disbelief as the platform erupted into chaos.

The Vietcong had made sure the Soviet was well guarded. They could never let such an important man fall into enemy hands. And they hadn't.

Nine of his best men, dead, or worse, captured. And it had all been for nothing. It hadn't meant a damned thing.

10

Immediate Action

August 1970

"You know what they told us in training, about a hundred and ten years ago," Stine teased quietly, after Franco had lapsed into brooding silence. "No mission ever goes as planned. It *really* wasn't your fault."

Franco nodded after a moment, but he didn't say anything.

"Look, Tony, at least you went into that one with an intelligent plan," Mike Boss added, laying a hand on Franco's shoulder. "I remember a Brightlight we had to conduct on a wing and a prayer, all because some damn fool named Bison wanted to go play cowboys and Indians with the Vietcong."

"Hey!" Johnny Bison bellowed back from across their table. "You mean you didn't have a carefully laid and well-rehearsed plan for rescuing me? What kinda *mo-ron* goes rushing into a Brightlight without a solid game plan?"

"This kind," Boss admitted with a good-natured shrug, as he launched into their story.

Smoke flooded the crew compartment as the helo bucked and shivered unnaturally. The pilot, Hunter, glanced back at the rest of his team, his mouth a grim line.

"Jolly Roger, this is Wolfpack Three," he called into the radio. "We're hit!"

"They have big artillery down there! Stay out of the area!" a voice shimmering with static called back. As if they had a choice in the matter.

"Wolfpack Three, Jolly Roger," came the cool, dry voice of the controller at HQ. "Say your status, over."

"Jolly Roger, stand by," Hunter shot back tensely, his eyes flickering over the control panel. Static filled the circuit. The controller had a hot mike, and a group of people who'd stopped to gather around him at base operations could hear the two doorgunners returning fire with their M60 light machine guns.

"Jolly Roger, this is Wolfpack Three. We're hit pretty good. We're trailing fluids and a little smoke. The controls are starting to stick. I'm not sure how long I can hold it. We're heading southeast. I'll try to make it to Cau Mau."

"This is Wolfpack Two," another voice joined them. "I'm staying with him. He's all over the sky. Don't think he'll make it. Recommend you scramble a Brightlight team."

It was bad, if they were asking for that. Brightlight Teams, the small special operations reaction forces assigned to recover downed crewmen, bodies, and POWs, were scrambled in only the worst possible circumstances.

"Roger, Wolfpack, solid copy," the controller replied crisply. "We're on it."

"Jolly Roger, this is Wolfpack Three. I just lost . . ." The transmission was cut off sharply with a hiss of static.

"Wolfpack Three, say again," the controller snapped, boosting the gain on the mike.

"This is Wolfpack Two! Mayday! Mayday! Wolfpack Three just went down! He's just west of Thoi Binh! I have immediate cover! Request scramble fast movers and gunships! We're still taking groundfire! I need a Brightlight priority!"

"Wolfpack Two, this is Jolly Roger. We have two Cobras on the way. Brightlight will be airborne in ten mikes. We'll do our best to get you some fast movers."

"This is Wolfpack Two. Wolfpack Three is upright in a paddy. He's hit pretty hard, but there's no fire onboard. There's a lot of smoke. The V are on the ground and they'll be able to see the smoke for miles. We need air cover fast, or I won't be able to keep them away!"

"This is Jolly Roger. Good copy. Any sign of survivors?"

"This is Wolfpack Two. That's affirmative! I see at least two survivors!"

"This is Jolly Roger, good copy. Stay airborne until the gunships arrive."

"This is Wolfpack Two. I have a platoon-sized element of VC closing from the west. How about that air cover?"

"Air cover is at least fifteen minutes out. Hang on!"

"Negative. They'll have them by then. I can't wait! I'm going into the crash site!"

"Negative! Negative!" the controller snapped. "Wolfpack Two, stay airborne and wait for cover! Acknowledge, over!" There was a dead silence on the other end, and the controller's heart sank into his boots. "Wolfpack Two, did you copy my last, over?" Silence.

Wolfpack Two descended quickly and flared just beyond the wreckage of the first helicopter. It was SOP for the survivors to move beyond the nose of the downed aircraft by fifty meters. Day or night, this allowed recovery crews to concentrate their rescue efforts in one spot, and if close air support was needed in a tight situation, the chance of friendly casualties would more likely be minimized. As Wolfpack Two touched down, the crewmen in the back jumped out to assist the survivors.

The two doorgunners from the back of the downed helo were grabbed from the middle of the paddy and dragged toward Wolfpack Two. Small arms fire cracked all around as the VC closed in on them.

"Where are the others?" one of the rescuers screamed over the noise of the rotors and gunfire.

"It's gonna burn!" the Wolfpack Three survivor shouted back in panic. "We can't help them now! It's too late! I think they're dead!"

The VC had closed to within three hundred meters of the crash site. Both helos were under fire. It was time to get out with what they had.

"Get in! Get in!" the pilot screamed. As the men scrambled aboard, the helo lurched forward and banked a hard left, showing the VC the belly of the aircraft. At this rate they were going to absorb rounds, and it was better to do it in a less critical area of the hull. The weight of the two additional men made the helo less agile, and it was heavy, too slow in climbing out.

"Wolfpack Two is airborne with two survivors," the pilot called over the radio. Static rushed in and overwhelmed the transmission. The controller went dead white.

"Wolfpack Two, this is Jolly Roger. Say again your status." Silence. "Wolfpack Two, Wolfpack Two, say again your status! Wolfpack Two, this is Jolly Roger, over!"

The only reply was the soft, deathly hiss of radio static.

Lieutenant Mike Boss entered the tactical operations center taut with tension and adrenaline. Less than two minutes before, he'd heard that there was a helo down. He ran to the TOC, knowing his men would do the same. Boss quickly spotted Doc Johnson, the Platoon Chief, who waved him over to a group of men huddled around a table.

"What do we have, Hammer?" the lieutenant asked, in a voice clipped with a faint trace of anxiety. His Chief had earned that nickname through uncommon skill and precision with an M60 light machine gun.

"One, maybe two Army slicks down, east edge of the U Minh. Bad area." That from the New

Yorker. "The second helo went into the first crash site, picked up two survivors, got airborne, and then their signal was lost," Hammer replied crisply, sticking to the facts as he knew them.

The senior officer and TOC watchstanders crowded around the two SEALs and tried to break in.

"We need your SEALs to . . ."

"Wait!" Boss barked at the officer, holding up a hand and cutting him off without breaking eye contact with the Chief. He didn't need anyone to task him. What he needed most were as many facts as he could get, and he needed them fast. The tension in the air was palpable; clearly there was more to this than a couple of downed helos. "How long were the second helo's radio transmissions before they went off the air?" he asked Johnson.

"Less than ten seconds."

"Enemy?"

"Second helo reported a platoon-sized element closing in from the west."

"Okay, Hammer, get the whole platoon jocked up ASAP. Split each squad in two. One half goes heavy, the other half goes light. Light groups will be four-man fire teams ready to haul bodies. Take crowbars and fire axes. We'll need thermite with those teams," Boss snapped, spitting out his orders in a rapid-fire stream. Turning at last to the other men in the room, he glanced quickly at a map on the conference table.

"Where are they, exactly?" he asked them.

"Here." One of them pointed quickly.

"Paddies all around," Boss murmured thoughtfully, "so forget going heavy with 40-mm, Chief.

Mud's too soft now for positive detonation. Go heavy with 7.62. It's all open, so go in heavy with smoke grenades, especially Willy Peter."

"How about a few LAWs?" Hammer asked him with a raised eyebrow. The anti-armor warheads would work against any bunkers they encountered.

"Good idea. Three per heavy-fire team," Boss shot back. "How many men were on those helos?"

"Six on the first bird, five on number two. One more thing, Lieutenant . . . Bison was on the first bird." Their eyes met and held briefly, and Hammer turned on his heel and left for the platoon hut.

So that was it. Boss looked back at the men he'd come to know well, all pilots and aircrew from the SEAWOLF Navy Hueys that flew in direct support of the SEALs.

"Is that true?" he asked them quietly.

"I'm afraid so," Shaddock nodded. "They were going on an Army aerial recon of this area right here," he said, pointing at the map. "You know how badly Bison's been wanting to work that area. He went along for the ride. One of his classmates from the Academy went down in a Black Pony OV-10 there eight months ago. He's been wanting to go in there and bloody the V ever since."

Boss knew Bison well. The Commanding Officer of the SEAWOLVES had pulled them out of a lot of hot spots during his tour. Boss's SEAL Team TWO platoon owed him and the other pilots their lives several times over. It went without saying that Boss and the other SEALs would stop at nothing to get Bison or any of the SEAWOLF aircrew out.

"How many helos you got up right now?" Boss asked Shaddock, the senior officer among them.

"We have four slicks and two gunships. There are two Snakes en route. The Army diverted them, and they should be on station anytime. They can fly cover and hopefully keep the V off the crash site until we get there."

"What's your flight time?"

"Just under twenty mikes."

"Crank 'em up!" the SEAL snapped. "We'll meet you on the pad in less than five."

Boss left the TOC with a map and ran to the team hut. The SEALs were scrambling to throw on their uniforms and equipment. No one wasted any time throwing on camo face paint or taking care of the small points they would have applied to a deliberate and carefully planned stealth operation. This mission was reactive, the worst kind. They were going in right on the crash site. The VC knew a force would be coming for those crews. They would probably wait and use the downed helos as bait in order to bag more Americans. They'd done it before.

The SEAL platoon had gone to the aid of downed helos before, but this time it was different. Bison was down. And the VC were going to pay a heavy price for trying to pick him up. Bait or no bait, this one wasn't going to be a quiet SEAL stalk through the jungle, sneaking and avoiding contact. They were going head to head with the VC to save Bison and the others who were down.

"Frag order in two minutes!" Boss shouted, gathering in his SEALs with his eyes. They'd cleaned and stowed all their web gear and reloaded ammunition after the last operation. In the event of a reaction operation like this one, the men were im-

mediately ready to throw on their gear, get a quick
fragmentation order, load the helos, and launch.
The entire process took only minutes, each one of
which counted against the crash survivors.

Still strapping on the last of their gear, the SEALs
listened to the quick brief as Boss pointed to a map
tacked onto the wall of the hut.

"Two Army Slicks flying visual recon over this
area," the lieutenant began. "One was hit and went
down here. There were six men onboard the first
bird, five Army, one Navy." He paused for a second and his mouth set into a grim line. "Bison was
on that bird."

Someone swore in the back.

"The second bird picked up two survivors. Then
radio comms were lost. There were five on that
helo originally, so that makes seven pax as their
count now. We should be looking for four at the
first site. We have to assume the second helo went
down near the first, but we don't know that for a
fact. A platoon-sized enemy force was reported by
the second bird to be in the immediate area, and it
was an Army bird doing the reporting. Army platoons are about thirty to forty men. Expect a lot of
VC. We can guess that they'll use the helos as bait.
We're going in hot and we're going in right on the
sites. Initial passes will be our leader's recon to confirm the situation, then we'll make our approaches
from the best direction we have. If we have only
one bird down, my squad goes on the deck."

"I thought there were two down," Art Jones
frowned. He was a lieutenant, junior grade, the
other SEAL platoon officer.

"The second bird might still be airborne; they

might just have lost their radios. We'll know when
we get up there. If we have two birds down, we'll
go for one at a time. My squad will go in first on
the site most likely to be overrun, and then yours
will follow, A. J.," Boss nodded to the other officer.
"That way we commit to only one at a time and
hold one of our squads in reserve at all times.

"The SEAWOLVES will put us in at a hover," he
continued as fast as he could, anxiety gnawing at
his vitals, "and we'll jump off the skids. They're
our ride home, and we don't need them sitting in
the paddies picking up lead on the deck. They're
harder to hit in the air, and it'll be one more distraction for the V. When the squads hit the deck,
the three-man fire teams will position themselves
between the rescuers and the enemy. Just keep
their heads down for us. The four-man team will
go in light and move to pick up everyone on the
ground. Remember that the survivors will try to
move to about fifty meters in front of the nose of
the aircraft. That's where we'll pull them to when
we call for extraction, but read the situation on the
ground. If you have any cover from the paddies,
use it. We'll count heads and check the wreckage
if necessary.

"Watch for fire and live ordnance on the helos.
Last man out will use two thermite grenades, one
in the cockpit and one in the crew compartment.
Don't toss in the thermites until the extraction birds
are on the deck, picking us up. That way any fire
will be minimized until we're about ready for liftoff. Don't worry about the radios or recovery of
documents. We're going in to save people and recover bodies, so don't waste time on anything else.

There's nothing else in those helos worth risking your lives for."

He was shooting information at them as fast as he could, tension in the hard set of his jaw. Every minute they delayed was ticking against them and the survivors, but they couldn't afford to go in completely blind.

"If we get caught on the ground," he muttered, "don't expect to waltz out. There'll be casualties from the helos, and there's nothing but open rice paddies full of mud. We'll never sneak out. Once we get in, we set up like the Alamo. Make every round count, keep the radios up and call in air strikes until the VC have been bled enough to let the helos come get us. We leave no one behind. No one." Boss turned toward the two radiomen in the platoon.

"Take two extra Prick-77s, extra batteries, and a couple of extra handsets. If we get on the ground, the radios are our only link out."

"Already got them here, boss," one of the men replied.

"Good," he nodded back. "Questions?"

No one spoke up. There were a hundred details everyone wanted answers to, but there was no more information to be had. For their sakes and the sakes of the men on the ground, the SEALs had to launch *now*.

"Get a commo check with the helos and everybody load! Move!" Boss snapped. The SEALs scrambled and sprinted for the helo pad. The SEA-WOLF Hueys were ready for liftoff. They piled in, doorgunners last. Several people from the TOC gathered to watch the launch, and one of them ran directly up to the lead helo and found Boss, who took off his headset to listen to him. He wound up having to grab the man's head and pull him closer so that he could hear him over the rotor noise.

"The second helo is down," the man screamed, "about five hundred meters from the first! Everyone is alive, but they have injuries! They have a radio and one of the doorguns! They're holding their position, but they say the VC are pressing them! They think the VC may already have overrun the first crash site!"

"Got it!" Boss yelled back. "Stand clear! We're outta here!" He put his headset back on, and the helo was airborne ten seconds later. The others were in close pursuit. The SEAWOLVES pulled a hard right bank and powered to full throttle directly for the crash sites.

The armada flew in at over a thousand feet to avoid ground fire en route. The pilots established communications with the Army Cobra gunships, which were pumping out ordnance at a steady rate to keep the VC away from the downed birds. The Cobras knew it would take time for the SEAWOLVES to arrive, and they tried to hoard as much ammo as they could. They didn't dare run out, not yet. An OV-10 forward air controller was en route to the site and would get there before the SEAWOLVES did. And a flight of F-4 Phantoms were being scrambled to support the site, but they wouldn't be arriving for another half hour or more.

"Ten minutes out!" Boss shouted back to the SEALs in the crew compartment of his helo, relaying the report from the lead pilot, Hector Gomez.

"The Snakes are keeping the VC off the second

helo, but the first site is in serious trouble," the pilot shot back to Boss, taking the report off the intercom. "Wolfpack Two says we should go in on the first downed helo. The VC are too close to get good rocket coverage. The first crash site is still responding with machine gun fire, but they're about to be overrun. Wolfpack Two says he can hold out a little longer."

"Roger!" Boss nodded sharply. He took off his headset and put his head close to the other three SEALs, who leaned in so that they could hear his voice as he shouted.

"We're going in on the first crash site! It's gonna be close! The V are almost there! Be ready for a close fight!" he screamed. The SEALs continued to ready their weapons and equipment.

"Five minutes!" one of the crewmen shouted back to them. The pilots frantically motioned Boss to get back on the headset. He did, and instantly wished he hadn't.

"They took it! Wolfpack Two and the Snakes just reported that the VC overran the first crashsite," Gomez announced, his voice thick with impotent anger. His co-pilot slammed his fist against the side of the aircraft, hard, swearing. "We'll divert you to the second one," he continued, as calmly as he could manage.

Boss looked at his men, took a deep breath and let it out slowly. *No way*, he thought. *That isn't the way it's gonna go down. Not for Bison. No way!*

"No!" the SEAL called to the pilots, startling them. "Negative! You put us in on the first site! I want my team on the first crash site, you got that?!"

Gomez turned and looked at him. "They got him, Mike," he muttered, his features twisted with barely suppressed rage. "It's too late."

"Listen to me, damn it! Look for the biggest group of VC by the first downed helo and land right on top of 'em, you got that?! You land this thing down hard, right on top of them! Do it!"

"Mike, I . . ."

"Hector, I know what I'm doing! Trust me, damn it! There isn't time to argue about this! Put this thing down on the biggest group of V near the hull of the first aircraft! Don't argue with me, just do it!"

The pilot adjusted his harness and turned forward.

"Okay, man, okay! You got it! Hang on in the back! I'm dropping down to the deck! We'll come out of the east! Anyone who tries to hit us will have the sun in his eyes! Touchdown ain't gonna be gentle, so get ready!"

Boss ripped off his headset and turned back to his team.

"The V just took the first crash site!" he shouted. "We're not gonna let 'em hold it! We're getting it back! We're going in right on top of 'em! Kill every VC you can, starting the moment we hit the deck! Don't let any of them get away! Use controlled bursts and watch for survivors! Don't let them drag one of our guys off!"

Boss saw his rage and determination reflected in the faces of his men. It was time. The 'Cong were about to find out who owned the block. Nothing else mattered. There were no politics involved, no strategic goals. The air armada was going to the aid of someone they all knew, for one simple reason. The man trapped on the ground with the Army crews would have done it for them.

In garrison and in the rear, a lot of people hated SEALs. They were arrogant and aggressive, and partied hard and stood out too much, anathema to the rank and file conformists. But this was the type of moment for which they were created. Boss's platoon brandished wall-to-wall firepower, and right now they were itching to use it. In this mood there was no force on the face of the earth that could stand toe-to-toe with them.

Choirboys they weren't. No mercy to the enemy. Make 'em pay.

The SEALs felt the helo drop fast, then accelerate as it flew ten feet off the ground. It was a gut-wrenching roller coaster ride as the helos barely skimmed the tops of the dikes and slipped through the narrow gaps between the treetops. The trail helos fell in close behind. Boss's heavy three-man team inside the second helo flew echelon right and mirrored every move the lead bird made. The other two passenger Hueys flew on the deck further back, and the gunships flew on the flanks. It was virtuoso piloting, and nerve-wracking if you were a passenger.

"One minute!" a crewman screamed. The door-gunners peered intently over the barrels of their weapons, waiting for the first glimpse of targets they knew were just seconds away. There was a slight bank left, and Boss made one last intercom call to the pilot before dropping the headset.

"Sat Cong! Get the Bison back!" Boss and his men mounted the skids, two on each side, as the helo continued at top speed. They hung on for their lives.

If there were survivors from the first crash site, the VC would pull them out and torture them, openly taunting the Cobras overhead. Their actions would be savage. They might kill the survivors on the spot in a spectacularly brutal way while the Cobra pilots looked on, powerless to stop them. Or they might drag them off into the jungle. In the meantime, they would have their fun. The survivors still had a slim chance, but only if Boss's team did what the VC would never expect. They had to come crashing through the front door, dive right in on top of them, and be quicker on the draw.

Gomez saw the smoke from the wreckage and guided on it. He timed his approach perfectly, waiting until just after a Cobra flew a low pass over the site. The OV-10 had just arrived and was helping them keep the VC off the second site with what little ammunition he had left. Gomez didn't see the crash site until the last moment. He opted to stay low on the deck and pop up over a paddy dike at the last moment. The maneuver caught the VC totally off guard. The sound of the approaching SEAWOLVES had been masked by the Cobra's last firing run.

There were about a dozen Vietcong swarming around the hull of the first wreckage like buzzards on a carcass. A half-dozen additional VC grouped about fifty meters in front of the nose of the downed bird. Gomez went right for that cluster, flaring harder than he'd ever tried to before. On the far skid, one of the SEALs caught two VC across the thighs with a long burst from his CAR-15. Both guerrillas dropped in pain.

The pilot nearly lost control and hit the ground hard, skidding forward ten feet. He narrowly missed the cluster of VC, causing them to scatter in all directions. They left two limp human forms at their original spot.

The SEALs were thrown from the skids before they could jump. The helo had made a controlled crash, and Boss rolled several feet before he recovered. He shook his head to clear it, and tasted blood from a cut lip where his CAR-15 had hit him on impact. Two VC were running less than ten feet away, frantically trying to scramble out of the area, but both slipped in the mud. Boss cut them down with three short bursts of automatic fire.

He turned toward the limp American figures on the ground in front of the SEAWOLF. They were bloodied and sprawled out, their hands tied behind their backs. Gunfire came from the other side of the helo. The second helo in the squad set down three hundred meters in front of the lead. His heavy three-man squad ran to cover at the top of the nearby dike and began laying down suppressing fire. Two VC were trying to run along the top of the dike. One of the doorgunners on the SEAWOLF took them out and threw them over the berm.

The VC were running away from the crash site and taking heavy casualties. Boss ran over to the downed crewmen. They'd been severely beaten. Both were alive, but only one was conscious. Neither man was Bison.

"Security on me!" Boss yelled, and the other three SEALs in his group rallied to his side, firing at targets as they moved, covering him. One of the men stirred to consciousness, and Boss cupped the man's battered face in his hands. "Where are the other two survivors?" he asked, having to shout over the din of rotor and gunfire.

"They're . . . still in the bird," the crewman rasped.

As he turned to the wreckage of the bird, Boss spotted a couple of VC still struggling to get out. The two injured crew were picked up and carried back to the SEAWOLF, and the helo lifted off. Boss focused on the wreckage. Several of the fleeing VC had items they'd pilfered from the helo. Two or three of them tried to stand and fight, but the Americans cut them down with accurate and continuous fire. If there were other survivors in the crashed helo, the SEALs didn't want to spray the hull with stray rounds.

One VC reached inside the pilot's cockpit door on the crashed helo with a .45-caliber handgun.

"No!" Boss screamed, and plugged him with three quick shots. The VC took them high in the chest, and the .45 flew five feet out of his hand and stuck in the mud. He crumpled to the ground. Boss sprinted toward the hull, and his men spread out at his heels. A VC sprang out of the crashed bird and ran head-on into one of the SEALs. The American gave him a vertical buttstroke with his rifle, knocking him down. The 'Cong hit the mud and tried to roll away, and the SEAL gave him a five-round burst at point-blank range.

As Boss reached the helo, he saw two bodies still strapped into the pilot and co-pilot seats. Both were limp and bloody. One coughed, the other was motionless.

"Johnny!" Boss yelled, a wide grin splitting his features. The one who'd been coughing rolled his head toward the SEAL.

"Hey . . . sailor . . . got a light?" Bison coughed weakly.

"Hang on, amigo. We'll get you out." Boss started gently probing for broken ribs and internal injuries. "Does it hurt much?" he asked.

"Only . . . when I laugh," Bison rasped with the faint ghost of a smile. "I think I broke . . . both legs. Check the pilot. I'll be okay."

One of Boss's men ripped the other door off with a crowbar and checked the unconscious man for a pulse.

"He's alive!" he said excitedly.

"Okay, call the bird back in," Boss nodded, unable to keep from smiling. "Don't pull them out until the helo is on final; that way we won't hurt them any sooner than we have to. Stay next to the skin of the aircraft for cover. That'll help the gunships bring in ordnance a little closer to keep the V away. Make sure the gunships know we have three guys up on the dike over there. Everything else is bad guys and safe to shoot."

The radioman called for extraction and relayed the message. The two victims were slowly pried out of their seats and laid gently on the ground. As they waited for the helo to land, Bison spoke.

"That 'Cong . . . was going to put a round in my head . . . with my own .45. Thanks, Mike . . . I knew you'd come."

"Shut up, you moron," Boss said, with as much

sarcasm as he could muster. "What are you doin' upfront here, anyhow? You got a license to fly Army birds? What are you, Billy Badass or somethin'? You think I got nothin' better to do than come swoopin' into VC war parties to extract your shiny white butt? I oughta break your arms to match your legs!"

Bison managed a feeble grin. They shot him up with morphine to ease the pain. A SEAWOLF flared in hot, and two crewmen helped the SEALs carry the injured pilots to the helo. It was almost over. As the SEAWOLF took off again, another came in and picked up the heavy squad from the dike. Then they pulled pitch in time to see the first pass from the F-4s lay down a wall of napalm two hundred meters from the second crash site. Boss sent the second squad, led by A. J., into the second site, and they made another clean sweep as the VC absorbed as much remaining fire as all the combined force could lay out. In less than five minutes, the remaining personnel were all recovered, the thermite grenades creating two huge burning wreckages as a monument to VC gunnery expertise.

As the VC unit melted into the U Minh Forest to lick its wounds, there were two less American aircrew with them to suffer in tiger cages in the mosquito-infested swamp. The SEALs flew back to base to downstage and reload. It didn't take the VC long to figure out that it had been the Green Faces who'd struck them and inflicted such carnage. They hid and tried to avoid them, knowing they couldn't afford many more engagements like that.

It wasn't often that they were the hunted. They

Salt and Pepper

September 1970

"Well, for a wing-and-a-prayer operation, that one obviously didn't go too badly," Joshua Marco sighed. "I had one that got really screwed up in the planning stage, but somehow it turned out all right in spite of itself. 'No mission ever goes as planned,' like you said, but sometimes that can be a good thing, especially if you can take charge in the field, away from the brass. And if there's one thing we do well, it's bobbin' and weavin'."

"Frankly, we're not exactly sure who they are," the intel man shrugged, making a broad gesture with his full coffee cup and sloshing a bit over the sides. The SEAL advisor, Lieutenant Joshua Marco, frowned and tried not to be distracted by the spreading stain on the other man's khaki safari shirt. Talbot shifted his impressive girth in his pale green vinyl high-backed chair, and Marco settled in to hear a long story. "They could be any of a number of people, and the intelligence has been clouded by some operations of our own."

The mix of photographs was supplemented by the album of POWs and MIAs on the shabby metal desk. The intelligence photographs were almost all 35-mm blowups. None were very good, certainly not good enough to make a positive identification, although a few bore a striking resemblance to each other. The physical evidence wasn't at all convincing, but Marco knew the pair existed.

"We've used various code words in reference to this issue over the years," Talbot yawned, leaning back in his chair, "but everyone knows them as Salt and Pepper. One guy is white, one is black. I know you have background from some of your professional dealings, but let me give you a little more insight.

"We know that Americans who've been captured by the VC and NVA have been tortured and survive today under extremely harsh conditions, when they survive at all. Many have died in captivity, especially the ones in the jungle camps in South Vietnam, Cambodia, and Laos. We know a lot of this from debriefing escapees. These two factors alone have caused several POWs to bend to the will of their captors and give in to one degree or another. Some have signed confessions for war crimes that have been dreamed up and composed by the Vietcong. Others have signed propaganda leaflets that end up being distributed in the villages controlled by the government and American bases nearby. Some have even been used in propaganda broadcasts. We're sure that most of the POWs have

attempted to the best of their ability to resist helping the communists."

"*Most*," the SEAL muttered. "That's the key
word."

"Absolutely," Talbot nodded, running a hand
through his nearly nonexistent gray hair. "There
are a few exceptions. We have a lot of suspicion
that a few Americans have crossed over. They
could have turned after extensive mistreatment, or
it could have been voluntary. Whatever the case,
there are red-blooded American boys fighting
alongside the NVA and VC right now. One of these
guys is a white six-footer nicknamed 'Porkchop' for
the big, bushy sideburns he wears to cover burn-
marks on his face. He specializes in stealing Allied
vehicles, mainly by flagging them down on roads
and hijacking them at gunpoint. Works mainly in
II Corps."

Marco had heard rumors about him from a SEAL
platoon member who'd worked a few operations
out of Nha Trang.

"There's another one, a lot more dangerous,
nicknamed 'Tex' for his accent. He works mostly
in III and IV Corps and strolls into a base, plants
explosive charges, and leaves. Hasn't been caught,
although a lot of Army MPs recall stopping and
talking to him. Always had a good cover story and
was able to bluff his way out." That one Marco had
never heard of.

"What about the 'Phantom Blooper'?"

"Ah, yes, the Phantom Blooper. I see you've
heard of him. Almost everyone up north here has.
He works harassment on I Corps against U.S. bases. His modus operandi is his legendary skill with

an M79 40-mm grenade launcher," Talbot drawled ironically. "He's reportedly an American, but it's hard to pin that one down. A good VC or NVA could use the weapon as well, but a few Long-Range Recon Patrols have reported seeing a white man among the VC, carrying an M79. You see, that's part of our problem."

"How's that?"

"Well, we've had a lot of HUMINT on the guys we think are defectors. Some of the information comes from villagers. Those are hard to pin down because they're not specific enough to get an accurate description, only a time and place and general information. Descriptions of the men are too poor to match with what we have. Then there are the field reports from various American recon teams. They're all over the place, and as you know from working MACV-SOG operations, that includes North and South Vietnam, Laos, and Cambodia. We have reports from Marine Force and Battalion Recon, Special Forces projects like Delta, Rangers, LRRPs, spike teams from SOG, Australia and New Zealand SAS . . . you name it. They've seen non-indigs out there running the trails with the VC and NVA. Now, who are they? That's where it gets even cloudier.

"The SOG Recon Teams and some of the others often wear NVA and VC uniforms, weapons and equipment to patrol in the bush. They use indig personnel trained to act like enemy soldiers. Hell, eventually some of the American recon teams are going to run into each other or see each other from concealed positions. They report what they see, and the reports obviously make it look like armed

Americans are running with the communists."

"That's got to account for a lot of the reports," Marco noted.

"Oh, it definitely does," the spook agreed, "and Uncle Sam would love to be able to blow it all off with those simple explanations. But going public about covert operations we're running into countries we're not supposed to set foot in would be political suicide. That'll never happen. A second reason for the sightings is the fact that there are foreign advisors assisting the NVA and VC. Some are communist reporters who accompany enemy combat patrols, and some are actual combat advisors. Cubans, Russians, East Europeans—you name it. We've even killed several of them."

"Captured any?" Marco asked with the lifted eyebrow that was his hallmark. He'd heard a rumor about another SEAL, a PRU advisor who'd supposedly been involved in the snatch of a Soviet advisor the year before.

"Do yourself a favor, don't get me started on that story," the other man grumbled, shaking his head so hard his jowls flapped. "Then there's always the other reason for the sightings," he said crisply, changing the subject, rearranging the papers on his desk with studied indifference. "We know for a fact through other intelligence sources that some Americans really *are* running with the NVA and VC. Some of them are so brazen that they take R&R in some of the coastal bases right among the GIs. This is really a pretty embarrassing situation waiting for a place to happen. The Pentagon doesn't want it to get that far."

"If that's the case, you must have some definite

suspects," the SEAL murmured thoughtfully.

"We have our suspicions. I'll give you a few examples. Early in the war, a USMC driver was captured very near Da Nang, right near Camp Black Rock, as a matter of fact. He was held in the transient jungle camps the VC have for Americans in I Corps along with a Recon Marine and a Green Beret officer. Over time, more prisoners were captured and held with them. The Recon and the Green Beret died in captivity because of malnutrition, beatings and mistreatment, but the USMC driver caved in to the VC and started running with them. He started with propaganda. Now he runs on their patrols; more often than not he uses a megaphone outside a firebase camp to try to get others to defect. He's been seen on the trails in black pajamas and uniforms carrying an AK47. Some of the released American POWs who knew him have reported his activities. And he works up north here.

"Another is a black guy who dropped out of the 1st Infantry Division and runs around in III Corps. He does odd jobs for the VC and has a Vietnamese wife, but doesn't fight for them. There are a whole bunch of possible suspects all over the country for this 'Salt and Pepper' thing, but a dozen or so cases are real strong. We even had one Navy corpsman who ran operations with Marine Recon up here in I Corps. In 1967, his group conducted a static line parachute insertion for a mission. They got a little scattered and screwed up, but the corpsman definitely steered away from the group. He was never found, and when the Corps investigated, they found he'd prepared all the gear he'd left behind to be turned over. He apparently had a Vietnamese girlfriend we think was VC. He may be part of the Salt and Pepper team. A lot of guys are suspect."

"Well, if so many recon teams have seen these guys out there, haven't any made contact?" the SEAL asked archly.

"Oh, it's happened already. In 1968, a ten-man Marine Recon patrol from 1st Force ran across one of these guys. The recon patrol was taking a break at a stream to fill canteens and eat some C rations. The Marines had set security and were using only hand and arm signals, to stay quiet. Suddenly, this white guy in a green VC uniform popped out of the brush on the other side of the stream, with one of his VC buddies right behind him. They looked at each other for a minute, dumbfounded, and then the Marines heard more Viet voices. The recon guys initiated contact, hitting the white guy, who went down and yelled for help in English. The team didn't have time to snatch him; they barely made it out of the AO with their own skins. They had a heavy contact, and one of them was killed. In the debrief, four Marines said they'd managed to get a good look at the guy, and the one who'd initiated contact was sure he'd hit him. They identified him as the USMC driver captured by the VC in 1965."

"Did they kill him?"

"Don't know," the CIA man shrugged. He went on. "The Australian SAS has even had a few run-ins way down in III Corps. A year ago, one small patrol caught five VC tracking them. One of the trackers was white. They fired them up but didn't have a chance to check for casualties. And in January, another SAS patrol spotted a Caucasian

carrying an M-2 Carbine with a radioman close behind. The men were with a group of VC. Again,
they were outnumbered and couldn't verify the
kill."

The story about the defectors connected with information he'd heard from a friend in SEAL Team
ONE who'd run missions in Laos. Only a handful
of SEALs had conducted missions based out of the
CIA base at Long Tien as part of a secret detachment. There wasn't a lot of ocean or swamp in
Laos, and not many SEALs had been there. But one
team claimed to have seen a Caucasian traveling
with an NVA unit on the Ho Chi Minh Trail.

Marco also remembered hearing about another
Marine patrol that supposedly did capture a defector. He was wearing a Marine uniform with a
weird red sash, like that of a beauty contestant,
possibly as an identifier to other communist forces.
The Marines, as the story went, beat him to death.

"But we want to get our hands on these two
guys specifically," Talbot was saying. Marco forced
his attention back to the conversation. "Of all the
possible defectors, these two are doing the most
damage. That's where you come in."

The SEAL officer leaned back and consciously re-
laxed; he wanted to be able to remember every
word that would be said from then on. Whatever
he was getting into wasn't likely to be recordable
in any other way.

"We have intelligence from several sources
which indicate that Salt and Pepper are with the
NVA north of the DMZ right now, resting and pre-
paring for further operations in I Corps." The
Agency man pushed the map closer to the SEAL.

Marco leaned forward and studied the spot the other man was tapping with a pudgy finger.

"You already know the location of Dong Hoi, and you know it's a major way station and base of operations for the NVA in the southern portion of North Vietnam. You also know it's located on the coast. The city sits on the north side of the Giang River, which flows into the Gulf of Tonkin. There's an airfield located just north of the city, and the whole area is an armed camp."

Marco blinked at Talbot incredulously. There were thousands of NVA in that area, maybe even ten thousand or more. Trying to get a small team into that would be a beautiful and noble way to commit suicide.

"You've got to be out of your mind," the SEAL muttered. "How the hell do you expect us to get in there?"

"You're only half the solution. Here's what we've got planned so far. We have two locations we think these guys are holing up. Actually, I'm the only one who knows about the second one. Everyone else thinks Salt and Pepper are at the airfield in this bunker complex right here," Talbot said quietly, pointing at the overhead tactical reconnaissance photographs. "A plan has been developed for that contingency. The whole thing is being run by MACV-SOG, as you know. I work for the operations department. Because of my special intelligence connections, they wanted me to give you the brief. We have a SOG team of three Americans and several indig that we put together for this mission. We're going to HALO them into the airfield and try a snatch."

HALO stood for "high altitude, low open," a specialized method of military freefall where the team jumps at altitude on oxygen, falls to about three thousand feet, and parachutes the rest of the way in. Marco let out a rare sardonic laugh, openly contemptuous of such an incredibly stupid idea.

"You're certifiable!" the SEAL sneered. "I can't believe you actually found three Green Berets who would buy into such a harebrained scheme!"

"Before you laugh, listen to the plan. We all know there's no quiet way into the airfield. So we plan to give the NVA a big surprise. The hit will go down at the end of the day, when all the enemy soldiers are settling in for the night. That way, if the HALO team is hit hard on the ground, the darkness will help them evade. And the NVA won't exactly be fresh and rosy after a full day's work; they'll be tired going into a chase.

"Now, we'll load the team up in Guam on a C-141," Talbot continued, gesturing with a pudgy hand. "They take off with a bunch of B-52s. The B-52s fly in cells of three. You can't really tell them apart from a C-141 Starlifter high in the sky, either visually or on radar. They'll go in and bomb the airfield at Dong Hoi, just as we've done with them all over the North Vietnamese panhandle for years. There's a bombing halt right now, but occasionally we hit them to remind them we can still do it, whenever and wherever we want. The White House has approved this strike in retaliation for the gunning down of one of our unarmed reconnaissance jets yesterday.

"The SOG team will be in the C-141 in the last cell of three B-52s in trail. The team will jump after the last bombs are released. They'll still be jumping in a little daylight, so it'll be easier for them to see each other in the air for grouping. The indig were handpicked for the op, but they don't have as many jumps under their belts as the Green Berets do, and they'll need that extra advantage. They'll be in the air as the bombs impact.

"Then, just after the airfield has been solidly pummeled, the team opens low and lands right on the site." Again with the hand gestures. "The dust won't even have settled. Their objective is to land right outside the bunker entrance. We've done this a few times before, and it's worked pretty well in large base camps in Laos and Cambodia. In the thick of the jungle, the bombs make an instant parachute landing zone. The NVA on the site will all still be in shock from the massive bombing, still cowering in their bunkers if they've got any sense at all. Most we've seen on other sites are walking around dazed in the smoke and rubble, bleeding from their ears, noses, and mouths, almost deaf, with mild concussions. It's easy to snatch a few prisoners to interrogate. We usually send in helos on those sites for immediate extraction. This team will hit the bunker at the airfield moments after the last bombs explode, try to snatch Salt and Pepper and get out, using the smoke, fire, and confusion as cover."

Marco was genuinely impressed. He still thought it was a suicide mission, but something this bold just might work, once. Not at a site as heavily defended as Dong Hoi, though.

"I still don't see the tie-in with me and my men," Marco hedged.

"Well, the airfield is near the coast. We can't pick up the HALO team by helicopter after the op, like we normally do. The helos would never get in or out. There's too much anti-aircraft artillery, and helo assaults into North Vietnam are tantamount to an invasion. The North Vietnamese would scream blue political murder. Too hard for the politicians. We'll take the team out by boat, where we have some deniability. And we think we'll need a reception team that can go to their assistance if things get too hot. That's where you and your boys come in."

It could be done, Marco thought. He knew of other teams that had conducted cross-beach operations in the North. The B-52s would stir the hornets' nest, but the NVA would be diverted from watching the coast. The plan was a classic example of special operations' "soft-and-hard" team concept. One group pre-stages by sneaking in. The other goes in hard, guns blazing. Each compliments the other and provides a certain redundancy.

"Okay, count us in," he nodded. "I think my part of the mission can be done. But I want it understood that my guys can get onto the beach and a little inland to help out or receive. I'm talking half a mile inland in an area like Dong Hoi. That's it. If the HALO team gets in trouble at the airfield or further than a half mile in from the sea, we can't get to them. It would be suicide, and I don't do kamikaze missions. The other thing is that I'm going to have to go ashore. Getting clearance for that is well above my pay grade. That's your department."

"Fair enough," the agent grinned. "Leave those details to me."

"Now, that's target one. You said you had another target."

Jason nodded and smiled a little less. "That's what I said." He rose from his chair and started to pace back and forth in the cramped office. "I have an independent source. A female agent who's passed me some good stuff over the last two years. I've kept her to myself, and she's never been compromised. I'm afraid to give her up to my superiors."

"Okay, so what's she got?"

"What she's got is a report from a relative of hers who lives in a village outside Dong Hoi called Phu Hoi. It's extremely close to the water and directly east of the airfield. A small, cozy fishing village. There's just a single unpaved road that runs to Highway 1. It sits among the dunes in the coastal lowlands and can be easily isolated." He glanced over at the SEAL, who nodded.

"Salt and Pepper have used Dong Hoi as a recuperation site before. Both Salt and Pepper have been seen in Phu Hoi, when they're in the area. They relax on the beach and flirt with the village girls. Real celebrities. Well, the reports I've been getting lately say that the white guy spends his nights with one of them and goes to the airfield during the day."

Marco sat up and looked at the map. It was too sweet to believe. He quirked an eyebrow. The CIA man smiled thinly as he saw the SEAL's interest piqued.

"How good is that intel?" Marco asked him.

"I think it's rock solid. My informant has never let me down in the two years I've collected from her. And no one else knows about this latest tidbit but me . . . and now you."

"My friend, I think we can do this one. Salt and Pepper captured." The SEAL's eyes glazed over for a brief moment in thought, and then his mouth hardened into a thin line. "That's the only part I can't guarantee. A snatch can go bad at any time. The harder the site, the less likely the capture."

"We know that. The HALO team leader said the same thing."

"So you know what the alternative is?"

"Yeah, I know," Jason said, without a trace of emotion. "But let me make it clear: if you can't bring them out, no one wants to see or hear anything about them again. Ever."

Their eyes met and held. Marco had killed a few men in the heat of battle. He'd even killed a few on SOG missions that weren't in the jungle . . . a little more cold-blooded and deliberate. Each was necessary to complete the mission and survive. He'd accepted that. He was a warrior, and that was combat.

But this time it would be different. Americans were rarely sanctioned to go on "Kit Kats," the code word for MACV-SOG missions into North Vietnam. This wasn't a recon mission or a hit against a communist officer; the targets were other Americans. They were sending a message over to the other side. The brass didn't really expect or even particularly want Salt and Pepper to be captured and brought back alive. They wanted the job done right, and they wanted an American to pull the trigger.

He knew how hard it usually was to get authorization to go into North Vietnam, but Jason had acted as if it would be as easy as renewing a driver's license. They wanted Salt and Pepper eliminated. Badly. And as usual, they were leaving the dirty work to SEALs and Green Berets.

"Okay," Marco said quietly after a moment. "We're in. We're in all the way."

The detailed planning, training, and staging for the mission took five days. Marco met only one man from the HALO team, the OIC, Elson Bridges. He was a former enlisted Green Beret who'd had three tours in Vietnam, one of them with SOG. Marco knew him by reputation. Bridges had been on several missions over the fence in Laos. He'd even been in North Vietnam. Once he and the legendary Dick Meadows had staged from the carrier *Intrepid* with a team and gone in to rescue a downed Navy A-1 pilot. They'd nearly succeeded, coming within a hundred yards of the man before he was captured. The NVA caught the team in a firefight, and the Americans managed to make it back in one piece with no casualties.

On this operation, the HALO team would literally be on the run from the time they hit the bunker on the airfield until they made it to the beach. Marco didn't have any intention of letting them down. Signals and procedures were established for link-up. Then the Special Forces man was gone; he and his men were temporarily moved to Guam.

Marco had one more surprise dumped in his lap.

He'd been debating a means to accomplish his mission if one or both of the defectors showed up in the village. Closing on the village during the day wasn't even worth considering, and at night it would be extremely difficult. If he could get next to the men, he might be able to use a shotgun with silent shells. It was an impressive weapon, but it required close range. The team would be on a cross-border mission, and for the sake of deniability they had to go in sterile. The shotgun he was contemplating taking in was a specialized weapon and couldn't be readily identified as American.

The best minds in MACV-SOG went to work on the problem, but none of the ideas they had were feasible. The CIA thought that if the team couldn't get close enough to the village, it might be possible to lure at least one of the defectors out into the open. A sniper team could possibly assure that the men didn't escape. SEALs hadn't really worked much to develop that particular skill for their roles in Vietnam, so they were going to have to dig up an actual sniper team. There were a lot of good snipers in country, most Army and Marine. The Agency had a few independent shooters, but they wouldn't be allowed to be used on this mission by the MACV-SOG chain of command.

Since they planned on swimming in on the last leg of the beach insertion, a Marine Corps team that could handle the water seemed to be the most viable option. Marco interviewed and screened five available teams and selected one.

The NCO in charge of the pair, Garner, had been trained by a Marine sniper known as "White Feather" for the bird's feather he always wore in his cap. White Feather was a living legend, the best the Marine Corps ever fielded in Vietnam. Anyone trained by him would be steady under pressure. The spotter was also very experienced. Between the two of them, they had a hundred and twenty-three kills. That said it all. And both of them swam like fish.

Once selected, the men were briefed, but they weren't told the mission was going to be in New York, the term used for North Vietnam by MACV-SOG PSYOPS men. They only knew they would be deep in enemy territory, and they could pretty much guess it wouldn't be in South Vietnam. The idea was accepted with an indifference born of obvious experience.

A plan was constructed and rehearsed. The Marines weren't told about the B-52 strike or the Green Beret HALO mission. They only needed to know the bare facts.

They spent several hours on a known distance range at Coral Beach, where SOG had firearms and demolition ranges, just to verify their "dope," the detailed information used to calculate the trajectory of their match-grade ammunition when mated with a specific weapon, shooter, and optics. They had a specific lot of match-grade ammunition transferred and held at the SOG ammunition bunkers at Spanish Beach nearby.

Sterile equipment didn't have to be taken along for the sniping. There would be few if any shots fired from their weapons, and no evidence would be left behind to be traced. All the figures for the dope would be studied in detail, and the projected winds in the target area were forecast.

The Marines wouldn't be using noise suppressors for the operation; they'd be working in the vast open area next to the sea among sand dunes, and accuracy and distance would count for a lot more than noise suppression. The shooter used a model 70 Winchester .30-06 Springfield sniper rifle, specially crafted to USMC combat standards. The weapon and shooter could put a target down at over eleven hundred yards under ideal conditions.

The second man would spot the rounds for the shooter. It was a job that took even more skill and experience, since his readings of the wind, range and other conditions were all the shooter had to go on to enable him to adjust for the shot. Waterproofing the weaponry became a key factor, especially for the Marines.

The insertion would be a cakewalk, but Marco decided they'd have to go in the night before and lay up for a day. That made everyone who'd approved the mission extremely uncomfortable, but there was no other way. Everything had to revolve around the best time for the HALO team to jump in, and that was at last light. And Marco and his team had to be in place before the bombing in order to make the snatch at the village.

The team rehearsed literally burying themselves in the sand dunes, and the Marine snipers proved their worth with brilliant suggestions on keeping concealed. Their other operations had made the Marines masters of the art. They also taught Marco to avoid movements that would give their location away. There was one they called "gophering," the bobbing of the head up and down as a prone stalker looked around. The movements had to be careful, slow, and controlled to remain concealed. Patience was the biggest asset they had, a lesson White Feather had continually pounded into them during training.

The mission was finally launched. Marco's sea team, called an "Action Team" in SOG terms, loaded and went north on SOG-operated PTFs. Several American and Philippine maintenance crews saw them off. The Philippine wrench-turners were under contract through a company called the Eastern Construction Company, a CIA front that worked throughout Vietnam. Its men did actual construction, but insurgency specialists were sprinkled throughout the organization.

From over the horizon east of Dong Hoi, the boats moved in slowly toward the North Vietnamese coastline. It took several hours to complete the final leg of the insertion. The team finally slipped into the water two thousand yards offshore and surface-swam to the breakers. They moved slowly through the water, laden with weaponry and ordnance, the Marines dragging their bagged weapons and equipment in floating packages behind the group. Outside the surf zone, two Vietnamese scout swimmers moved in and reconned the beach, and the team was signaled ashore.

The rest of the night was spent carefully moving in on the village and selecting a position from which they could observe, yet remain undetected. They covered their tracks behind them as they moved. Finally, two hours before dawn, they buried each other in the dunes.

Throughout the next day, it was almost impossible to stay hidden. The activity around the village was substantial. Remaining absolutely still became a brutal test of self-control as the hours passed. Marco had lain in ambush in water all night on numerous missions, but he'd never tried to do it in sand before. It made more of a difference than he would have thought possible, and he gained more respect for the Marine long gunners with every grueling hour.

Time passed with aching slowness until mid-afternoon, when a Russian jeep pulled into the village. Three men climbed out, two NVA soldiers and a Caucasian with sandy blond hair in an olive drab military uniform, not American. The villagers greeted him warmly, and a gorgeous woman with waist-length black hair flew into his arms and led him into her hootch. Marco felt his blood run hot. The intelligence had been right. Salt was within his grasp.

You're mine, he thought.

But he and his men would never be able to close on the hut before the bomb strike. It was too great a distance through too much open terrain. The daylight was working against them. They were four hundred meters from the hut. When the first bombs hit, the villagers would hear the strike and scramble, and Salt would likely bolt in his jeep. Marco couldn't get up and move fast enough to get to him before he took off. It looked like it would be up to the snipers. When he was finally finished calculating the odds, he whispered to the spotter next to him.

"You guys know you're it. We'll never be able to sneak up to the hut in broad daylight before the bombs hit. The only shot you'll have is after the B-52 strike impacts the airfield."

The Marines nearly came unglued.

"*What* strike?" the spotter hissed.

"Couldn't tell you before. There's more to this mission than our part. Don't worry, though. The bombs are only a diversion."

"Lieutenant, have you ever been around a B-52 strike?" the Marine whispered harshly. "The ground shakes. This close to the airfield, we're going to feel the shock waves. That guy will be up and gone before we can take a clean shot. It's only about four hundred yards, but with the ground shaking, we won't have a steady shot! The sight picture is going to be screwed!"

Marco went dead white. He couldn't believe he hadn't thought of it before. Christ, what a stupid mistake! He should never have kept the rest of the mission from the snipers. They were in this together, and now his greater concern for operational security had doomed the mission.

He had to come up with a solution. He couldn't let Salt get out of the village alive.

"Okay, okay, listen up," Marco hissed. "What's happened can't be helped. Here's the new plan. I'm going to take the others, crawl between the dunes, and close on the village. You'll see us as we move, because we'll have to start about thirty minutes before the bombs fall, and it'll still be light. All you have to do is put the guy down when he shows. Just put him down. I'll close with the team and finish the job. If I don't make it back, there's another team coming out from the airfield. Link up with them and get out to the PTFs. If the NVA chase us, we'll head south, then out to the beach for a PTF pickup. That will lure them away from you guys. Remember, all you have to do is knock him down." Marco passed them the recognition signals for the HALO team linkup.

When the sun hit the horizon, Marco slowly rose from his position and let sand pour off his body. He crawled up a nearby dune. There was no sign of activity nearby except for the village. He checked his watch. The Archlight strike would hit in forty minutes, and he wanted to be ready. He moved to each man and signaled them out of their hidden positions in the sand. The men slowly formed into a tight perimeter.

"No matter what happens, you put the guy down," Marco whispered to the Marine sniper team as he and his men headed out. A steady breeze came in from the sea. It didn't carry their scent toward the village, mercifully; they would have heard from half the animal population of North Vietnam if it had. Unfortunately it meant the snipers would have to fire in a crosswind, making the shot even more difficult. Things weren't shaping up well on this mission, and Marco knew he'd have to get in close. He and his men were two hundred yards away from the target hut when they heard the first explosions on the airfield to the west.

The earth shook and the airfield erupted with brilliant fire. No parachutes could be seen in the air. Marco took off for the road at a dead run. The ground was still shaking, and the SEAL fell down twice as the sands shifted treacherously beneath him. His legs were weak from their twelve-hour sojourn in the sand, and he hadn't counted on that. Damn. There were a lot of things he should have counted on, a lot of mistakes he was making on this mission. And there would be plenty of time to kick himself in the head for them later, if he lived.

Salt emerged from the hut and looked toward the airfield. He bellowed to his two NVA body-guards, and they all bolted for the jeep. *Damn it!* They had about a hundred and fifty yards to go, and the snipers hadn't taken their shot yet. If Salt and the NVA made it into the jeep, it would be almost impossible for the Marines to hit him on the move as the ground shook in a hot crosswind.

They made it to the jeep and started it up. Marco had another hundred yards to go, and the enemy were focused on the airfield. In the fading light, they couldn't see Marco and his men sprinting to-ward the road ahead of them. The SEAL made a quick calculation. It looked like they were already too late; they weren't going to make it to the road in time to meet the jeep. Where was the damned sniper shot?

A crack rang out, and Salt slumped forward on the passenger side of the jeep. The driver pushed on for another thirty yards, then slowed the vehi-cle, obviously uncertain as to what had happened. Marco continued to close in on them.

At seventy-five yards, he could see the horror on the faces of the NVA as they realized their com-panion had been shot. The driver frantically worked the gearshift, but it was too late. Marco and the two SOG Vietnamese bore down on the jeep and riddled the three bodies with a full magazine each. Panting heavily, Marco grabbed the defector by the hair and pulled him down to the ground while his Viets made sure the others were dead. They took up security positions around him after that.

The SEAL pulled out a Browning Hi-Power and pointed it in the face of the defector. The blond man was fighting to draw in each shallow breath. Dying.

"How's it feel to be on the other side now?" Marco asked him, not really interested in his answer. "Who are you?"

The American focused and tried to reply.

"Question is . . . who are you?" He fell into a violent coughing fit, blood streaming out of his mouth. He looked like a fish out of water, trying to breathe. Just before Salt faded, Marco saw his eyes widen with the realization that he'd been gunned down by another American. Clearly, he'd never expected that.

The sniper round had taken him high in the chest, and was probably non-survivable. All in all, not a bad shot, considering the conditions. Marco and the Nungs had simply nailed the coffin shut.

Once he confirmed the defector's death, they left the scene and moved out. The NVA would be combing the area soon from the airfield to the sea. They couldn't be burdened with the body, so they left it to save their own lives. They had to focus on meeting and assisting the HALO team. They circled west, then back east to the sniper position. The villagers stood clear and dared not pursue as darkness closed in.

Marco and the team found the Marines in the dark and confirmed the kill. They picked up and moved several hundred yards north. Twenty minutes later, the HALO team arrived on a dead run, followed closely by an NVA search party which didn't last long.

The linkup went as planned, but the team had bad news. Pepper wasn't at the bunker. The HALO team had landed perfectly, kicked in the door, and killed half a dozen NVA officers. They also thought they might have killed a senior ChiCom officer, judging by his different uniform. They took fifteen seconds to throw maps and documents in waterproof bags, then ran as hard as they could for the sea. They'd been at the bunker for less than a minute. Good hit, no Pepper.

The combined team moved straight for the water, with the snipers behind the HALO team and the frogmen in the rear. Everyone swam out through the surf, the exhausted HALO team using UDT lifejackets to help them stay afloat while the frogmen helped them through the breakers. The boats picked them up about a thousand yards offshore. They sped south before the North Vietnamese could recover enough to scramble their patrol boats.

Marco was never able to identify the American defector. The light had been bad, the American was covered with blood, and his features had been contorted in agony. The SEAL had seen him for only a few seconds, but he'd verified the kill. SOG wished he'd been able to bring the body out, but knew that was a pipe dream. Marco had thought about taking fingerprints, but in all likelihood they would have been erased by the pounding surf. And any photos taken from their hide site during the day would have been likely to give away their position. All the brass had was Marco's description.

In the years that followed as the war wound down, other reports persisted of defectors working for the other side. But never again a pair, one black, one white.

=12=

Dragon's Jaw

May 1972

"Yeah, that was an embarassing screw-up," Marco admitted. "But at least it all worked out in the end."

"It just doesn't always matter how well you plan a mission," Art Jones murmured thoughtfully. "I was in Grenada with John Tindle, Steve Horn, and Rick Raydon, and after two heated engagements we ended up having to evade a superior enemy force and hide in the jungle until darkness fell. I took three rounds as we ran for cover during the second firefight. The first two bullets blew off equipment I carried, and the third shattered a bone in my forearm. And that was my drinkin' mug hand. I suppose it could have been a lot worse. But Grenada almost killed me, and it did kill four other SEALs we all knew well." His eyes hardened as he remembered friends he'd never see again this side of death.

"Well, A. J., they can't *all* be as pretty as the

Dragon's Jaw," Marco drawled teasingly after a moment's silence. "I mean, you *only* helped pull down the most obnoxiously unconquerable military target in North Vietnam."

"I did that, didn't I?" A. J. smirked, letting his mood lighten again. No sense dragging everybody down; he wasn't the only one of them who'd lost friends in Grenada. "Yeah, I guess they can't all be as pretty as the Dragon's Jaw."

Art Jones quietly studied his team in the calm before the storm. They sat in the helo, tense, expectant, waiting. The noise of the rotor made conversation almost impossible, which suited him well enough.

Dick Gilbert looked too eager. He and John Tindle were the support team; they'd ride the insertion and extraction helicopter to assist as swimmers if any of the commandos were wounded, and they'd provide fire support during an emergency or normal extraction. Frankly, A. J. didn't want Gilbert anywhere near the ground if it could be avoided. The man was unhinged.

He boasted frequently of having the highest body count in the teams. On his second tour in country, he made a bet with another SEAL that he would run more operations during their six-month tour. Gilbert and the others went on R & R halfway through the tour, but unlike the other SEALs, Gilbert found another SEAL platoon in the Delta and ran missions with them for several days. He won the bet, spilling his secret only as he and his teammate boarded the plane for the return back to the Silver Strand at the end of the tour. His teammate didn't take the news too well. Gilbert wore the broken nose as a badge of honor. They were almost thrown into the brig because of the fight.

Now Gilbert had a bet that he would be the last SEAL in country. As insane as he obviously was, A. J. had serious doubts about bringing him on the mission at all. He was just crazy enough to get off the chopper in North Vietnam and never come home. Hell, he would probably see it as a heaven-sent challenge. He'd wander all over the North, killing NVA in onesies and twosies, picking them off slowly and quietly. He could live off the land forever and use combat resupply, taking the weapons and ammunition of his victims.

No, Gilbert was better off in the helo. But his multiple tours and combat experience would be valuable if the ground team had to have heavy backup. The mission was too risky for them not to have him along. A. J. only prayed that the quiet, taciturn Tindle would be able to steady him and keep him in the support role they'd been assigned to. Tindle and Gilbert both stared out the window of the helo. Tindle was lost in his thoughts, and Gilbert was fidgeting with anticipation, running a hand over his short light brown hair, his ice-blue eyes flickering with barely contained violence.

Petty Officer Mark Sloan had been an obvious choice for second in command on the mission. He and A. J. had been working together for months at An Hoa, where the few remaining SEAL advisors in country had all been moved. They were comfortable together in the field and under fire, and they worked well as a unit. Sloan sat calmly enough, worrying at a thumbnail, dark eyes narrowed in thought, a slight frown creasing his brow.

A. J. hadn't worked with either of the Vietnamese commandos who rounded out the team, but he had no doubts as to their ability. He'd handpicked both of them from the "Earth Angel" project originally run by MACV-SOG and carried through when MACV-SOG was renamed the Strategic Technical Directorate Assistance Team 158. Both Van and Trinh had been North Vietnamese soldiers. Now they worked for the South, trained agents who were sent back into the North on specific short-term exploitation operations. Van was dressed for his mission as an NVA officer, and Trinh was disguised as a noncommissioned officer. For the area they would be going into, they would both be invaluable.

The target area was one of the most heavily defended in North Vietnam, all because of the bridge. The infamous Dragon's Jaw was located three miles north of Thanh Hoa and seventy miles south of Hanoi on the main highway, Route 1. It was the main artery that fed the highway and rail line across the Song Ma River, which emptied into the Gulf of Tonkin ten miles to the southeast.

Of the nearly one hundred tactical targets CINC-PAC had drawn up to be taken out, the Dragon's Jaw was number fourteen. The bridge had been attacked several times since 1965, with massive amounts of American firepower, and always unsuccessfully. It had been damaged, twisted, charred, gouged, even temporarily put out of commission, but it had always been rebuilt. Now it stood as a living testament to the determination of their opponent, a powerful semi-fortress of steel through-truss spans and concrete abutments, complacent, mocking the Americans with its continued existence. The Dragon's Jaw had become more than a tactical target. It had become a legend, a symbol of the futility of the conflict.

Since the Easter Offensive in April of 1972, when the North Vietnamese had steamrolled over the border with heavy armor and artillery, the gloves had come off once again. The bombing halt President Johnson had called back in 1968 was officially over, and the Defense Department was cleared to hit the North with significant airpower. The Thanh Hoa Bridge was one of the first targets on the list.

The Americans had to cut the line that fed the armor and infantry the NVA were throwing into the South, and the Dragon's Jaw was one of the main links. By now, laser-guided bombs, or "smart bombs," were in theater, and everyone was itching to use them. No longer held to seven-hundred-and-fifty and one-thousand-pound ordnance, the LGBs were in the two-thousand and three-thousand-pound class. It was time to do some serious damage to the supply artery.

On April 27, the first strike had used chaff and cover planes in a highly orchestrated raid, and had produced serious damage, but the bridge still stood. Then the administration had authorized Operation Linebacker I on May 10, and that was when A. J. and his team had been pulled in.

The first LGB strike was on the right track, but they still encountered heavy AA, and smoke and dust from the first bombs on target obscured the bridge for follow-up aircraft. The target had to be illuminated by laser energy so that the bomb could ride the energy beam to its impact point. The aircraft worked together, one illuminating the target and one dropping the smart bomb in a technique called "buddy lasing." But once the smoke and dust flew, lasing from the air was difficult to impossible. The North Vietnamese knew the aircraft would be back, and they knew about LGBs, thanks to their Soviet advisors. They burned the fields all around the area and helped thicken the constant haze around the objective to make it as difficult as possible for the Americans.

There was one other possibility. A ground team could take in a hand-held lasing device and illuminate the target from the ground. The devices were new, delicate, and large enough to be cumbersome, but it could be done. A. J. had participated in some experimental tests at the Navy's China Lakes Weapons Test Center in 1971 after his first tour in Vietnam, never expecting to actually be in on such a mission. He had knowledge of the devices and the LGB mission profiles, which required considerable training. When Linebacker I was initiated, his name showed up on a list of those few special operations men who knew how to ground-lase.

And STADT 158 knew that the best way for a ground team to get out of such a hot area was to take the river out to the Gulf. It would require a lot of swimming and small boat work. They might have to hide during the day and swim out at night. The best men for that kind of movement would be combat swimmers. Navy SEALs.

A. J. had the dubious honor of being selected for the mission because he was a top-ranking SEAL, he'd trained for laser operations, and he was in theater and immediately available. Hardly the sort of honor one could refuse, but A. J. had his doubts about the mission. He would need every tactic and trick he'd ever learned in order to pull it off, and it would be a crapshoot even then. He was on his own this time as far as coming up with a plan and executing it, and the laser mission team was given only two days to train for the operation.

And now, here we are in the "Wing-and-a-Prayer" School of Operations, the SEAL thought dryly. Like it or not, there was no more time to plan this. They were inserting from this helo, right now, because he'd considered and tossed out about a half-dozen other options for insertion. This was the best he had.

The commandos were going in sterile, no name tapes, no dogtags. There weren't even American labels inside their uniforms. The AK47s they carried were NVA standard, and they would blend with the sounds of the enemy's weaponry in a firefight. It would minimize the chances of their being pinpointed, and A. J. hoped a few enemy soldiers would panic and pick each other off in the confusion.

The team tried not to gear up too heavily, but it was hard to draw the line. They intended to avoid contact at all costs; it would only get them killed. They wanted to go light, but if they had to fight, there would be no rescue helos streaming to their aid. They would be completely on their own. They had to have enough ordnance to break contact and run. They carried a couple of white phosphorous and CS grenades of foreign manufacture for deniability.

The inbound flight path of the helicopters was electrifying. The aircraft dropped to fifty feet above the sea, splitting apart and scattering two miles from the coast. There was little small boat traffic where they intended to cross the coast, several miles north of the mouth of the Song Ma River. As they crossed the coastline, they flew separate routes, saturating the area in their search for the fictitious downed airman. The commandos' HH-53 continued inland like the rest, but penetrated slightly further. The pilot was looking for a spot just over five miles upriver from the bridge. At that point, both the Song Ma and Song Chu Rivers came together in a pronounced fork.

By the time they crossed the coast, the sun was already fading in the western sky beyond the mountains. The insertion was supposed to take place just after sunset, and the darkening sky helped cover the activities of all the SAR helos. For the next few minutes there would be nothing to do but wait.

Finally the helo bucked and swerved, throwing the men in back tightly against their harnesses. The halts and hovers would make them appear to be searching for the downed aviator. A quick, whispered transmission burst over the airwaves on an SAR frequency, but the pilots couldn't make it out. Probably one of the pre-recorded "come get me" messages, but real enough to be unsettling.

"Three minutes!" shouted one of the crewmen, holding up three fingers in the darkened red light of the cabin. A. J.'s teammates were stationed

around the deck, harnessed in gunner's belts
clipped into attachment points on the deck. They
were able to move, but the harnesses would keep
them from falling out of the helo during an erratic
maneuver. The rear ramp was dropped, and the
miniguns were manned as they had been since the
helo had crossed the coast. Each of the six-
thousand-round-per minute guns had been test-
fired into the sea on the inbound leg. The tail ramp
was still slightly down. The hot exhaust and damp
night air mixed with the scent of the lush terrain.

"One minute!"

The HH-53 suddenly crossed the Song Ma River
and banked sharply left, facing downriver. It flared
violently in the now-total darkness, coming to a
hover thirty feet above the water. The team was
ready, standing along the port bulkhead and hanging onto any handhold they could find. A. J. was
the first man in the file, standing on the hinge of
the ramp.

"Go! Go!" the crewman shouted, gesturing
wildly out the aft of the helo. Without hesitation,
A. J. leaped out into the darkness. His heart
plunged with the shock of falling. Crossing and ex-
tending his legs, he kept his eyes straight ahead
and clutched the rucksack with the laser tightly to
his chest. The others were right behind him. It was
a slow count of four before A. J. hit the water.

It was shockingly cool . . . muddy, but strangely
enough, it felt better than the sweat and hot flush
of anticipation. It was a relief to be in and on the
ground, and as soon as he bobbed to the surface,
he settled down for the mission. It was good to be
in on deck once again. *Welcome to North Viet-*

nam, A. J., he thought to himself with a grim, tight-lipped smile.

The HH-53 had come to a full hover. As soon as it had come out of the flare, the pilot had allowed it to drift forward for a count of five, then nosed it forward, gave power, and rose to move out of the area. A few seconds later it was gone.

A. J. and his men assembled silently in the water. The noise from the helo faded away quickly, and overwhelming silence followed in its wake. The two Vietnamese swam around behind A. J., and Sloan took up the rear. Sloan was carrying the crucial second laser, to be used as a backup, if necessary.

The current was perfect; it would easily take them south toward the bridge by dawn. The men wouldn't have to swim hard to make it to the target area before first light. The fact that their equipment was rigged for buoyancy would make it even easier. They pulled camouflage netting from their pockets. The large gaps in the netting permitted swimmers to see through it easily, but from over twenty-five meters away, their netted heads looked like flotsam in the water. Even though it was completely dark, they left nothing to chance. If they were discovered, they would never make it out alive.

As the team swam slowly and quietly southeast, they passed a large island in the middle of the river. A. J. knew the bridge was only about three miles beyond the south end of the island. Enemy positions peppered each bank. The defenses thickened as the men closed on the target area. A. J. didn't want to try to swim past the bridge the next day while the strike was being executed, so he was planning to try to swim past the structure that night and set up to the south. That would give them a fighting chance to escape to the sea once the deed was done. And it would give them a chance to conduct a leader's reconnaissance of the target from the water, always an essential part of any operation.

They had SAR radios and no others; they had to go in light. *Moonbeam*, the ELINT C-130 flying off the coast, would keep the team located by monitoring the signals of the small transponders the SEALs both carried. They had no plans to contact the strike aircraft as they were inbound, and the lasers took up all the space and weight the team could handle on the long swim. This wasn't like a jungle patrol by a heavily laden Ranger or Special Forces team. The long distance swim, even with the current, would be an all-night affair. Before the pickup in twenty four hours, the men would have to swim nearly fifteen miles. They had to stay light and rely on concealment and stealth. The SAR radios would be used only for extraction. The plan called for the men to be set up for a specific time on the thirteenth. There would be no second chance. Either they'd succeed, or the method would never be attempted again.

The commandos swam in a loose formation. It was dark, but the Americans had night vision equipment, and some of that equipment had been captured by the North Vietnamese during the war. Their Soviet advisors had doubtless provided them with similar technology as well. A. J. had to plan for the possibility that sentries near the bridge would be scanning the waters for enemy sappers with that.

Fires marked several enemy encampments along the bank. They added to the haze in the vicinity of the bridge, and that would hinder the lasing from the air. The swimmers drifted slowly toward the target. The water was cool from the spring rains.

Two hours later they reached the bridge. It was vast, imposing, cold-looking. The four men paired up and whispered their final farewells. Then the two Vietnamese drifted toward the southern shore, away from the SEALs.

That was all part of A. J.'s plan. He'd allowed the Vietnamese to "discover" that he and Sloan were going to establish their position upriver from the bridge. He'd concealed the truth from them in case they were captured, or worse. They might be double agents. A. J. had no intention of making a mistake that could cost them the mission or their lives. If the Earth Angels compromised the laser mission, the North Vietnamese were still going to have to scour the countryside for the SEALs.

Lasing from the ground was going to be incredibly difficult; A. J. had no illusions about that. It wouldn't be safe to leave the water for a lasing position. Even then, there was a lot of traffic around the bridge. They stood a good chance of being compromised by their movements alone.

He had to have a diversion. There would have to be a distraction in order for them to pull it off. The Earth Angel pair were meant to be that distraction. They were supposed to penetrate an ammunition storage nearby and start a large fire. It was hoped that some of the ammunition would go up in the smoke. At the very least, if they could start the fire, a lot of communist soldiers would have to be drawn off to stop the loss of ammunition, so greatly needed against the attacking American pilots. At worst, the pair would be discovered and captured and create a stir outside the area A. J. planned to set up in. Cold as he knew it sounded, that was good enough for him.

The fire they started might help obscure the target to the aircraft lasing systems. But it was still the best solution he'd been able to come up with.

The Earth Angel pair swam into the darkness, leaving the SEALs on their own. The Americans drifted and became as silent as possible as they approached the structure. The Dragon's Jaw was a dark and mystic shadow against the blackened sky. The SEALs made sure the nets covered them and their equipment and drifted on easily. They deflated their air bladders slightly and sank as low in the water as they could manage.

The bridge was a beehive of enemy activity. Trucks streamed south with men and supplies. There were hundreds of guards and construction workers all around them. A. J. took a deep breath to steady himself and continued. They paused briefly below the main pilings in the middle of the river, studying the structure of the bridge and its surrounding terrain and defenses. Suddenly a small spark drifted down and hit the water ten feet away. A North Vietnamese soldier had just finished a cigarette. A. J.'s breath caught in his throat and he froze in place, his heart hammering wildly. After a few seconds he regained his composure and signaled Sloan silently to follow him past the bridge and toward the north shore.

The two made for land in the area A. J. had previously selected. They found shallow water and had to move downriver to avoid enemy activity and barren bank. Finally they held up near a small overhang. Observations and instructions flew back and forth in whispers so quiet they could barely hear each other. It was obvious they'd have to move inland to a better spot. A. J. hated the thought, but he knew it had to be done. During his planning, he'd selected two areas inland on either side of the river to lase from. He decided to try the primary site he'd selected on the north side, the bank they were on.

They swam out slowly into the center of the river and floated several hundred yards downriver beyond the ferry point. There was a clear spot on the bank with enough foliage to allow them to move ashore. They crawled out of the water on all fours until they were fifty meters inland, cradling their AK47s in the crooks of their elbows, and dragging their rucksacks. A. J. risked raising himself to one knee and peered intently into the darkness. They were clear, so far. A dirt road lay in front of them.

"We're going for high ground," A. J. whispered. Sloan nodded, and they slipped across the road and went into the bush. Slowly they made their way up the large hill on the north side of the river, using every depression and bit of vegetation for concealment. They had to stop frequently to avoid the enemy troops who swarmed over the area.

Finally they selected a spot about six hundred meters from the river with a clear field of observation of the bridge. That put them within the fragmentation radius of the laser bombs, but A. J. wanted to be sure. There would be no second chance. They hadn't quite made it to the top of the hill. A. J. knew the NVA had all the high points laced with AAA. He and Sloan pulled into a shallow depression and pulled all the available scrub brush in around them. Each move was agonizingly slow and deliberate.

It took A. J. almost an hour to remove the laser, the battery pack, and all the components of the device from their four protective layers of plastic. He also removed Sloan's laser and placed it nearby. Using his K-bar knife, he slowly and silently dug a furrow into the ground, building a mound to lay the devices against. Once he'd finished, the men lay still, hardly daring to breathe, watching the North Vietnamese in their normal rounds of mundane activities. Neither could sleep, under the circumstances.

Dawn broke at last, and the men readjusted their camouflage to cover themselves. They were badly exposed, and they felt naked in the heart of all the NVA. They were forced to lay deathly still. The sun rose and began to roast them. They'd forgotten to unzip their wetsuit tops before they'd settled into their position, and now they didn't dare move. Sheer willpower kept them from wiping away the sweat that was running down into their eyes.

A. J. repeatedly looked over the devices and the setup, moving only his eyes. He also kept an eye on the bridge. Sloan was curled up next to him, facing the opposite direction for security. Half an hour to go. He felt his pulse quicken as the minutes counted down.

Ten minutes before the first aircraft was supposed to arrive, the sounds of shouting and gunfire came from an area near the ammunition storage targeted by the Earth Angels. Smoke billowed over the palm trees and more gunfire erupted. Two explosions fireballed skyward within five minutes of showtime. A. J. smiled. The Earth Angel distraction would help them get back to the water regardless of the outcome of the operation, and the blasts and smoke might help the inbound planes identify the target more quickly.

Two minutes. A. J. turned his head slowly.

"Get ready," he told his partner. "It's time to burn the bridge."

"Let's do it and get the hell out of here!" Sloan hissed nervously, sweat pouring over him as much from fear as from the heat. As A. J. turned the device on and sighted once more, Sloan scanned the area and covered him.

"Come on, boys," A. J. rasped at the unknowing aircrews. "Come and get it."

All hell broke loose, right on schedule. All the anti-aircraft guns in the area began blasting skyward. The air filled with the scream of jets, and a huge blast shook the bridge. Smoke and dust from the explosion obscured part of the target, but the laser that A. J. had directed at it was aimed at another section. A second bomb hit the exact spot their laser was illuminating, and the span whined and screeched. The western end fell twenty feet, but didn't completely detach to hit the water. It dangled stubbornly, as if refusing to grant its destroyers that final satisfaction.

The Dragon's Jaw was out of commission. The two SEALs watched, a little stunned by the success of the ploy, then glanced at each other and clenched their fists in celebration. A. J. pulled the pin on a thermite grenade he'd set next to the units, and he glanced back at Sloan.

"Go! Go!" he hissed loudly. The other SEAL got to his knees, scanned the horizon quickly, and nodded to A. J. They were clear. Sloan turned and moved out.

A. J. glanced down to make sure the thermite grenade was in good position against the laser MULEs and let the spoon fly off. He pulled his hand back as if he'd burned it, jumped up, and raced after his partner. The thermite grenade ignited in a brilliant flash and burned so intensely it melted the MULEs in less than a minute.

Even in the confusion of the airstrike and Earth Angel fire, the thermite grenade drew the attention of a North Vietnamese soldier, who shouted at the pair. Suddenly the SEALs found themselves under sporadic fire from above and behind them. They kept running, using ravines and vegetation to cover their movements. As they plowed through a series of bushes, they ran headlong into three NVA soldiers who were scrambling up the hill.

Sloan literally crashed into the first NVA. Too close to fire on him, the SEAL gave him a horizontal butt stroke with the metal stock of his AK47, then brought the weapon around and laced the other two at point-blank range with half a dozen shots. A. J. turned and fired on the soldier who'd been knocked unconscious from the blow. The SEALs each fell to one knee facing opposite directions, fighting to quiet their breathing as they scanned the area. All around them, NVA continued to shoot at the aircraft, and confusion reigned. A. J. and Sloan picked up and moved out fast.

They reached the water and immediately slid in. Tugging the nets over their heads, they floated steadily toward the middle of the river. The NVA continued to fire into the air, dotting the hills on both banks. A few were searching the area the SEALs had lased the bridge from. The frogmen hastily strapped on their fins and kicked steadily toward the sea, letting the swift river current carry them along. They would have to put some distance between themselves and the NVA quickly. If there was one thing the NVA were good at, it was organizing searches for downed pilots and small recon teams in the jungle.

The Earth Angel team wouldn't be trying to move to the river. They'd be traveling in the opposite direction on a mission A. J. wasn't privy to. The Earth Angels were supposed to be picked up in a week, if they survived. For now they'd served their purpose, and they'd be leading any search parties away from the SEALs.

A. J. and Sloan continued to swim, passing several small boats on the water. Twice they had to stop along the bank, drag themselves out of the water and slip around concentrations of enemy soldiers. It took them the entire day to drift to the sea, but by the time the sun touched the horizon, they were two miles upriver from the coast. Pickup was preset for just after dark.

The recovery was built around simplicity. The pair would either steal a small boat or swim toward the sea. A. J. nixed the boat idea after seeing all the NVA activity after the lasing. They stood a better chance swimming under their nets. The idea worked. They reached the mouth of the river just as darkness fell.

They both lit off their strobelights with infrared filters and held them out of the water. In the safety and grip of the open sea, they could finally let themselves relax a little.

Half an hour later, they heard the pounding of a large helo inbound from the east. A. J. began to give short transmissions from his SAR radio to vector them in. The helo flew low and headed right for the mouth of the river.

The crew immediately picked up the flashing strobes and made a sweeping turn, approaching and slowing. Two heads peering out of a side hatch vectored the pilot directly over the pair. Twenty feet before they reached them, they threw a large bag out of the helo. Ropes unraveled from the deployment bag as it hit the water and was dragged toward the SEALs. The spray of the saltwater from the massive HH-53 rotors stung their eyes and blinded them. They grabbed blindly for the ropes and found them, feeding them through their hands until they reached the harnesses at the end. Strapping themselves in, they turned off the strobelights, the signal to the helo that they were set to go.

The helo lifted off slowly, then picked up speed and headed out to sea in the darkness. The pair dangled below the gigantic bird, turning their backs to the wind to ease the sting of their eyes, hanging spread-eagled to stabilize their flight. The fierce gale stripped the water from their uniforms in sheets.

Exhausted, shaking, physically and emotionally drained, A. J. was still aware of a profound sense of contentment. They had done the impossible. The Dragon's Jaw was cracked.

The bridge remained closed until another laser mission dropped the structure into the water permanently in October 1972. The North Vietnamese spent the rest of the war desperately attempting to resurrect it.

They never succeeded.

=====13=====

Last Man Out

May 1975

"And it was the last good thing to happen in a long war," A. J. concluded. "Sometimes I still can't believe we all made it out."

"Even crazy Dick Gilbert made it," Tony Franco murmured, shaking his head. "Who'd have ever seen that one coming?"

"You know, I hear he had a bet on with another SEAL that he'd be the last frogman to leave Vietnam," Nick Stine smirked. "He'd foam at the mouth if he ever heard otherwise...."

The word came down as it had many times before. The operation had to be executed immediately.

The White House wanted a small, quiet run. No publicity, no problems. The Teams had to move, and move quickly. The United States was still in shock over the fall of Phnom Penh and Saigon. Operation Eagle Pull on April 12, 1975, the massive helicopter evacuation of the capital of Cambodia,

277

became a prelude to catastrophe. Two weeks later, the United States evacuated over seven thousand refugees and Americans from South Vietnam using helicopters and boats as the North Vietnamese rolled over the South in a massive conventional blitzkrieg. The nightmare evacuation mission, Operation Frequent Wind, was supposed to be the final tragic chapter in the conflict. But it was not to be.

Both evacuation operations had been chaotic. The number of Americans and refugees saved was nothing short of a miracle, but many more were left behind. The fall of Saigon was a bitter defeat after all the American blood that had been shed in Vietnam.

Nick Stine had been in the Philippines when word came about the mission. Stine was now master chief petty officer of UDT 11, the senior enlisted man in the command. He and his commanding officer, Gary Dennison, had gone to Subic Bay to congratulate the two UDT platoons that had participated in Frequent Wind. They'd performed well under the most harrowing conditions imaginable.

Stine was proud of their efforts during the evacuation. They'd been forced to board and search dozens of small craft as they'd fled the communist advance. Many of them were young, inexperienced, just out of BUD/S training; but they'd managed to stay calm under fire. Stine and Dennison were there to compile information and submit awards for at least a few of them.

Then the other shoe dropped. The *Mayaguez* operation.

It was the second week in May, days after the fall of Saigon. On the twelfth, an American merchant ship had been seized by rogue communists off the coast of Cambodia. The ship and crew were taken to a small island off the mainland called Koh Tang. American aircraft were able to isolate the position and keep the communists from taking their prisoners to the mainland. Delta Platoon from SEAL Team ONE and a platoon from UDT 11 had been scrambled from Subic Bay for a rescue operation, but in the end, the task force commander from the Carrier Battle Group *Coral Sea* elected to use only Marines in a totally conventional response.

The frogmen had argued that the location of the captured crew was unknown and thus a clandestine reconnaisance was needed, one which appeared to be tailor-made for them. Their recommendations fell on deaf ears.

A ground force of Air Force air police were rushed to Thailand to stage for the mission, but most of the unit died in a freak and tragic plane crash. Marines were immediately brought in from Okinawa and staged out of Thailand. The captured American ship, anchored off the island, was boarded and recaptured without a shot being fired. Two Navy destroyers towed it to sea in the early hours of the operation. An eminently predictable conventional American daylight assault of the island turned into a nightmare. A reinforced company of Marines was heavily engaged and pinned down by the Khmer Rouge. The Mayaguez crew was released by the Cambodians from another location on the mainland shortly after the Marines were inserted onto the island.

The fight on Koh Tang cost the Leathernecks dearly. Eighteen men never made it back. Another fifty were wounded. Nearly a dozen HH and CH-53 helicopters were shot down. And the whole situation could have been avoided.

The SEALs and UDT men could have quietly determined whether or not the captured crew was on the island, making an invasion unnecessary. And their recon would have indicated the size and disposition of the enemy force, intelligence unknown when the mission was launched. The Marines landed in broad daylight with incomplete intelligence using predictable American methods because they were told resistance would be minimal.

To make matters worse, the same "conventional" commanders who'd ordered the raid tried to order the frogmen on to Koh Tang after the battle to try to recover Marine bodies, unarmed, in broad daylight. The commanders were going to ask the communists nicely not to intervene. Dennison told the Admiral, not so nicely, that there was no way in hell he or his men would execute such a ludicrous plan.

The crew was released and the ship recaptured, but the cost was heavy. If it hadn't been for the efforts of a handful of helicopter crewmen who'd gained experience in aerial combat in Southeast Asia, the Marines on Koh Tang would have been slaughtered to a man.

Now a second mission had emerged, and CINC-PAC was painfully aware of the need for stealth and finesse. The publicity generated by the loss of

Cambodia and South Vietnam had created a huge public outcry. The *Mayaguez* incident had added fuel to the fire. The United States couldn't afford anything more. This new operation had to be carried out quickly, quietly, and flawlessly, with a reasonable amount of deniability and absolutely no headlines. This mission was tailor-made for frogmen, and CINCPAC wasn't planning on a repeat performance of the events on Koh Tang.

The mission call had gone out late at night, and most of the frogmen in that dull gray briefing room had been rousted out of bars and loud nightspots in Olongapo. The heavy silence and absolute seriousness that lay over them now like a pall was crushing by comparison. Dennison gathered them all in with his eyes and shattered the tense silence with his dry quiet voice.

"We have a full muster. The time on my mark is 0216 local . . . mark, 0216. Gentlemen, this briefing is classified top secret NOFORN. You must be absolutely careful of your actions and especially your talk outside this room from this point on. This mission is very high-priority. We *cannot* afford to let information about the mission reach agents still working for the communists. The Vietnamese are *good*, and their agent nets are still active around this base with all the civilian workers. This mission is being driven all the way from the White House. You won't see anything higher-priority in your lifetime." Dennison paused briefly to let his words sink in, then continued.

"Situation . . . a lot of CIA sources and their families were unable to make it out of Vietnam when it fell. There were literally hundreds who were left behind. It no longer matters why or how . . . the country will be arguing that one out for years to come, but it happened. We now have covert reports that some of them are assembled and need to be extracted . . . quickly and quietly."

"I don't understand," Stine frowned. "It was just a few days ago that we abandoned the entire country. The CIA and everyone knew the place was falling. A blind man could've seen it coming. They had plenty of time to get at least some of their people out, but they obviously didn't. So why is the White House making a big deal about them now?"

"All the operational information and this mission, a clandestine evacuation, are being set up from the inside by an American," Dennison replied. "He's still in country. He's still in Vietnam."

There was a low whistle in the back of the room, and Stine swore quietly under his breath.

"This is a reaction to a situation neither we nor the White House control," Dennison said coolly. "What happened before the fall of Saigon can no longer be changed. Either we act on this operation, or things are going to get a lot worse for a lot of people."

More Americans left behind. The thought raced around the room, reflected in the grim faces of the men around him. Dennison continued.

"The American's name is Tucker Gouggleman. He's a former CIA paramilitary agent who went back in to Vietnam at the end to get as many people out as he could, because the Agency and the State Department weren't doing squat. He wasn't supposed to be there, and the Agency says he knows way too much. He'll be scarfed up if some-

one doesn't go in there and get him, fast. And if
the Vietnamese do manage to get their hands on him,
their communist allies will get a huge intelligence
bonus. Neither the Agency nor the United States
can afford that. This man worked covert operations. We're talking about handing over a tremendous amount of information and intelligence . . .
events, names, places, dates, all of the greatest sen-
sitivity, and not just in the Vietnam arena. Worse,
he knows a tremendous amount about the agent
nets we had in country when Saigon fell. Some of
them might be able to go to ground and hide from
the communists, but if they capture Gouggleman,
they'll torture him. We all know nobody can hold
up against the best interrogators Hanoi and Moscow have. If they get everything out of him, the
communists will roll up a lot of people we couldn't
get out. There won't be anyplace for them to hide.
The communists will take out the agents, their families, and anyone else they know.

"Everyone in the government is screaming for
not acting fast enough to get the agents out of
South Vietnam when it fell. The Vietnamese agents
were the ones who took the risks, and they served
us well. Already there are reports out of Cambodia
of mass murders the communists are conducting in
their own country. How long before Vietnam goes
the same way? The United States simply didn't do
enough to help in the evacuation of South Vietnam
and Cambodia.

"Now add the bloody *Mayaguez* rescue to the list.
We all know the casualties the Marines took at Koh
Tang. The White House wants action on this evac-
uation Gouggleman is driving, and they want it

yesterday. And they don't want a Marine amphibious or helicopter assault with a cast of thousands. They want it fast, they want it small, and they want it quiet. We've been tasked to go back in and get Gouggleman out, along with anyone he brings to the extraction site. But above all, we *have* to get Gouggleman the hell out of there.

"Right now he's insisting that we take out several people he's been able to locate and hide. The last report we received, and that was forty-eight hours ago, he still hadn't been caught by the NVA. But it's just a matter of time. This is a race, gentlemen, and we have to act now or a lot of people are going to lose."

The room was quiet for a moment as everyone drank that in.

"So, why both a SEAL platoon and a UDT platoon, sir?" asked Tim Colder, the LT(JG) SEAL Delta Platoon OIC.

"Our mission is to go in under cover of darkness to a beach landing site. I've been assigned as the task unit commander. We're going into a country that became entirely communist a few days ago, and if it's a trap, we'll need gunslingers and firepower. That's your platoon, Lieutenant. I expect the SEAL platoon to be the security element for this operation. That includes scout swimmers and beach landing site security."

Dennison turned to the UDT platoon.

"As for the UDT platoon, there's nobody better in the water than you guys. We're going to stage and launch off the submarine *Grayback,* and you guys are a lot more familiar with it than the SEAL platoon. You've used it on lockout/lock-in missions dozens of times, and you've done a lot of wet deck launches and recoveries. In addition, your platoon has conducted scores of small boat operations. It'll take a lot of skill to handle those boats if the surf is rough. The navigation has to be flawless to find the BLS at night. We also need you to personally handle and safeguard the refugees while the SEALs pull security."

"Why not use SDVs off *Grayback*? Sam Elson, one of the more experienced UDT men, asked thoughtfully. Dennison recognized him as an old hand with the SDV, one of the men who was rumored to have conducted photo reconnaissance of ships and defenses in Haiphong Harbor.

"We won't need SDVs to get in on this one, and we have to bring the agents and their families out on the surface. There will probably be a lot of them, more than SDVs could ever carry. They're not frogmen and they can't scuba, remember that. They'll be scared and out of their element."

"How many boats are we talking, sir?"

"We're talking a small armada. Ten boats. I know you're not used to operations of this size, so we're going to keep it simple and take it by the numbers. But we have to work fast. And I know this could all seem like one big setup. Believe me, I have the same feelings, and I've been over this repeatedly with the brass already. If it makes you feel any better, I'm going to be right there with you. I won't send you in on any beach I wouldn't go on myself. If it *is* a trap, they'll have to catch us, and you know how hard that is on cross-beach operations. We'll set this one up so that we have the best chance to win. And we will."

*   *   *

The Team planned and trained for thirty-six hours,
then loaded *Grayback* and put to sea. One more
communication had come out of the country from
Gouggleman, and the time and place of the evacuation were set. Gouggleman's movements were
highly restricted, and the original BLS had to be
modified by several miles. *Grayback* would be the
only vessel in immediate support. All other warships would have to stay away from the Vietnamese coast, or they'd risk tipping off an operation in
progress. There would be no close air support or
helicopter gunships on call. This mission called for
a small, elite force of deadly shadows. Grayback
steamed west as fast as she could toward the Vietnamese coastline.

On the night of the operation, the submarine approached the drop site submerged underwater,
closing slowly and cautiously. Eighteen miles out
to sea, there was no boat traffic in sight. The fall of
South Vietnam had interrupted the usual flow of
thousands of indigenous fighting vessels blanket-
ing the coast. The communists were tightening the
noose around all those attempting to flee the new
regime. No small boat activity would be allowed
until Hanoi had established firm control.

The U.S.S. *Grayback* was an old submarine, one
of a handful of diesel subs left in the modern nuclear Navy. Real submariners drove nukes . . . but
you could never convince *Grayback*'s proud crew of
that. They relished their special operations role.

But the diesel boats were never considered
choice duty in the underwater service, and association with UDT/SEALs and other special opera-

tions forces tended to be last on the hit parade, thus the UDT familiarity with *Grayback.*

It was one of the many reasons the United States couldn't execute special operations as well as Britain or even the Israelis. UDT/SEALs, Green Berets, and others were all well trained, but they were never equipped with the best support, nor were special operations officers ever groomed for or promoted to top positions. Just as in the *Mayaguez* incident, the top task force officers, unfamiliar with special operations capabilities, often brushed them aside in the crunch.

Grayback had the same general shape and size of other conventional subs, except for one very unique feature that stood out like a nose wart. A pair of identical Regulus missile tubes sat complacently on the bow, two large humps that had been converted into two massive lockout/lock-in chambers for combat swimmers. The vessel could launch a large number of frogmen underwater or on the ocean's surface. During the latter stages of the war, *Grayback* had stalked the North and South Vietnamese coasts during covert and clandestine operations. On more than one occasion, it had gone into Southern Chinese waters. *Grayback* was a small piece of the special operations history of the Vietnam War.

The submarine surfaced after the immediate area off the coast had been thoroughly checked. The frogmen on board needed only a few rehearsals to conduct the launch in minimal time. *Grayback* surfaced quickly, and the command was given to the UDT and SEALs to launch. The huge bay hatch to one of the Regulus tubes yawned open, and frogmen poured out of it and onto the deck. Ten black rubber boats were rolled out and assembled on the deck, and the main tubes were inflated in seconds using compressed air cylinders.

Within fourteen minutes, Dennison gave the all-clear, and the submarine rigged for dive. As the frogmen climbed into the boats with their weapons and equipment, the *Grayback* flooded its ballast tanks and began to fall away into the ink-black sea.

The boats were linked together to form a cohesive unit, after which the frogmen signaled the submarine with a small infrared light. It made a complete circle, doubling back and coming up on the boats again slowly. Its periscope pierced the surface, snagged a towline stretched between the boats and started towing them closer to shore.

The boats were towed at eight knots to a point five miles off the Vietnamese coast. The submarine and an airborne early warning aircraft had given no indication that the Vietnamese had aircraft on strip alert or patrol boats active along the coast. Everything pointed to a no-ambush situation, so far. At that point, a final set of light signals was exchanged with the periscope, and the frogmen cut their way free of the sub. The Grayback stayed in the area, awaiting their return and watching their backs against coastal patrol boats.

The miniature armada moved steadily toward the coast, slowing to four knots at the two-mile point. GM1 Anderson and PR1 Braddock carefully plotted and followed their navigation route. Both of them knew this coastline intimately; they'd served in UDT Det Charlie and worked off the coast in submarines. The navigation took them

north of the BLS by a little over a mile, a pre-
planned offset. If they'd navigated directly for the
site, it would have been a lot harder to locate
against the nondescript background. The offset let
them know with certainty that they'd have to head
south to find the BLS. This was the most critical
point in the operation. If it was a trap, North Vietnamese soldiers would be waiting in ambush
along the sand dunes.

About two thousand yards from the beach, the
boats turned and headed south along the coast.
They passed several points they recognized from
their chart study. EN1 Mark Sloan verified their
location, having worked the same areas as an
LDNN and MACV-SOG advisor during training
missions on this same stretch of beach. Everything
was quiet. The boats finally reached a point just
north of the tentative BLS and stopped. Five scout
swimmers slid into the water and swam quietly off
toward the light-colored sand of the beach. Their
OIC was Art Jones. During a prior tour in country
as a STADT 158 advisor, he'd learned to speak
Vietnamese. The skill might well come in handy for
the link-up.

They'd decided to beef up the normal two-man
scout swimmer group to a team of five. If it turned
out to be a trap, the five-man team would give
them a little more security and firepower. And five
well-trained men could still move quietly enough
in the dunes. The boats tied off together, and all
the engines remained idling. If they stopped an engine, it might not restart, and this was no place for
engine trouble. Twice they moved back against the
current to remain on station.

The scout swimmers stopped just outside the surf zone. The beach was empty. They moved low into the surf until they felt sand beneath their feet, and they scanned the beach and all around the dunes. Still no sign of life. At a signal from A. J. they took off their fins and crawled up to the water's edge. The surf continued to break around them, foaming up to the white sand. They lay at the water's edge for two minutes until they were certain that there was no one in the immediate vicinity. Another signal brought the five of them up to their knees, and they sprinted across the open beach to the first sand dunes. The beach was wide open.

They dropped to their knees as they reached the dune. For another minute or two they watched and listened for enemy patrols. Nothing yet. They'd come ashore five hundred yards north of the intended extraction site. It would allow them to slip silently through the dunes down to where the refugees should be, a much better tactic than trying to cross the beach at the extraction point. If the Vietnamese were waiting in ambush, the SEALs would back off, move away to the north again, and slide back into the water to escape. The boats would be warned, and the frogmen would depart Vietnam for good.

The five SEALs slipped along the dunes like coastal fog. They moved together with two men out front and several feet away from each other, a technique called "double point," until the last two hundred meters. Then the points converged and one man covered the other, ten meters at a time. This cut their movement in half, and also their chances of detection from the front if things went badly. Their movement was slow and deliberate. They used the darkness of the sparse vegetation and shadows to their best advantage.

Suddenly they heard noise coming from about a hundred meters away. They cocked their heads, straining to catch every sound on the wind. There was definitely someone out there. From seventy-five meters out, they could hear about half a dozen people, maybe more, in front of them. Definitely not a military unit. They had to be the refugees.

Staying about seventy-five meters out, the SEALs circled the area slowly and cautiously. They wanted to make sure the group was alone. If the enemy were there, they might be using the refugees as bait. After forty-five minutes of quiet and careful reconnaissance, they were sure the group was alone. They approached from the rear, knowing the refugees would be focused toward the sea.

The first SEAL scared the refugees enough for them to make an audible collective gasp. They were obviously scared out of their wits, and with good reason. They started to rise when they realized the huge, fierce-looking men were Americans. The SEALs did their best to stop them, restricting their movement and speaking to them to calm them. They appeared to be two families, a ragtag collection of males and females, young and old. A. J. understood their fear completely. They were risking their lives to leave the country. And if any of them had worked for the Agency, the lot of them would be tortured and slaughtered by the communists if they were caught.

"Where's Gouggleman?" A. J. whispered, glancing at the faces around him.

"We don't know," one of them whispered back, his eyes wild. "He went back for one more family and missed the contact with us this evening!"

A. J. froze for a moment, waiting for his heart to start beating again. The V almost certainly had Gouggleman. If so, the team was running out of time. They had to get everyone out of the area immediately.

The SEALs used an infrared light to signal the boats from the bottom of the last dune before the open beach. Security had been established to each flank, and a lookout watched the land behind them. The boats took ten minutes to arrive, moving slowly to avoid creating a visible wake. During that time the refugees were organized into boatloads and lined up. As the boats came ashore, each beached side by side in a specific order. Bowmen jumped out and pulled the nose of each craft solidly up to the beach. They held tension on the lines as the SEALs and UDT jumped out. The SEALs fanned out in three different directions, putting firepower on the flanks and even more on a security position landward, all within hand grenade range of the refugees.

Dennison and two UDT men from each boat came to A. J. and received a quick brief and the breakdown of the refugees. In one boatload after another, the refugees were escorted in a run across the open beach to the waiting boats. As they were being helped into the craft, Dennison suddenly saw the lights and heard the trucks. He turned to see what it was.

Several vehicles were speeding into the area. They'd turned off the coastal road only a few hundred meters to the west. This one wasn't a coincidence; the Vietnamese were launching a search of the area. Gouggleman must have been captured and tortured into revealing the location of the extraction site. Dennison felt sick; the man's reckless courage deserved a better end. The SEAL shook himself out of his thoughts. He had to move his men out quickly.

Dennison and A. J. immediately called in the security positions to the water's edge. If the operation was discovered, they would hold off the communists until the boats were away, then swim to sea for pickup. No one would be left in the dunes to share Gouggleman's fate; Dennison promised himself that much. The vehicles stopped only three hundred meters away, and he could pick out clearly the sounds of a search being hastily organized.

The boats were readied, and Dennison signaled for each of the security teams to embark. Head counts in each boat were being conducted as quickly as possible. Dogs started to bark and bay in the dunes. A few minutes at most before the Vietnamese stumbled onto the BLS.

The last of the SEALs climbed into the boats, and the bowmen pushed the craft off into the water. Master Chief Stine was the last man off the beach. He turned and looked back, a final check to verify the head count. Suddenly he was struck by an overwhelming sensation. It paralyzed him, shot through his limbs like lightning, froze him in place. His mind reeled back twenty-one years in time to his first mission near Haiphong, when he'd helped put intelligence agents ashore. Now he was pulling agents and their families out. The country, the war, his experiences, the friends who'd died, the men he'd killed, the emotions he'd felt all came flooding forward in a rush, almost crippling him. He suddenly felt a huge lump in his throat and wanted to vomit. His eyes watered.

Someone hissed his name sharply and extended a hand. He snapped out of his thoughts, swallowing hard, and waded out quickly into waist-deep water. Stine grabbed the hand of his fellow teammate, like so many hands that had always been there in the chaos and senselessness of all the battles. The grasp was strong, steadying, the solid grip of another frogman. It was Dennison, his Commanding Officer and one of his closest friends. Dennison helped him into the boat, and they were off.

The boats turned and glided out to sea, careful not to open their throttles more than halfway. They still had to avoid stirring up the water and pinpointing their location. Flashlights could be seen among the dunes on shore, but the sounds of the dogs and the search were drowned by the surf and the ocean. The frogmen and their special cargo melted into the darkness and out to sea. Although there were ill-defined footprints in the sand, the communists never really knew whether or not the Americans had been there.

"Jesus," Dave Stone breathed, as soon as Stine finished the tale. "Did they ever find out exactly what happened to Gouggleman?"

"Yeah," Stine muttered. "It's the kind of story

you'd almost rather not hear about. He was captured and held in Hoi Chi Prison outside Saigon. The communist Vietnamese tortured him, with assistance from the KGB and GRU. Washington knew he was alive, but at that point they were powerless to help him. No rescue would have been possible. So they requested his release through diplomatic channels, and you can imagine how effective *that* was. His body was returned to the United States in September 1977."

"Christ," Tony Franco shook his head. "I wouldn't wish that on my worst enemy."

"On my worst enemy, I might," Mike Boss admitted lightly. "But not on anyone with that kind of integrity."

"The man was a twentieth-century Regulus," Dave Stone said quietly.

"A who?" Boss asked him with a raised eyebrow.

"Rome passed a death sentence over Regulus during the Punic Wars. And he returned to Rome anyway, knowing that they were going to stick him in a barrel lined with arrows and push him off a cliff. It was a matter of honor for him to return and carry out his sentence. Unlike Regulus, Gouggleman had a slim chance to escape the fate that finally claimed him. But he had to have known that all the odds were against him."

"And he went anyway," Boss concluded.

"Exactly," Stone nodded solemnly. "And because he did, several families made it out that would have been trapped there without him. Those children had a chance to grow up. I don't know if he found any comfort in that thought, but I hope he did." He raised his beer mug, and the others followed suit. "A toast to Tucker Gouggleman. Maybe a hundred men of his caliber are seen in a century, and probably less."

They raised their glasses and drained them dry as they had a hundred times before, for friends, for comrades-in-arms, for other warriors who'd earned their respect. For those who'd fought the good fight and lost, or won, depending on how you looked at it. For those whose sacrifices were probably destined to go unsung, for those a nation wouldn't know to mourn. They raised their glasses and drained them dry for Tucker Gouggleman, and for others they'd known and fought with in hellish battles in every corner of the world. There would be more battles and more reunions to come. And those who survived to find themselves back in Coronado on the Fourth of July would drain their glasses again, for others.

Appendix:
The Dark Side of the Cold War

Vietnam was never an isolated guerrilla war. It was a pivotal struggle in the cold war of superpowers, and its importance in that context has seldom been recognized. For SEALs and others who fight in covert actions, the dark side is always their killing field. Vietnam was a big one.

The evidence was absolutely conclusive as far as anyone who actually fought in Vietnam was concerned, but the White House and the diplomats in the State Department would never have admitted it. There were foreign communist trainers, advisors, and combat troops accompanying the Vietcong and NVA into battle against U.S. forces in Vietnam. It was a matter of national policy to keep such tidbits of information from the battle zone low-profile in the news. Who the information was supposed to be kept from was never very clear. But it didn't take a rocket scientist to piece together the motives of the Ivy League Washingtonians. The war in Southeast Asia was supposed to be one more "brushfire war" pitting eastern communists against the West; the 1960s saw dozens of them. But they didn't see anything like Vietnam.

In the East, the man on the street had no say in what his government did on the sly, had no knowledge of it and didn't care. They went with the party line; it was safer than asking too many questions. Western democracy theoretically meant the people had a say in what their government became involved in. But if their government kept the facts from them, there was no way they could voice informed concerns to their politicians.

East and West were right in the middle of a major conflict in Laos, Cambodia, and Vietnam. The politicians would never admit it, but the troops in the field knew the sound of 122-mm communist rockets produced in China and the sight of green tracers made in the Eastern Bloc. The munitions were a message from communists worldwide to every American soldier in the fight, and they got your attention a lot faster than a White House press release.

As far as the United States was concerned, Vietnam should have been a small, controllable brush war. Just turn up the pressure of the West's foremost military power little by little and most of the brush wars would be contained or snuffed out. In Vietnam, the United States had drawn a distinct line. The guys on the other side just hadn't cared to step across it. All they wanted to do was reach across that line and jab at the Yankees until they crumbled. And the North Vietnamese didn't play by the same rulebook that Uncle Sam did. Hanoi had a hell of a lot of help from fellow communists on any given day. They'd do whatever it took to get the job done, and they were good at focusing on their goals.

The soldiers in the field who dodged the VC snipers could tell you firsthand just how different Vietnam was from other guerrilla wars. It went well beyond communist material support or technical assistance to the VC and NVA forces. The Soviets and Chinese could resupply them for years and tie up the United States. Over time, such a war would drain the resources of the Americans considerably. Social programs at home would suffer. But most of all, the morale of the people would erode tremendously. The more casualties, the faster the erosion.

In time, the American public might begin to question the ethics of its own government. And that could be the beginning of the end of American intervention abroad, an end well worth the strong support of other communist nations.

The White House was trying to conduct a war without encouraging another "Thanksgiving Surprise." The Chinese had crossed the Yalu River and entered the Korean conflict in 1950, and they could easily do it again in Vietnam.

But the ChiComs were already there, in massive numbers, as advisors and technicians and even soldiers who covered the backs of the VC and NVA. And the ChiComs were only part of the foreign advisory and assistance connection.

In the middle of 1966, North Korea had sent twenty-five to fifty pilots to North Vietnam to act as trainers and advisors. In addition, those same fighter pilots flew air-to-air combat missions against Americans. This wasn't an unusual arrangement between communist nations. The North Koreans actively sought ways to season their forces into combat veterans, and they hated the Americans intensely.

It was in South Korean interests to make sure the United States took the North Korean threat seriously, so they never hesitated to leak information on the North. According to South Korean sources North Korea talked Egypt into allowing their pilots to fly against the Israelis during the Six-Day War in June 1967.

Earlier that year a North Korean defector confirmed to U.S. intelligence the presence of the North Korean fighter pilot group in North Vietnam. He also confirmed the fact that North Koreans were running with NVA in the field, broadcasting propaganda targeted against South Korean ROK troops participating in the conflict. Numerous Korean language transmissions had been taped by Allied forces prior to that admission. The North Koreans weren't there in large numbers, but they were definitely there and throwing lead downrange.

Then there were the Cubans. As early as 1965, Cuba had admitted training Vietcong cadre in guerrilla operations. Cuba had a lot of experience in such operations throughout Latin America. And they'd met American-trained commandos in combat at the Bay of Pigs and in scores of commando raids which the CIA sponsored against Havana. In fact, East Coast frogmen from UDT trained Cuban

exiles in CIA bases throughout Florida to conduct
such hit-and-run operations.

Early in the war, several Cubans lost their lives
manning SAM sites around the Vietnamese countryside. Two Cuban propaganda specialists toured
North Vietnam and guerrilla bases in Laos and
Cambodia in 1965. Marta Rojas and Raul Valdes
Vivo were given access to several American POWs
being held by the VC in South Vietnam. The POWs
included four Special Forces NCOs captured when
their camp at Hiep Hoa was overrun in a VC attack
in late 1963. Franco had met one of the Green Berets after he'd managed to escape from captivity,
evading the VC for four days before he was finally
picked up by Allied forces.

By mid-1966, Cuba had sent Major Julio Garcia
Olivera, a six-foot-six-inch, thirty-eight-year-old
missile expert, as Ambassador to North Vietnam.
Olivera was trained by experts in the Soviet Union
from 1961 to 1963, but his diplomatic training and
credentials up to that point were far less impressive. In fact, they were nonexistent. The CIA had a
huge dossier on him. He was in Hanoi to help coordinate SAM site effectiveness using Cuban
launching missiles, diplomatically, no doubt.

But the most flagrant involvement by Cuba was
its assignment of a Cuban intelligence officer reportedly named Fernando Vecino Alegrit. While
assigned to Hanoi, Alegrit and a few of his side-
kicks interrogated and personally tortured a handpicked dozen American POWs. "Fidel," as he was
nicknamed by the POWs, terrorized the men at the
Cua Loc prison camp, called "The Zoo," from August 1967 to August 1968. He administered some

of the most savage treatment experienced by the
POWs up to that time and was directly responsible
for beating one USAF officer into a catatonic state.
The American later died in captivity because the
Vietnamese refused to release him and let him get
the care he required. Instead they separated him
from the other POWs, who'd taken to force-feeding
the man to keep him alive. In appreciation for his
support, Alegrit was driven to and from the prison
camp daily in his own vehicle, compliments of the
Vietnamese communists, while the Viet camp commander rode a bicycle.

All the while, the communists proclaimed to the
world that they had a policy of "humane and le-
nient treatment" toward their captives. A lot of
SEALs and Special Forces men prayed for the day
the gloves would come off and they would be allowed to hunt the Cuban intelligence officer down.

The Soviets were by far the biggest material con-
tributors to the protracted war effort. They had
provided a constant flow of major military and ec-
onomic aid to the North Vietnamese for years. As
early as 1961, Soviet advisors were spotted with
Pathet Lao guerrillas in Laos. Soviet piloted aircraft
conducted resupply to numerous Pathet Lao base
camps in north central Laos. In one bizarre story,
a Soviet helicopter crew flew several American
POWs to freedom when they were released as part
of the Laotian cease-fire in August 1962. The POWs
included one Green Beret captured with three of
his teammates when the indigenous unit they were
advising was overrun. Two of his friends had died,
he believed, from wounds suffered during the capture. And the third, an officer, was killed in an es-

cape attempt. The Soviet helo crew had apparently been quite cordial to the released POWs, even giving them a few Salem cigarettes during the flight out.

Before 1965, Moscow coordinated utilization of Soviet and Eastern Bloc technicians in numerous projects throughout the North. Several reports indicated that Soviet submarines assisted in ferrying supplies to VC guerrillas in the southern tip of Vietnam throughout 1964. Soviet intelligence trawlers trailed US aircraft carriers in the Tonkin Gulf and were stationed off the end of the runway at Guam to send early warning of American B-52 airstrikes when they were launched. Coupled with other intelligence, this assisted greatly in placing anti-aircraft batteries at their highest level of alert.

Nineteen sixty-five turned out to be a major watershed year for active combat participation by the other foreign communists. That was the year the Soviets became directly involved. By that time, hundreds if not thousands of Soviets were actively engaged alongside the North Vietnamese. Hanoi barely registered an air force in 1964, but a year later they were able to wage an aggressive campaign against American fighter pilots in the skies. And they were actually winning some of those engagements. It was hardly a shock to anyone involved that most of the fighter pilots they encountered weren't Vietnamese.

The most promising North Vietnamese pilots were being trained in the Soviet Union at least as early as 1965, as reported by the Soviet newspapers *Pravda* and *Red Star*. While some Soviet pilots were vectored in aerial combat against Americans, the biggest support they supplied was the addition of SA-2 surface-to-air missiles manned by Soviet crews. By July it had become impossible to avoid foreign casualties. On July 24 an American plane was hit by a Soviet SAM, and three days later there was an unsuccessful attempt at retaliation. On August 12 another aircraft was hit by a SAM, and more retribution raids were ordered. Defense Department officials knew that Russian soldiers were killed in at least some of the SAM site attacks.

Although the SA-2 was used extensively throughout the war, the effectiveness of the missile could be minimized. The Soviets poured military aid into Indonesia until 1966 in the hopes of drawing them into their sphere of influence. There, CIA operatives managed to break into a warehouse holding several SA-2s, and they stole the guidance system from one of the missiles. Careful study of the weapon allowed countermeasures to be developed which allowed U.S. bombers a greater survivability rate.

In the meantime, the Americans struck missile sites at many locations in North Vietnam. It annoyed American pilots no end to see Soviet ships resupplying the North Vietnamese without opposition. But it was infinitely more frustrating receiving small arms fire from those same Soviet crews while their ships were in port. A few American pilots took it upon themselves to return that fire, against all orders, and they paid the price when they returned to base after formal complaints had been lodged through diplomatic channels.

The secret fighting between the superpowers continued to escalate. In July 1966, an American

command and control aircraft, a C-47D, was shot
down by a Soviet-piloted MIG while flying in Laos.
The incident was kept as quiet as possible by U.S.
authorities. By that point the Soviets had openly
admitted that they were sending military advisors
to help the North. Colonel Vladimir Naumov and
Colonel Nikita Karatzupa were two of the officers
sent to assist. The veteran border guards set up a
training camp on the North Vietnamese border to
train their counterparts.

In 1967, one SEAL platoon reportedly came in
contact with a Soviet advisor during an operation.
The group had set up a surveillance post along a
waterway in a remote area of Kien Giang Province.
During the second day of their mission, several
sampans quietly drifted into view. Sitting in the
bow of the lead boat was a big Caucasian with an
AK47. The SEALs turned the site into an immediate
ambush and opened up at a distance of less than
fifty yards. The Caucasian was the first to be hit,
and he tumbled headfirst off the bow. The SEALs
were outnumbered and outgunned. They fought a
running firefight to the extraction point, but they
all made it out in one piece. Intelligence later reported that the man they'd killed had been a Soviet
advisor. They were ordered to keep the incident
quiet.

The Soviets also used helicopters to ferry VIPs
and supplies from Haiphong and Hanoi to bases
in western North Vietnam, Laos, and Cambodia.
Reports had come from several MACV-SOG spike
teams, small American-indigenous recon teams
which penetrated the borders, that the Soviet helos

flew at night, turning on their lights only in the last minute before landing.

The blatant use of the helos got the attention of the top brass, and they decided to conduct their own special strike. In October 1967, an Air Force strike hit six Soviet helos as they sat parked on the tarmac at an airfield thirty miles west of Hanoi. All six were destroyed on the ground. Four were MI-4s, and the other two were the huge MI-6, capable of carrying a hundred and twenty combat troops. Moscow had only built thirty of those, and they were less than delighted about losing two of them. But they'd used the transports to resupply remote sites—too effectively, as far as the United States was concerned.

The Soviets became more audacious in their activities. Support of other regional communist insurgencies became a part of the package deal. Beginning in 1967, MI-8 helicopters were flying blacked out to resupply communist guerrillas in the northern part of Thailand. They were flying in from bases in western North Vietnam and Laos, and there was little doubt in anyone's mind as to who was at the controls. Flying blacked out through the Karst Mountains and jungle took experienced pilots.

In March of 1968, the secret war took a turn for the worst. The CIA's top secret mountaintop site in Laos, Lima Site 85, fell in an attack by NVA regulars who swarmed the site. The defenders were surprised by NVA commandos who scaled a sheer cliff to begin the attack and gave the edge to the regulars who followed. It was rumored that a handful of Soviet *Spetznaz* commandos, expert in mountain operations, had led the NVA commando force and made the assault possible. The loss of the site compromised the USAF Strategic Air Command's top secret TSQ-81 Skyspot radar, which enhanced a bomber's ability to conduct all-weather bombing. It also compromised a lot of radio encryption devices used by the Americans. And the loss of that equipment, combined with the loss of the equipment on board the U.S.S. *Pueblo*, doubtless allowed the Soviets to unscramble a lot of American military communications and counter the United States ability to conduct surprise operations.

The Chinese provided the lion's share of men on the ground. Where the Chinese lacked technology and sophisticated equipment, they had manpower to provide. As early as May 1962, the Chinese provided the NVA with several battalions of soldiers during the battle for Nam Tha in northern Laos. Thousands of Chinese remained from then on to support the war through road construction and bomb damage repair along the Ho Chi Minh Trail. This massive effort, along with Chinese anti-aircraft batteries, kept the trail open during periods of heavy U.S. bombing. Tens of thousands more ChiComs manned anti-aircraft batteries in North Vietnam. Chinese gunners manning the sites regularly hit U.S. aircraft, and in turn, American munitions killed and wounded a lot of Chinese.

Although allegations flew back and forth across diplomatic channels, no concrete evidence of ChiCom involvement was produced until May of 1964. During that month, a Chinese engineering officer and a noncommissioned officer were both cap-

tured in an ambush sprung by Meo guerrillas near
Phongsaly, Laos. The support of the guerrillas was
being managed by the CIA using a handful of
American paramilitary operatives. The 1964 capture was led by an Army Special Forces major on
loan to the Agency, and the captives were dis-
played to the international press as proof of active
Chinese unit involvement in the war. By May of
1965, thousands of Chinese were supporting the
communist Pathet Lao and NVA based out of the
Sam Neua area. Up to fifteen Chinese army battalions were reported in Laos, and the reports didn't
stop there.

In December 1964, a village priest near Binh Gia,
South Vietnam, reported seeing eleven ChiCom
soldiers and one European traveling with a Vietcong unit. In the skies over North Vietnam,
ChiCom pilots reportedly downed two F-105 Thunderchiefs in April 1965. The MIG-15 and MIG-17
aircraft used in the battle had been given to the
North Vietnamese by the Chinese just after the
Tonkin Gulf incident in August 1964.

By May of 1966, fighting between the Americans
and Chinese had worsened. Four ChiCom MIG-17s
jumped a flight of U.S. fighters and an RB-66 supporting a bombing strike. The Chinese didn't
bother to deny the attack. They insisted that the
attack had taken place over Chinese territory. One
MIG was downed by U.S. fighters, but that wasn't
the first loss on either side. In April of the previous
year, a USN KA3B went down in Chinese waters,
and the crew was lost. Hot pursuit near the North
Vietnam/China border sometimes spilled over into
Chinese territory, and God help the pilot that sur-

vived a shootdown over ChiCom areas.

Nineteen sixty-seven was the decisive year for Chinese involvement. At the rate of confrontation, the Chinese and Americans were very near a repeat of the Korean War. They were as close to openly engaging in all-out war as two nations could possibly be. To the men on the firing line, there was little difference. In March, estimates of Chinese soldiers in North Vietnam stood at over thirty thousand. The Soviets and Chinese, never the closest of friends, had temporarily patched up their differences so that the Soviets could send military supplies by rail through Chinese territory.

The Americans had their own plans for dealing with that. SEALs, Special Forces, and a few Agency paramilitary men were training Nationalist Chinese in Taiwan to conduct operations in mainland China, targeting the rail system. Other armed indigenous recon teams were being trained by Americans, and they penetrated up to two hundred miles into southern China from bases in Laos. The teams were mainly composed of Yao tribesmen who lived in large numbers in China, Vietnam, Laos, Thailand, and Burma. They were tasked with surveillance, tapping into telephone lines when it was possible. Normally they'd stay in for three to four months at a time, keeping radio contact with aircraft flying along the border and with a base at Nam Lieu. The operations kept the Chinese busy and forced them to expend men and equipment guarding their own coastline and borders, diverting assets away from the Vietnam battlefields.

The United States should have gone a lot further. Too many of the war supplies were coming by rail from the Soviets and Chinese. A few well-trained saboteurs could easily have reached the Sino-Soviet border, picked off Soviet and Chinese border guards and created a massive flashpoint between the two traditional enemies. That would have been the quickest way to divert massive assets from both major communist suppliers to Vietnam. The borders would have closed down and the rail supplies would have been seriously interrupted while the two giants traded slugs. But as a solution it was too unconventional ever to have been acceptable to the State Department.

The Chinese MIGs rotated between bases in North Vietnam and southern China. They knew the U.S. wouldn't violate their airspace, and when a few American planes strayed or were lured across the border, they paid the ultimate price. There would be no search-and-rescue (SAR) missions authorized for the aircrews who went down in Chinese territory. In August, 1967, two USN A-6A attack aircraft were shot down in southern China. At least one of the pilots was captured by the Chinese. The monsoon rains finally slowed the air war down and gave the two sides a chance to cool off once again. But in the South, captured documents and prisoners near Loc Ninh and other locations indicated the Chinese were continuing their advisory role on the ground.

This was nothing like the media interpretation of Vietnam. The Vietnamese weren't a bunch of ragtag peasants who farmed by day and took potshots at the Yankees by night. This was an all-out war fought by seasoned professionals. They had years of experience, and they were supported and supplied by a host of foreign nationals. They were given all the weapons, ordnance and assistance they could handle. The United States had drawn a line in Vietnam, and a union of communist nations had risen to answer the challenge.

But the United States wasn't a passive western nation bearing the brunt of communist design. The Americans were the central western players on the Cold War stage, and they kept up an aggressive series of intelligence programs to monitor the latest developments in the communist countries. And they were directing covert operations to that purpose.

One of the long-term operations included flying electronic warfare aircraft along the borders of communist countries to gather intelligence on early warning and defense systems. Sometimes these aircraft would feint or actually penetrate the borders to produce a response by the communist nation's interception system. The operations were dangerous and didn't always go as planned. In April of 1950, a Navy Privateer intelligence gatherer with ten men aboard was destroyed by Soviet fighters over the Baltic Sea. A trawler crewman later confided to an American prisoner who was released by the Soviets that eight of those crewmen survived and were captured. Rumors persisted for years about survivors of the aircraft being held in the Soviet gulag system. Two were reportedly seen in camps near Taishet in late 1953.

On November 6, 1951, a Navy Neptune intelligence gathering plane was downed off Siberia with another ten men. An Air Force RB-29 reconnaissance plane was lost over the Sea of Japan on June

13, 1952, with at least one survivor believed captured. He was later seen in a Soviet hospital near Magadan. Another Air Force RB-29 was downed on October 7, 1952, near Japan by the Soviets.

Two more aircraft were lost in 1958. One was an American EC-130 which was shot down by Soviets after it crossed the border of Armenia in September. It was believed that at least eleven of the seventeen crew members survived and parachuted into Soviet territory to be captured.

And one of the more memorable incidents was that of Francis Gary Powers in May 1960. Basically, the United States had been flying spy planes over Soviet territory and lying about it. Powers was downed and captured by the Soviets in a U-2 aircraft and exposed in a trim for all the world to witness. He was convicted and imprisoned, but later traded in a spy exchange. He was lucky. He made it out alive.

On July 1 of the same year, an Air Force RB-57 was shot down by the Soviets in the Barents Sea. Two crewmen were captured and miraculously released. In January 1964, the United States lost a T-39, and in March, an RB-66. Both had been over East Germany and were shot down by the Soviets. All the crewmen were captured and later released.

But in April of 1969, a Navy EC-121 with thirty-one military men onboard was shot down by the North Koreans. This followed the capture of the U.S. Navy intelligence ship *Pueblo* and its crew a year before. *Pueblo*'s crew were tortured mercilessly by the communists before they were finally released. The North Koreans, just like other com-

munist nations, hit the Americans when and where
opportunities came up.

And those who were captured never anticipated
being given a closed communist trial, sentenced,
and held in a prison system that may as well have
been on Mars. For all anyone in the West would
ever know, they had fallen off the face of the earth.
A few feeble State Department queries and protests
in diplomatic notes would never bring them back,
and the U.S. government would never admit to the
missions or make the missing soldiers a national
priority. No commando force would ever be dispatched to find and rescue them. They were on
their own. The United States registered at least a
hundred and five casualties of these actions up until 1969. Only the communists knew how many
they had captured and were holding prisoner.

There will be other wars waged half in shadow.
When the call goes out, it will be quick and unexpected. The Nick Stines and other veterans of the
Teams realize it has always been up to them to prepare the next generation of SEALs. They can't afford to fail their teammates.

And they never have.

Glossary

A6A Attack Aircraft (USN)—the Grumman Intruder two-seater carrier-borne all-weather strike and attack aircraft; capable of carrying up to 18,000 pounds of underwing ordnance, the Intruder can fly at speeds of over 600 mph and cover distances of over 1,000 miles.

AKL-44—Light Cargo Ship (#44); the class of small cargo ship converted to a reconnaissance ship and reclassified as Environmental Research Ships (AGERs).

Black Pony OV-10—Light Attack Squadron 4 (The Black Ponies) were a group of fourteen Rockwell OV-10A Bronco aircraft assigned to supplement the helicopter gunships of the Navy Seawolves.

COSVN—Central Office of South Vietnam, the national-level communist party leadership for South Vietnam that took its orders from the Communist leaders in Hanoi and oversaw Vietcong operations in the south.

C-141 Starlifter—a turbofan-powered, four-engine, long-range cargo plane capable of carrying a crew of four and over 95,000 pounds of cargo more than 2,900 miles without refueling.

C-4 Explosives—the standard explosive used for general demolitions in the U.S. military; C-4, or Composition 4, is an RDX-based, off-white, malleable, plastic explosive that can be formed over irregular targets and is 1.34 times more powerful than TNT.

C-47D—a twin-engine, propeller-driven cargo plane with one of the longest service records of any aircraft of its type. When armed with three 7.62mm miniguns, the C-47D became the AC-47 gunship, better known as "Puff the Magic Dragon."

Flechette Rounds—shotgun-like anti-personnel, multiple projectile rounds that launch a swarm of roughly one-inch long finned steel darts.

F-105 Thunderchiefs—single-seat, single-engined, long-range tactical fighter bombers; over 5,000 pounds of underwing stores gave the Thunderchief a heavy attack capability and the aircraft flew over 75 percent of the USAF assault missions in the Vietnam War.

GRU—Glavnoe Razvedyvatelnoye Upravlanie (or Main Intelligence

Directorate), the primary Soviet military intelligence; responsible for external espionage only, the GRU also controls the majority of the military *Spetznaz* forces.

HALO—High Altitude, Low Opening; military skydiving where the parachutist free falls from a high altitude and opens his parachute after a long delay.

HH53—Rescue and Recovery version of the Sikorsky S-65 heavy assault/transport helicopter. The HH-53, generally referred to as the "Super Jolly Green Giant," was armed with up to three 7.62mm miniguns, a crew of three, and up to thirty-eight combat-equipped troops.

Hueys—the common name for the entire family of UH-1A through N helicopters; derived from the designation UH, for Utility Helicopter.

HUMINT—HUman INTelligence; military information obtained from a human source such as prisoners, travelers, agents, defectors, and refugees.

Ithaca—the Ithaca Model 37 featherlight 12-gauge shotgun, the standard pump-action shotgun of the SEALs during the Vietnam War; Ithacas were modified for the Teams with an extended magazine (8 round capacity) and a Duckbill muzzle attachment.

Kit-Kats—penetration operations by indigenous agents deep behind enemy lines.

MACV Recondo—Military Assistance Command Vietnam Recondo School; a specialized training base at Nah Trang Vietnam giving a three-week, 310-hour course in wartime patroling techniques unique to the Southeast Asia area.

MAW-A1—Multi-purpose Assault Weapon; an 83mm reloadable rocket launcher that uses a built-in 9mm spotting rifle to aim an armor-defeating or concrete-shattering high explosive rocket with a very high first-round hit capability.

Meo Guerrillas—Meo (Humong) tribesmen in Laos who operated as an anti-communist guerrilla force patterned on the Pathet Lao; the group was trained and supported by CIA elements and operated under the command of Laotian Colonel Vang Pao.

M-79 grenade launcher—the first 40mm grenade launcher; the M79 resembles a large, single-barrel shotgun and can fire a wide variety of ammunition including high explosive fragmentation, smoke, illuminating, buckshot, and others; the weapon is intended to fill in the gap between the farthest distance a hand grenade can be thrown and the shortest range of a small mortar.

Pathet Lao (also Pathet Lao)—indigenous communist guerrilla forces in Laos under the influence of Prince Souvannouvong, half-brother to Prince Souvana Phouma, the Laotian leader of the 1960s and early 1970s.

RB-57—a twin-engined reconnaissance version of the B57 bomber that can fly at speeds exceeding 550 mph for over 2,000 miles.

RB-66—a twin-engine reconnaissance/bomber nicknamed The Destroyer.

RPG-2 Rocket Launcher—Ruchnoi Protnivotankovi Granatometi; a smoothbore, muzzle-loaded recoilless gun firing an overbore (warhead larger in diameter than barrel), fin-stabilized high-explosive armor piercing shell instead of a true rocket; produced in the Soviet Union from the German Panzerfaust design, it was also made by the communist Chinese as the Type 56 and the North Vietnamese as the B-40.

SAR—Search And Rescue; specially trained groups of personnel along with specialized equipment for locating and recovering personnel in distress on land or at sea.

SA-2 (also **SA-2 SAM**)—the general designation for the Soviet-designed surface-to-air missile (SAM); the SA-2 was intended to attack high-altitude bombers and could deliver its 286-lb HE warhead up to 31 miles at speeds of up to Mach 3.5.

SDV—Swimmer (later SEAL) Delivery Vehicle; a small wet-type submarine with a crew of two (pilot, navigator) capable of transporting up to four fully-equipped SEALs.

Seawolf—the common name for the members of Helicopter Attack Squadron (Light) 3, also known as HA(L)-3; working closely with Navy Special Warfare units gave the Seawolves a unique feel for what the SEALs needed in the way of air support, and they were able to supply those needs with valor.

SIGINT—SIGnals INTelligence; military information gathered from intercepting and analyzing enemy electromagnetic signals and communications; normally subdivided into ELINT (ELectronic INTelligence) and COMINT (COMmunications INTelligence).

SR-71 Spyplane—commonly called the "Blackbird," this titanium-hulled aircraft is able to cruise at an altitude of 82,000 feet at speeds of up to 1,190 mph and can continuously photograph the ground under its flight path with high resolution cameras.

Stoner 63 Assault Rifle—the Stoner 63 system was a series of weapons, including a carbine, rifle, automatic rifle, and several types of belt-fed machine gun that could be assembled on a single receiver; chambered for the same 5.56mm round used in the M16A1, the Stoner system was most often seen in SEAL hands in the form of a light, belt-fed machine gun.

TSQ-81 Skyspot Radar—a modified SAC radar system intended to direct and control jet fighters and bombers while also providing radar-controlled bomb release points; this system allows accurate bombing attacks in all weather conditions.

XM148—a 40mm grenade launcher that fits underneath the barrel of an M16-series rifle; the somewhat fragile nature of the XM148 caused it to be removed from service and replaced with the M203 grenade launcher.